NIGHTSHADE

Also by Annalena McAfee

The Spoiler
Hame

Annalena McAfee

NIGHTSHADE

Harvill *Secker*

LONDON

1 3 5 7 9 10 8 6 4 2

Harvill Secker, an imprint of Vintage,
20 Vauxhall Bridge Road,
London SW1V 2SA

Harvill Secker is part of the Penguin Random House group of companies
whose addresses can be found at global.penguinrandomhouse.com

 Penguin
Random House
UK

First published by Harvill Secker in 2020

A CIP catalogue record for this book is available from the British Library

penguin.co.uk/vintage

ISBN 9781787301948

Typeset in 14/18.5 pt Columbus MT Pro
by Integra Software Services Pvt. Ltd, Pondicherry

Printed and bound in Great Britain by Clays Ltd, Elcograf S.p.A.

Penguin Random House is committed to a sustainable future for
our business, our readers and our planet. This book is made
from Forest Stewardship Council® certified paper.

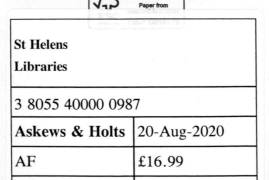

To Jane Maud and Mary Kaye Schilling

As a man is, so he sees.

    William Blake, letter to the Reverend Dr J Trusler (1799)

1

Night. Winter. A city street. Eve's footsteps echo as she walks along the broad pavement past sepulchral buildings – Georgian, stuccoed and porticoed – flanking a central garden. Wreaths of greenery on every door brag of good taste and festive fellowship but the houses are mostly in darkness. At number 19, the lights are on in the second floor, the master bedroom, giving the closed red curtains a visceral sheen. Three doors on, the ground-floor windows flicker blue – someone's watching late-night news, dozing in comfort before grim dispatches from a disintegrating world – while in the basement a night lamp's sickly amber glow filters through slatted blinds.

Further on, at number 31, the first-floor drawing room is shamelessly bright – ugly abstracts and clunky sculpture on glaring display. A tall ficus, with viridian leaves so glossy they could be artificial, is hung with strings of coloured lights and mirrored baubles – silver planets spinning in a twinkling solar system. The room is an empty set; the actors have left the stage. This is an industrious street and they keep early hours. But at number 43 they will still be up. Kristof always said, evoking the jazz pianist Thelonious Monk, that the world got more interesting round midnight.

And there he is, framed in the right panel of the ground-floor window's illuminated triptych. He's in profile, sitting in the leather armchair by the carved oak bookcase he and Eve bought in Berlin. In one hand is a glass of red wine, in the other a remote, which he's pointing towards the sound system, summoning Monk, Coltrane or Evans. Lined up on the bookshelves above him are scores of Christmas cards – the usual miscellany of bad art, poor printing and disingenuous greetings penned under pressure, testimony to a rich social life and a mostly functional extended family. Opposite him, in the left panel, also in profile, gripping her own glass of wine, is his new lover: the redhead, coiled and complacent as a marmalade cat in the armchair, entirely at home. Between them, flaring from a large terracotta pot on the bureau, centred in the middle panel, are the massed crimson tongues of poinsettia, the Christmas flower.

The front-door wreath – holly leaves, red berries, silver-sprayed pine cones – puts her in mind of those East End funeral arrangements: cushions of chrysan-themums spelling out 'Dad', 'Mum' or 'Nan'. This one could, it occurs to her in a moment of grim fancy, spell out 'Eve' – a spiky floral tribute to her, the not-so-dearly, not-quite departed. It's barely five months since she walked away from this house and the marriage. Kristof has wasted no time.

In the darkness of the street, she shivers, and her breath is an icy cloudscape on the night air. She tucks her chin into her scarf and gazes through the window at the radiant tableau. It could be a Vermeer: a luminous domestic interior. Her husband, her house, her life. Once. She turns away into the gloom, skirting the locked garden of shadowy evergreen shrubs and skeletal trees ringed by spear-tipped railings. She used to have a key to this private place, like all the residents in this street, and in early spring she would sit on the bench under the fleshy buds of magnolia. Now the garden is barred to her, like the house she lived in for twenty years.

It took a lifetime to build and a second to wreck. Family life. That was the first to go. Then dignity and, with that, reputation. All the rest followed into the vortex. Only her work remains. The boy caught her glance and held it. Freeze-frame, then rewind. If she could, she would spool all the way back to the beginning, more than three decades ago – before the boy was even born – to her own thirties and the start of the family life she has so resolutely destroyed.

She flexes her gloved hands deep in the warmth of her pockets and walks on, hoping this stocktaking – all she has lost, all she has left – will calm her racing mind.

To her younger self in the distant, urgent days post-art school, slumming it in New York's febrile Lower East Side, intent on making it in the arts scene, her relationship with

Kristof, ten years older and already a rising architectural star, seemed a kind of ending too – a happy ending: to confusion, to insecurity and loneliness, and to the hectic distractions that had almost derailed her teens and early twenties. That she was also saying goodbye to freedom and spontaneity didn't trouble her. She'd had enough of that. Choice was another tyranny. Wasn't there liberty in confinement? Fewer options meant greater clarity. Time to give contentment and partnership a go.

It's starting to rain. She rummages in her bag for her umbrella – an object she would never be seen with as a young woman. Too uncool. Let the hard rain fall. But at this risk-averse end of life, in a hostile landscape, you take shelter where you find it.

Better to think of the past, where the few snares encountered inflicted only flesh wounds. As an art student, her sole commitments were to pleasure and work. Creative, busy chaos was her medium. With the move to New York – three feral post-punks from hard-pressed seventies London let loose in a city where it was still possible to survive on ideas and a certain pugnacious style – she embraced pandemonium. Then, finally, after she moved back to Europe with Kristof, busy order became the rule. She was lucky with pregnancy – a few months' discomfort and inconvenience, followed by a Caesarean, barely impinged on her work.

One critic, a Marxist feminist, later wrote that 'mother-hood' launched Eve, guiding her from a formal retread of still life on canvas – 'an obsessive mimesis that holds a mirror up to nature and shows rather than tells' – through 'an oblique dialogue with botanical illustration' and 'skilful flirtations with genre' to a dynamic, 'multi-media exploration of life, freezing time and privileging perception over analysis, being over doing'. Eve bridled when she read the review – did they ever mention 'fatherhood' when discussing the work of male artists? But at least the critic seemed to be on her side. The review hadn't harmed her reputation, either.

The baby, though, did her best to disrupt it all. Nancy was an avid, picky consumer from the moment she first opened one baleful eye and wailed at the waiting world. In her early years, she was a night-time despot too, and Eve, hollow-eyed and guilty, despaired as she watched her contemporaries transformed from scratchy, work-fix-ated feminists into bovine Madonnas, dreamy and doting. Even Mara, crop-haired firebrand of the art school trium-virate, succumbed. Once she was back in London and had little Esme at her breast, conceived with the aid of an obliging gay male friend, Mara Novak turned into a placid nurturer as depicted by Raphael. She'd spent years making banners, Reclaiming the Night and marching to protest the patriarchy – for this? But then her Esme was a sleeper – 'straight through till 7 a.m.', the newly rumi-nant Mara would boast, as if her daughter's capacity for slumber somehow conferred moral superiority on *her*.

What did that say about Eve, up at least six times a night with her own howling infant? Not for nothing was sleep deprivation used as torture by repressive regimes. For a time, she even envied the execrable Wanda: the plain, neurotic room-mate, devoid of talent, who stayed on in New York to pursue her questionable career, declaring that her artworks and performances – a baffling series of self-obsessed happenings, 'aktions' and installations – were her progeny. She was grappling, she said, 'with woman's place in the universe'. An actual child would be a distraction, she said. She got something right, perhaps. She was the only one of the three who didn't have children. She was also the least talented. Look at her career, then look at theirs.

A car approaches, its headlights smouldering in the heavy rain, and sweeps past in a blur of brightness and pounding noise. Drum and bass? Grunge? Where's the pleasure in sealing yourself from the world in a metal box and subjecting your ears to bone-jarring decibels? The driver would be stone deaf within a decade. Eve catches her irritability – she sounds like an apoplectic matron from the Home Counties – and relents. Perhaps, for the driver, it's a means of reclaiming power. Taking back control, as that delusional political phrase has it. As for the compulsion to seal yourself from the world, Eve knows more about that than most.

In the early years of their relationship, Kristof paid lip service to her needs and did his best to ensure that there was always a studio available for her. Once the baby came along, though, Eve didn't have the mental space, let alone the time and energy, for creative work.

Those were the days of rage. As Kristof's public profile grew, she felt herself shrinking. So diminished was she by the incessant demands of domesticity that she felt she might as well take up residence in Nancy's doll's house. Would Kristof even notice? Finally, he intervened, sending a succession of dim and pretty au pairs to the rescue – a scented cavalry charge, with stuffed saddle-bags scattering mascara wands, lipsticks, used tissues and foolish magazines in its wake. The girls kept Nancy under control, or at least out of earshot, so successfully that sometimes it seemed it wasn't the child but the staff – all those tempestuous phone calls and tearful retreats to the bedroom – who were the real impediment to household peace and progress.

There are so many ways of measuring a life. Most people, imagining their deathbed inventories, are said to think in terms of relationships – love won or lost. For Eve, in these harrowing days, that's a reckoning too far. 'What will survive of us is love' was an unpersuasive line from a poet who, more convincingly, wrote 'Man hands on misery to man'. Velocity was another calculation – from the languorous slo-mo of childhood, cranking up to the adolescent's brisk, bright Super-8 narrative, accelerating on to the breathless blur of old age, swift as a blink-and-you'll-miss-it credit sequence. That's all folks!

There was altitude, too; heights ascended and depths plumbed, in terms of career, or emotions, or those relationships she didn't at this moment have the stomach to consider.

For Kristof, who spent his working life meticulously drawing to scale, she guessed this would be the chosen measure – the arc ascending, from post-hippy firm designing low-cost housing and community projects, to global practice with clients in high-rise property development, finance and government. The salary rise was vertical, too.

Real estate was another gauge – for her, the trajectory from childhood home, a mock-Tudor hutch incubating boredom and mediocrity in London's outer suburbs, to dingy student rooms in the inner city, then a turbulent shared house in the old Huguenot quarter, before the move to New York and a squalid sublet with Mara and Wanda above a funeral parlour in Alphabet City. From there, it was a few blocks south-west to her first home with Kristof, a sparsely furnished loft shared with nine others – musicians and artists – in a former Bowery 'dime museum'. By this measure, Delaunay Gardens, and all its entailed comforts, was her summit. It's downhill all the way – a headlong rush – from here.

A buzzing vibration startles her out of her thoughts. Her phone. She stops to retrieve it. A missed call from Ines

Alvaro in New York. Eve shuts off the phone and drops it back in her bag. Too late, Ines.

Though her own New York years had been fraught – creative drive and ambition butting against an indifferent world; the distracting Rubik's cube of relationships – Eve fought the return to London. Fought and lost. So they left bohemian New York for the bright aquarium of a serviced London duplex in one of Kristof's first 'cookie cutter' Thameside blocks, and from there it was a short hop – or a long Tube journey – to that Georgian villa glowering proprietorially over its shared central garden.

She walks on through the empty streets, black and glassy with rain, away from the stifling security of her past, towards an unfathomable future. Too late to turn back.

There were, over the years, ancillary acquisitions: the Devon cottage, their weekend bolt-hole, sold long ago; the unlamented chalet in Chamonix (she never mastered skiing and found the cold unbearable); the Tribeca penthouse, on the top floor of the building used by Kristof as his firm's US headquarters; and – she winces to think of it – the converted barn in Wales, her own secluded Eden. That was the hardest to let go.

At the barn, hidden in oak woods under the Black Mountains, she first attempted a more intimate engagement with her subject, growing annuals from seed in an

Edwardian glasshouse, planting them out on the five-acre smallholding, picking them – revelling in the godlike pleasures of scrutiny and selection – discarding inferior specimens and conveying the best of them to a Victorian draughtsman's table under the big north-facing window. Here she would draw and paint them, fixing their evanescent beauty in time, before their frail, broken forms were swept away to join their substandard compatriots on the compost heap, their immortality assured in her meticulous, radiant likenesses.

She wasn't, in fact, very good at the growing. The attrition rate, seed to seedling, was high. She lacked the patience and the commitment – her mothering style should have been an early warning – and it proved as difficult to find someone dependable to attend to the seedlings in her absence as it was to find reliable childcare. Still, there were some successes. Sweet peas, cosmos, larkspur, campion. Those paintings, translucent watercolour on vellum, were all now in private collections in Japan. But these days, someone else is tending, or supervising, Eve's patch in Wales. She wonders if that smug redhead in the window ever gets compost under her fingernails.

Eve cast herself out of the garden, like her original namesake, turning her back on Arcadia to wander naked in the wilderness with a compliant male. This was decluttering on an existential scale. She walked away from everything but her London studio. The derelict nineteenth-century canalside factory in the east of the city was bought and converted ten years ago by Kristof when their marriage was still viable: a fiftieth birthday gift to her, who had – he acknowledged – played complaisant, though not entirely uncomplaining, geisha to his nascent career.

The building, reconfigured, was cavernous enough to accommodate her work-in-progress – the monumental canvases, video equipment, tanks of preservatives, industrial refrigerators and drums of pigment – and what was once a warren of small back rooms (the accounts and administration offices of Bartlett's Sweet Factory) was now her home. The compact bedroom was designed by Kristof for her rare overnight stays, when work demanded it. It isn't quite a nun's cell – the double bed undermines that aesthetic – and for the last eight months it has been a perfectly adequate *mise en scène* for her affair. There's also a decent shower, a serviceable galley kitchen, an office, a laundry room and a small but well-equipped gym. The building's spatial ratio is just about right: 90 per cent work, 10 per cent life.

Tonight, having revisited her old existence – the parallel universe, one glance away, in which she still presides with Kristof over that teetering empire heaped with goods, property, friends, connections and public esteem – she is, days before Christmas, in the season of shameless excess, hurrying back to the stringent purity of the new.

There was pleasure to be had in exile, as Adam's Eve must have found. Paradise, all that ceaseless cud-chewing

11

happiness, must have been a bore, and the sudden curse of mortality would have given the days a fresh, sweet urgency. Only the stupid and incurious could fail to be stirred by the lurking perils of the wilderness. That first Eve listened to the serpent's sibilant arguments, weighed them up and made her choice. As for Adam, he barely came into it. He turned out to be a bit of a bore too.

No one talked twenty-first-century Eve into this. It's sheer accident, lucky misstep or catastrophic stumble, that she should be here – her eye pressed against the peephole, watching the diorama of her former world – rather than there, a figurine at ease in a familiar set, unaware that out there in the darkness, she has an audience. One fateful step, a delicious, tumbling surrender, and the old life was over, rushing past her as she plummeted. How easy it is to let go.

2

What is she hurrying back to? She slows down. Calamity can wait. She feels strangely dissociated, as if pacing a deserted film set, and she's eager for digression. Anything to take her mind off this enveloping sense of horror. She turns into the long street of artisan cottages, whose nineteenth-century residents – craftsmen, wet nurses, shop assistants, cooks – once worked to keep the residents of Delaunay Gardens in decorous ease. Today, Crecy Avenue is occupied by young professionals – medics, financial advisers, lawyers – working for the twenty-first-century inhabitants of Delaunay Gardens, maintaining their health, shepherding their funds and negotiating their divorce settlements.

They're pretty houses – neat country cottages transplanted to the city by a Victorian landowner with philanthropic urges and Gothic Revival tastes. Nancy and her dull husband Norbert had wanted to buy one. Kristof – always a soft touch – was keen to help but Eve managed to dissuade them. It was too close for comfort. Growing up should be about getting away. For Eve, growing old seemed to be about getting away too.

The rain has stopped. She shakes her umbrella, rolls it up and puts it back in her bag. Her steps quicken again and she realises she isn't hurrying, against all reason, towards her future, but trying to outpace her thoughts.

In Delaunay Gardens, apart from those discreet wreaths, the gaudy ficus in number 31 and that nasty poinsettia, you might fail to notice that Christmas was approaching. In Crecy Avenue, the young professionals have embraced the season, indulging their children, in a spirit of irony no doubt. Fairy lights wink, enbaubled trees shimmer and, in one window, the grinning head of Santa – the embodiment of stranger danger, sneaking into the bedrooms of sleeping innocents – is trapped in an illuminated snow globe.

Eve always loathed Christmas – fake cheer, tawdry decorations, enforced consumerism and gluttony – and disabused Nancy early of the Father Christmas myth. Some of the parents at nursery took Eve to task, saying that she was 'spoiling it for the other children' after Nancy became, briefly, an evangelising rationalist. The conventional view was that the more loving the parent, the more elaborate, and long-maintained, the lie. But as Eve has learned to her grievous cost, there are lies, and then there are lies.

She's nearing the Tube station now and life is stirring on the streets. The gaunt high-rise Lowry House, a damp-streaked thirty-storey monolith, looms over the north end of this prosperous quarter like a bad conscience. Up there is where today's equivalent of those nineteenth-century wet nurses, cooks and shop assistants live – the carers of other people's young and old; the dispensers of fast food, the pickers and packers in cavernous Internet retail warehouses. Some of the women who clean the houses in Delaunay Gardens and Crecy Avenue live there too.

Eve and Kristof visited the block once, looking for Marie, the young Vietnamese woman who looked after them in Delaunay Gardens for twelve years, sending most of her money home to her parents in Hanoi. Two and a half years ago, just after the Brexit vote, Marie, who had never taken a day off, failed to turn up to work for three days and wasn't answering her mobile. Around that time, a rather valuable Georg Jensen wine tray also disappeared. Eve was all for going to the police but Kristof suggested that they give Marie – after years of blameless service – the chance to explain herself and return the tray. They went together to Lowry House to confront her.

By night, the high-rise had a reputation for drug dealing and teenage gangs. In daylight, on a weekend morning, Kristof and Eve were met by children, clean and cheerful, playing football and riding bikes in the scrappy communal garden. In the lobby, predictably decorated with spray-painted graffiti, more small bikes and pushchairs were parked and a residents' association noticeboard displayed an invitation, in five languages, to a community lunch. There were adverts for a holiday play scheme and a music-hall night for pensioners, as well as handwritten notes offering free furniture and baby clothes. This was, by day at least, no Fagin's Den but the multilayered, child-friendly and functional 'sky village' Le Corbusier dreamed of.

Marie's flat – she shared it, she told them, with three cousins – was on the twenty-first floor. Kristof and Eve stepped into the lift, which was acrid with the smell of disinfectant. They were joined by two teenagers, maybe fifteen years old, pretty black girls, one in hijab and ankle-length skirt, the other with an exuberant Afro, cropped denims and a pink sweatshirt bearing the slogan 'Love'.

They chattered and giggled – about a particular boy at their school, as far as Eve could tell: 'he thinks he's so fit …' – all the way up to the eighteenth floor, where they stepped out and turned back to Kristof and Eve. 'Bye,' the girls said in unison, then they giggled again, giving the middle-aged strangers a little wave before the doors closed.

There were six shoes lined up neatly outside Marie's door – two pairs of men's trainers and a pair of ballet pumps. Eve and Kristof rang the bell. They could hear voices – panicked whispers, it seemed – and they stood there for a full five minutes before the door was finally opened. The frightened face of an older woman stared out at them through a four-inch crack secured by a chain.

'No. Marie's not here,' she said. 'Gone away.'

'Where?' Kristof asked.

'Holiday,' said the woman. Then she closed the door.

Marie had never been on holiday in the twelve years they'd known her. The following week Kristof learned that she'd been arrested on the Tube by immigration officials and deported back to Hanoi. Six months later they found the Jensen wine tray in the cellar. It had slipped down the back of the champagne rack.

Tonight, the concrete high-rise is *en fête*, a pulsating, perpendicular Vegas strip. It seems everyone here is celebrating the birth of Christ or anticipating the arrival of Santa Claus. In the windows of the lower-storey flats Eve sees flashing two-dimensional bells, glowing reindeer, glimmering snowmen, neon holly wreaths. Higher up, the outlines of these sparkling symbols of conviviality blur and merge, transforming Lowry House into a vertical City of Lights.

She remembers hearing, when she lived in New York, that the year-round Christmas lights decking the exteriors of slum buildings on the Lower East Side were a condition of tenancy, imposed by the buildings' landlords – the Hell's Angels; unlikely champions of the season of goodwill. Today, those buildings have gone, sold by the bikers, gutted and transformed into brownstones and condos fit for hedge-fund kings. The perennial fairy lights have vanished too.

In an unequal world, social ascent requires a degree of discretion – the more you have to shout about, the softer you should whisper. One of Mara's old boyfriends, a dialect coach to film actors, once explained the physiology of accent to Eve and said that the upper-class English drawl was achieved by minimal movement of lips and tongue, as if the speaker were attempting ventriloquism. Those aristocrats never needed to expend energy on articulation or projection – their servants approached, leaned in to hear their commands and hung on every mumbled word.

Delaunay Gardens has come up in the world since Eve and Kristof first moved there three decades ago with new-born Nancy. Then, there were neighbourhood shops selling fruit and vegetables, meat and fish, household hardware. In their place are circumspect boutiques with expensive clothing, scented candles and yoga mats arranged in stark, spot-lit displays like exhibits in a Cork Street gallery.

Gentrification. Or re-gentrification. Eve and Kristof were part of the late-twentieth-century revival. When they moved in, Delaunay Gardens was a shambolic ruin, briefly a squatters' collective, with graffiti inside and out, and, in one corner of the neglected central garden, the remains of a tree house above a patch of marijuana.

Near the Tube station is a single survivor of the old order. The family-run corner shop is still open, selling groceries, liquor and lottery tickets. The family has changed – once Bangladeshi, they are now Afghani – but the narrow aisles of tins and packets and the utilitarian window displays, tricked out for the season in a nod to local custom with copper caterpillar trails of dusty tinsel, seem just as they were when Eve and Kristof arrived.

Across the street, outside the Bull and Butcher – renamed the Bull and Broker – last orders have been called and groups of smokers shiver, sucking on their cigarettes and vape pipes in the chill. When was the last time she was in a pub? Certainly before the smoking ban.

She'd never been a smoker, apart from the occasional hit of cannabis. She lacked the commitment. Wanda, who smoked Gauloises, thinking they gave her a Françoise Hardy mystique, was always fussing about getting to late-night stores for fresh supplies. Eve's compulsions lay elsewhere. But she disapproves of the smoking ban on libertarian grounds – if people wish to wreck their health, let them. They pay enough tax on their drugs to finance their health care, as well as the health care of many of the sanctimonious non-smokers. She admires David Hockney not so much for his work – the later paintings are too garish, the line wilfully imprecise – but for his defiant insistence on lighting up wherever he chooses.

Judging by the group outside the pub, the young are still smoking and it continues to be an equal opportunities habit.

In Eve's teens and early twenties, most pubs were grimly masculine and inhospitable to unaccompanied women.

19

But the Railway Tavern became an unofficial extension of art college. Love affairs, student politics and even, it seemed for a time, global politics were determined over pints of cider in the wood-panelled gloom. Then they did their smoking indoors and the tobacco haze, occasionally spiced by marijuana fumes, was thought to be as intrinsic to the tavern's ambience as incense in High Mass, or dry ice in a production of *Phantom of the Opera*.

The old pub regulars, many of them ex-soldiers, survivors of the Second World War, looked on the co-ed art college crowd with contempt – 'They don't know they're born' was the accusation. 'They don't know they're going to die' seems to Eve nearer the mark. The veteran regulars were finally seen off when the new landlord brought in live bands to attract younger, higher-spending customers. These were the heady days of punk, when abuse, shouted over a three-chord guitar accompaniment, passed for style. Old soldiers who withstood Hitler and Mussolini at Normandy and Catania, finally retreated in the face of the Sex Pistols and X-Ray Spex.

This show reel of memories seems to be her only defence against a creeping, vaporous sense of fear. She walks down the steps to the Tube station and taps her card at the automatic barriers, which open obediently. Another innovation. Not a bad one. At a stately pace, the escalator draws her deeper towards the platform below, where the air is fetid as a mummy's tomb. That, at least, hasn't changed – it's as comfortingly foul and familiar as it was when she was in her teens, fleeing the claustrophobia of home for the galleries, clubs and concert halls of central London.

A gust is building, a warm wind machine ruffling her hair. The train rattles past, each window a bright frame of film reel with its own starring cast and complicated back-story, before creaking to a halt.

She spent so much of her youth on this subterranean network, the veins and arteries conveying corpuscular citizens to London's pulsing heart. In 1979, it inspired her first major work, the *Underground Florilegium* – much reproduced, copied and pirated – for which, referencing Harry Beck's classic 1930s Tube map, she replaced the names of stations with botanical paintings.

Reputationally, Eve has been cursed with connections – to Florian Kiš and his indelible, ubiquitous portrait of her, to Kristof, even to the despicable Wanda Wilson. Fame, as Florian used to say, was a cheap trick of the light. If Eve has any profile for her own work among a wider public, the *Underground Florilegium* is its source. But, just as the demeaning association with 'the famous' rankles – the idiocy of a public that gives esteem to a fraud like Wanda! – Eve resents being known for one piece of work completed when she was fresh out of college. The licensing fees, which continue to bring in a decent income, are small consolation.

She takes her seat in the carriage in a daze of dread. It's been tough to keep going, to stay true to her vision and continue to refine her skills in the face of that belittling public perception. She's lost count of the number of times people, introduced to her at events with Kristof, have said: 'Oh, I love your *Florilegium*!', or worse '... your Tube map!'

But tonight, returning to the studio and to the major work she has just completed, she's confident of creative vindication, at least. The years of struggle have paid off. It has come at a terrible cost but no one will deny the groundbreaking quality of her latest work; a departure, certainly, but also the summation of a lifelong exploration. All roads – intellectual, technical, aesthetic and emotional – led here.

In the *Underground Florilegium*, all those years ago, she used a salmon-pink dahlia to denote this Tube station. The same Marxist feminist critic who lauded her later work argued that the dahlia represented 'corporeal decay and a parody of the bourgeois conformity that defined the materially affluent, spiritually impoverished district in which the artist lives'. This critic knew as little about London as she did about Eve. But it would have been pointless, and a little ungracious, to respond that the *Florilegium* was completed more than a decade before Eve moved to the area, that she had no connection with Delaunay Gardens back then; that salmon pink was the only colour available to her at that moment, and that a stylised dahlia was a pleasurable challenge for a young artist striving to develop her skills.

She was twenty-one, footloose after graduating from art college and living in London's East End. She rarely travelled west, the direction of that dull outer borough where, after the divorce, her mother lived on alone in the half-timbered semi that had been the family home. Whole centuries passed, it seemed, civilisations rose and fell, while her mother remained the same, only dwindling in size, in that barren suburb until her death.

Eve was always an outsider, straining against the confines of family – 'like your father', her mother said, just before she died. That was only half true. Her father fled the family – Eve, her younger brother and their mother – only to set up an identical arrangement with his former secretary in another outer London borough, sixteen miles north-east.

The secretary, Sandra, was brash and bosomy, one of the grosser Toulouse-Lautrec *serveuses* transported to twentieth-century suburban London. She wore patent high heels, sweet perfume and gelatinous, cherry-hued lipstick that left traces, like smears of gingival blood, on her big yellow teeth. Sandra soon produced a son and daughter in direct riposte to her new husband's first family, but motherhood didn't curb her style. It wasn't loyalty to her own mother that made Eve recoil from her father's new wife. The woman was an embarrassment. Even in adulthood, Eve couldn't bear to be seen with her stepmother in public.

Eve was in her teens when her parents divorced, though the dress rehearsal ran for years – the shouting and tears, the long sulks in which she and her brother were carrier pigeons, conveying messages between two silent encampments before battle resumed. She was relieved when her father walked out of the family home for the last time, and if her mother retreated to bed, sobbing and railing for weeks on end, Eve barely noticed. She was already out of the door herself, with school – she was a formidably focused pupil – her Saturday job in a record shop, her boyfriend, and the attractions of London; she was constantly travelling eastwards to the city's nucleus.

Once at college, she extended her territory further east and north (though rarely as far as her father's new home). The outer western and northern suburbs were only scantily represented in the *Florilegium* and the south of the city was a blank, represented on her map with the words 'Terra Incognita'. And so it still was.

She used to think of travel as the necessary condition of a fully realised life, with a direct correlation between distance covered and knowledge acquired. She was disabused early, with brief excursions on the hippy trail, by the number of dimwits she met hitching across Europe to Greece, wandering India, millionaires compared to the locals, flamboyantly barefoot and searching for selves that weren't, in the end, worth finding, in that solipsistic transhumance of privileged youth. 'We are stardust, we are golden …'

She wanted grit not glitter, just as music segued from jangly acoustic introspection and bombastic stadium rock to punk – raw and, it seemed at the time, piercingly authentic. She took off for New York, hungry for transformative urban experience, keen to push boundaries, fuelled by generic rage and convinced that transplantation would make her a better artist. But the experiment produced limited creative results; its chief value lay in putting distance, psychically and geographically, between her and her family. It also, she sees now, put her safely beyond the reach of Florian Kiš.

Later, as Plus One, the trailing spouse of a successful husband, there were trips insulated by luxury – first-class travel, five-star hotels – all curiously diminishing to her sense of self, all interchangeable in memory. Sometimes, she wondered if she was going mad, a patronised patient in a secure psychiatric facility with 1000 thread-count bedlinen and a nightly pillow chocolate.

Now she feels her focus shrinking, homing in on childhood's delight in the proximate and miniature, in the quiet thrill of small steps, carefully observed. The protective curl of a petal, the gentle arc of filament and anther, the fat thrust of the pistil and its glans-like stamen. There's wisdom to be found here, too.

What flower might she use to replace the dahlia in an updated *Florilegium*? Not magnolia. That was already taken by the cheerless suburb of her childhood. A rusty chrysanthemum – the most lifeless bloom, native of garage forecourt and hospice? Coarse kniphofia, red-hot poker, with its fiery spikes? Then it comes to her and she smiles. Of course, the flaring tongues of poinsettia. The vulgar plant must have been his lover's choice. Kristof has better taste than that. What will it be next year, once the girl is truly entrenched? Blinking fairy lights and a shimmering nativity tableau?

Tonight, the train is bearing Eve east again, towards the studio – she resists the word 'home'. She can't bend her mind to the horrors that lie ahead. Instead, she steers her thoughts back, forty years ago, when she represented the studio's nearest Tube station, Stratford, in her *Underground Florilegium* with a sweet violet: 'referencing', one critic absurdly stated, 'the bard of the other Stratford, 130 miles west on the River Avon – "I know a bank where the wild thyme blows, / Where oxlips and the nodding violet grows."'

Then, the studio would still have been a factory, belching sugar-scented smoke from a Heath Robinson arrangement of tubes and funnels, disgorging, on long lines of rubber belts supervised by workers in overalls and hairnets, tooth-corroding confections for the nation's young. Eve had seen the archive photographs. Now the factory is silent, transformed into an austere temple of art; her sanctuary, a rebuke to greed, mediocrity and the season's ostentatious clichés.

3

She closes her eyes, lulled like a baby in a cradle, nightmares held at bay by the gentle swaying of the Tube carriage.

In February this year, two months before her show at the Sigmoid Gallery, a colour supplement journalist interviewing Eve in the studio observed that, for a painter of nature, 'there isn't much nature around'. Certainly, there was the current focus, the blaring twin klaxons of scarlet hippeastrum in a zinc pot, facing their giant mirror image, oil on canvas, leaning against the east wall. But the visitor gestured towards the glass and rusting steel, exposed brick and bare light bulbs; the teams of assistants self-importantly wrangling canvases, shifting ladders, arranging trailing wires, wheeling trolleys stacked with tubes of paints and jars of brushes, manoeuvring cameras; the computer and printers; vats of gesso, linseed oil, turpentine and preserving fluid, the microscope and magnifying glass; and the trays of dissecting tools set out on the long oak refectory table which bisected the room. Outside, through glazed triple-height windows, the canal gleamed with its viscous petroleum patina in the morning light.

'Not the natural habitat of a botanical artist,' he said.

Eve fixed him with one of her stares and said quietly: 'Really?'

She loathed the designation 'botanical artist' almost as much as she loathed that other reductive term: 'flower painter'. What's wrong with 'artist'? The journalist later wrote: 'At that moment, I felt eviscerated, a subject of the artist's cold scrutiny. Sepal, stamen, pistil … pinned, from seed to senescence, in a single forensic glance.'

Six months later, in August, all but one of the assistants had been banished. And only the Gerstein curator, Ines Alvaro, a brisk, importuning young woman who was organising Eve's big New York retrospective, and Hans, Eve's dealer, owner of the Rieger Gallery in Cork Street, would be admitted to the studio. By invitation only.

Ines had her own agenda and it was strictly business; the retrospective would be as much about building the curator's reputation as it would be about celebrating the work of Eve Laing. Hans, in his autumn-hued tweed suits, blinking behind tortoiseshell-framed glasses, never pried. If he had any curiosity about Eve's life, he never displayed it, and if ever some intimate detail was revealed, he would make a moue of distaste, take out his paisley silk handkerchief and apply it to the corners of his mouth. Prurience was kitsch. For Hans Rieger, as for Eve, the work was the thing.

At the next station, a young couple, teenagers, step into the carriage and slump on the seat opposite her, their arms linked, the girl's head resting on the boy's shoulder. Young immortals, confident in their beauty and love, oblivious of the hell that lies ahead.

Eve thinks again of her own first boyfriend. Memories of that time of stumbling innocence have been haunting her lately, like a snatch of a corny song she can't get out of her head. An earworm. Only this worm burrows into the soul.

When Eve first met him at a weekend art fair, they were both sixteen, still at school and still virgins, though they affected a swaggering worldliness that suggested otherwise. They were attracted, in that drab suburb, by each other's tentative maverick style. His army great-coat was too big for his lanky frame and his narrow feet were cartoonishly elongated by platform boots. She was a tomboy rocker, eyes ringed in sooty black, wearing a thrift-store leather jacket and patched denim.

They both had Saturday jobs – he waited tables in his father's restaurant, she worked at the record shop – but they would spend Sundays together roaming London's galleries and museums. It was, she realises now, an inchoate yearning for grandeur that took them on regular pilgrimages to the National Gallery, the Tate, the V&A, the Geffrye Museum, the Museum of Childhood (two cool teenagers faking an anthropologist's interest, as if their own childhoods were a distant country), the Wallace Collection (he loved the suits of armour; she feigned interest, though she preferred the Dutch still lifes).

They looked in the windows of fashionable boutiques, closed in those nominally God-fearing days, browsed street markets, went to the cinema and, when they could afford it, to rock concerts – once they'd paid for fares and tickets, they'd blown their budget and would share a single Coke or a juice, making it last all evening. Sometimes, they went to the Albert Hall – against the grain of their generation – and, stunned with pleasure, sat in the cheap seats to hear the big symphonies. More grandeur. Then he would travel with her on the Tube and walk her to her doorstep before getting the Underground back to his own family home, five stops away. Such quaint gallantry.

The most direct route to her house from the station took them through a large municipal park. When they started seeing each other it was winter and the park closed early. He would help her climb over the railings and, rather than risk the embarrassment of discovery in the porch of the family home, they would have their long farewell kiss under a magnolia tree at the park's northern exit before squeezing through a gap in the locked iron gates for a more formal farewell at her front door.

At first, their kisses were awkward under the bare branches of the tree. She knew what they were meant to do, or at least she thought she knew, but what exactly was she meant to feel? In the weeks that followed, small furry buds burst through twig tips, pale green shoots split grey bark, and leaves began their slow unfurling as the couple moved on to a ritual of mild fondling and she let him massage her breasts through her coat. It was an odd sensation, this urgent pummelling. She wasn't sure how to respond.

Later, she sat with him in the back row of the Prince Charles Cinema in Leicester Square and endured the same routine during a showing of *Emmanuelle*. She was mortified and repelled by the film – so much moist pink flesh, such animal sounds, funny when they weren't frightening – even as she submitted to her boyfriend's clammy kisses and kneading hands.

By the time the magnolia was coming into flower, the farewell rite was extended. He unbuttoned her coat and blouse, insinuated his hands under her bra and squeezed her breasts, skin on skin, as if testing fruit in a greengrocer's. His hands were cold and she tensed herself to avoid flinching. Soon he was pressing for more. She was ashamed of her innocence and knew she must submit, and pretend to enjoy her submission, if she was to attain full maturity. She learned from more worldly classmates – girls who arrived in school each Monday with fading love bites on their necks – that if you wanted a boyfriend, and all the freedom and independence that entailed, this was the bargain.

And so, under a full moon, beneath the tree's flushed pink candelabra, each thrusting bloom a fat spear tip, he guided her hand towards his zip. The layer of fabric beneath was parted and his penis, another pink bud, thick and fleshy, was unleashed. His muffled moans grew louder as she touched its silky heft. She knew, now, what to expect – she'd read the books, heard the accounts – but when he climaxed noisily, coating her hand with sticky warmth, she retched.

She sits on the Tube, lost in memory, eyes resting on the couple opposite. The girl glances up and returns Eve's gaze with a stare of frank contempt. Eve parries with a withering look of her own. The young are no match for the Gorgon glares of the old. The girl turns away and nestles deeper into the arm of her oblivious lover.

It took practice, sex. It wasn't like crack, or what they say about crack – one hit and you're hooked. Just as you had to work at cultivating a taste for alcohol and cigarettes, patience and discipline were required to overcome initial revulsion before you could move on to the intermediate stage of tolerance. Actual enjoyment was advanced level. And compulsion, she learned from those sophisticated classmates, before finding out for herself, was a whole other league. She got there, eventually; though not with Magnolia Boy. Poor kid. He was patient, kind, sincere. He didn't stand a chance.

Art school was the portal. At first, Eve lived in fear of being rumbled. Her libertinism was a pretence. She was a timid suburban schoolgirl on the loose, disguised as a free-spirited, hedgehog-haired punk in outlandish clothing, black eyeliner and permanent scowl. Before long, there was no pretence at all. She was the real thing, albeit the art student version, involving intellectual pretensions, sound personal hygiene and a preference for anguished pretty boy poets over mouthy proletarian nihilists, though she had her moments with a few of those.

How much time and energy did she expend on the pursuit of intimacy? It's clear, now, that hoggish youthful hormones were at work, tricked up to look like a quest for connection. Whatever its spur, the endless pursuit and flight was destabilising, the urge a ravening beast that consumed most of her late teens and twenties. From the distance of years, it looked frantic, foolish and such a waste of time. And Florian Kiš? Well, she was still working through that one.

The charismatic wild man of twentieth-century art, *monstre sacré* and keeper of the flame of figurative painting, Kiš was almost four decades older than her. She was a guileless student, awed to attend his life-drawing class. He asked her to sit for him and who could resist that invitation to immortality? Then, in a sustained campaign that in those days was called seduction, and would now be called harassment, he cajoled her into bed. As a lover he was vigorous, demanding, sometimes cruel. He was also fanatically elusive – he never gave her his phone number; she would be summoned to his ramshackle house in Mornington Crescent, sometimes late at night, by a scrawled message posted through her door by one of his henchmen.

Sexual infidelity, or profligacy, was as much an article of faith to him as the primacy of portraiture.

'The human clay is the only concern,' he said once, scoffing at the idea that he might join Eve at the opening of an exhibition of pottery.

And in his rough, deft hands, Eve was more malleable than mud. He educated her, told her how to dress (architectural lines, exquisite fabrics), what to read (Gombrich, Doerner, Shakespeare, Rochester, the French symbolists, the war poets, the metaphysicals), what to look at (the human form in all its variety, flesh puckered by emotion and experience) and how to look at it (the telling light, concealing shade, and the spaces in between). Abstract painting was 'infantile daubing', conceptual art 'the empty posturing of talentless nincompoops', ceramics was 'craft – mere women's work' – and video art and the entire pop culture movement was 'image harvesting: technology-assisted theft'. Eve wonders what he would have made of Wanda's new 'relational art'. Grand larceny? Robbery with violence?

Eve was enthralled by Florian and he caught her subjugation in his famous painting, *Girl with a Flower*, an oblique self-portrait, which he worked on over the nine months of their relationship. Naked, her blonde hair straggly and unwashed, her eyes huge, moist and wounded, she is sprawled on the floor by the artist's bare feet, which are rendered with more care and tenderness than her slender young body. Her flesh is given a livid blotchiness by thick impasto brushstrokes. Behind her, stacked facing the wall, are dozens of completed canvases. Her portrait, if it is spared one of his regular bonfires of inferior work, will join them there, in a Bluebeard's archive of lovers who made the grade. In her right hand, she holds a mauve pansy – 'heart's ease'.

She came to hate that picture, which smacked of the abattoir and conferred immortality not on her beautiful youthful self but on a time of confusion and idiotic vulnerability. She hated the fact that its fame, Florian's fame, had eclipsed any of her own achievements. Until now, perhaps.

Gently rocking with the rhythm of the train, the young couple sit entwined, an urban re-enactment of Pierre-Auguste Cot's *Springtime*, the Tube seat with its check upholstery standing in for a bosky swing. Let's see how they fare in Wintertime, this enraptured pair.

Eve thinks of the portfolio that never was: each lover must have cost her at least one decent painting. Her body of work was sacrificed for the demands of her restless, greedy flesh. That same hunger cost her old friend Mara her entire career. It was, however, no real loss. As a painter, Mara was a retro abstract expressionist, smearing pigment with a disgusted brio as if it were seepage from her psychic lesions, as if that hadn't been done before and just as badly. She turned to sculpture, producing giant geometric puzzles in welded steel. More abstract expressionism. You might admire the technical challenge and sheer effort involved, but her work never contributed much to the conversation. It was, though, one way to go if you couldn't actually draw.

Wanda Wilson took the other route. After a shaky start with her first performance piece in New York, the witless fairground sideshow *Love/Object*, Wanda's whipped and scarified body, its needs and wounds, became her subject, rendered in her own secretions. You broke her heart and you did her a favour. Every slight was immortalised in one of her masochistic enactments: your initials carved on her bleeding chest as she lay naked for five hours groaning on a bed of nails in a downtown gallery; a five-day hunger strike – also conducted naked – in a Perspex box in an uptown museum; publicly shaving her head and keening over an empty coffin on the steps of City Hall.

The couple are kissing now and there's an element of display in their frantic groping. Eve recoils and looks away. Nothing to see here. Her eyes glaze as she focuses instead on memory's inner gallery.

Who could forget, try though they might, Wanda's 'groundbreaking' show *The Curse* – the smell lingered in the nostrils for days – or *He Loves Me/He Loves Me Not*, for which she filmed herself plucking out her own pubic hair? She cast herself as the archetypal abused woman. Not abused enough, in Eve's view.

4

The teenagers uncouple at the next station and leave. The doors close again and on the platform, safely outside the sealed train, the girl turns and shoots Eve a farewell hostile glance. Eve smiles as the tube moves on and now she's staring at the window watching her own reflection, superimposed on the sliding sooty walls of the tunnel.

She had her own trials of the heart. Who didn't? But Florian Kiš was a good teacher. Those painful late-night visitations from other women had served a purpose. Who knows how many passed through there in her absence, but the first time he entertained another lover while Eve was in his studio, she was traumatised.

He was working on her portrait as she posed naked on the floor, when the doorbell rang. Handing her a woollen shawl, he sent her into the bathroom, where she locked the door and sat hunched on the toilet seat waiting, her bewilderment turning to horrified disbelief as she heard murmurs and muffled yelps of pleasure. Florian was making love to his visitor on the studio couch – the couch where Eve had lain with him earlier that evening and would do so again, hours after he had dismissed his visitor.

If Florian noticed Eve trembling when he finally called her from the bathroom to resume her pose, he might have put it down to the cold. She said nothing and later, when he tired of painting, they lay together once more on the couch, which was still scented and, she felt, warmed by another woman's body. Eve left the studio at 3 a.m., racked by anguish. How could she put herself through that pain and humiliation again? But she talked herself down. Extraordinary men don't play by ordinary rules. Would she swap unreadable, mercurial Florian for a transparently devoted chump? This was the price of proximity to genius.

The second time it happened, she was reconciled, comforting herself with the fact that it was *her* portrait he was painting, *her* body he was subjecting to his brilliant sustained gaze. The other women were meaningless; an itch scratched. She knew about them, the simple fact of their existence in Florian's life, but they knew nothing of her – he always directed them to the bathroom downstairs. Eve felt her complicity conferred additional status. She was Florian's co-conspirator and she became habituated, feeling no more than a passing squeamishness at a damp stain on the couch, an oddly familiar animalic scent, a stranger's beaded earring on the floor or the sight of a stray hair: long strands of blonde silk, paler and finer than hers; dull mid-length, mid-brown filaments; dark springy coils which seemed faintly pubic.

Sometimes, when the doorbell rang, she would grab a newspaper and a pen to occupy herself in the bathroom. By the time she'd finished the quick crossword, the visitor would have gone. Occasionally, she would speculate about Florian's Other Women, ascribing personalities and biographies on the basis of their fragrance. Jasmine conjured a lonely intellectual, a professor at the Royal College who kept cats for company; rose water, a vapid Home Counties girl with her own pony and a grace-and-favour job at an auctioneer's; musk, an earth mother with artistic ambitions and questionable sanitary habits. But those late-night visitors – Eve was exiled, uncomplaining, to the bathroom at least a dozen times – didn't even merit a thumbnail sketch; she had the greater part of him and posterity would know it.

Of course she came to resent the portrait, which fixed her in a moment that gave no hint of the fully realised artist she was to become. But the life lesson had been useful: there would always be another lover waiting in the wings, ready to step onstage and sweep her up for the next brief scene. She had no time for wound-licking.

The pursuit of love, or lust, became Eve's primary career in New York, financed by the *Underground Florilegium*, waitressing stints and a spell as a bartender in an underground club, where her knowledge of contemporary indie music, acquired – though she'd never admit it – at her Saturday job in a suburban record store, lent her a certain countercultural authority. She was embraced, for a time, by Warhol's late-period Factory set, who loved her British accent, were taken in by her fake punk credentials and invited her to join the twenty-four-hour party – costumed as for carnival – in rolling re-enactments of the Sack of Troy and the Fall of Rome. No party since deserved the name.

In between, somehow, she managed to paint – a small sequence of carnivorous plants, produced, miraculously, on the kitchen table of that chaotic Avenue B apartment. One critic later argued that here she'd moved into the realm of memoir, that the swollen, self-lubricating coils of the flesh-eating cobra lily, *Darlingtonia californica*, or the hairy traps of *Aldrovanda vesiculosa*, stood in for the snares of love. For a time, she wondered if they had a point. Now it seemed clear that the carnivorous series was her calculated nod to the New Wave, reflecting an anxiety that her fastidious botanical studies were insufficiently edgy for hip New York sensibilities.

Once she had prised herself away from Florian, she hurtled between adventures, occasionally misadventures, but there were no long shadows then in Eve's intimate life; free of Kiš, she was invulnerable, lacking Mara's susceptibility or Wanda's appetite for operatic misery. It astonished Eve when she realised that some of her New York encounters, lightly made and lightly left, should have caused such scouring resentment in Wanda, who wished to claim them as her own – Jorge, the Colombian guitarist with the meth habit; Bradley, the exquisite actor with exquisite self-regard whom Eve bedded as a thank-you for his thrilling Hamlet, only to find that without Shakespeare's ventriloquising, Bradley was a monosyllabic ass; then there was poor Mike, hapless, hopeless Mike, whom no one could have taken seriously, least of all Mike himself.

Here was a case of retrospective ardour: once Mike was lost to Aids, Wanda, who'd been dumped by him years before, recast him as her life's Grand Passion, the indispensable soulmate stolen then left on the trash heap. Kristof, another object of Wanda's romantic delusions, compounded the misery. Every artist needs a narrative. Even bad artists. In one recent interview, Wanda claimed she was a victim of PTSD – post-traumatic stress disorder. Eve laughed when she read it; a more accurate diagnosis would have been narcissistic personality disorder.

The warning signs had been there from the start, long before Eve decamped to New York with Mara and Wanda. Fresh from school, the three eighteen-year-olds had first met when they were assigned student accommodation together by the college. These middle-class white girls were so unalike, physically and temperamentally, in those distant monocultural days, that their differences could almost pass as diversity.

Mara, small, gamine and dark, a purposeful, jumpsuited doer, one of nature's entrepreneurs; Eve, tall and blonde, given to reflection, the cool perfectionist in rock-chick black; and needy, manipulative Wanda, chunky and bushy-haired, with a taste for ethnic jewellery and vivid scarves,

41

whose scatty nature could, in those days, be charitably described as 'kooky'. Eve and Wanda sized each other up like boxers before a prizefight. Mara was their referee. Wanda was envious of Eve's friendship with Mara and was always anxious that she was being excluded. Wanda was envious of Eve, period, as they said in New York.

When Eve's relationship with Florian Kiš became public knowledge, making her the object of prurient press attention, Wanda was insufferable – there were tantrums and tears, as if Eve's unasked-for fame consigned Wanda to further obscurity. Wanda's first suicide attempt – her unresponsive form slumped across the bed, the empty bottle of pills – followed closely on Eve's success with the *Underground Florilegium*. When Mara and Eve finally got their groggy flatmate to the hospital, she was threatened with a stomach pump. The sight of tubing designed, it seemed, for unblocking industrial drains, had the effect of intravenous adrenalin. Wanda confessed that she'd taken two pills and thrown the rest down the sink – the grogginess was a sham, setting the tone for her future career.

Eve gazes up at the Tube map – *her* Tube map, in the eyes of a few idiots who credited her with Beck's original work. The graphic skills wouldn't have been beyond her, at least.

What expertise could Wanda claim? A flair for banal Grand Guignol? As a flatmate, she had a genius for possessiveness, even about her groceries. She marked milk bottles to catch out any visitors who dared to slip a slug in a cup of coffee. She concealed cheese and biscuits under her pillow in case a flatmate came back late and hungry.

'Ever thought of making one of your installations out of this?' Eve suggested. 'A gallery full of half-empty milk bottles scored with black lines? Or a site-specific work here in your bedroom, where spectators are encouraged to rummage through your knicker drawer for concealed snacks?'

Mara, whose kindness, it struck Eve now, was nothing more than a refusal to make difficult choices, was the household arbitrator, on call during the long cold war, on twenty-four-hour fire watch when things heated up. Somehow, during Eve's own low point, physically and emotionally, in London when it was finally over with Florian, Mara persuaded her that the move to New York with them would be a good idea.

'It's the patriarchy that's the problem,' she said. 'Dividing and ruling … We don't need them. There's strength in solidarity. We're a team, us three.'

It could never have worked. In the late-seventies saturnalia of the Lower East Side, groceries were the least of it. Eve turned sorrow into anger and entered the sexual fray as if intent on retribution. She set fires around the city and walked away without a backward glance. Wanda, though, spent her life looking over her shoulder and raining curses on those who, in her view, never loved her enough. This towering sense of grievance she went on to call her art.

Eve, once she was free of Florian's prescriptions – 'Flowers?' he would say, one shaggy eyebrow raised mockingly. 'Again? Where's the flesh? Where's the blood and shit? The *life*?' – got back on track. Her subject matter transcended the merely personal. Why contort yourself, fixing your eye on the umbilical peephole, when you could stretch out and explore the entire biosphere? In love, too, why limit the focus? She laughed later to hear from Mara of her daughter Esme's solemn declaration at eighteen, seven years before she changed course and embarked on her programme of radical body modification, that she was 'polyamorous'. Weren't we all, in the sixties and seventies?

Then came the plague years and the brutal cull of so many friends and lovers. Mike succumbed – spawning another self-referential performance from Wanda, who hadn't spoken to him for three years. Eve knew it was time to get out. When she met Kristof, the timing was perfect. It was Wanda who introduced them – she'd bedded him herself at a warehouse party and earmarked him for her own purposes; he'd slept with her a couple of times, mildly amused by her work, but later confessed to Eve that he'd been repelled by her. When Kristof finally got together with Eve, Wanda took it hard and there was a second suicide attempt – the real thing this time, with a hardcore stomach pump – after Eve told her frankly about Kristof's feelings. Maybe, as Mara said, Eve had been too brutal. But Wanda was looking for fresh material for her work and Eve had obliged. They hadn't spoken since – the only communication over the years had been Wanda's terse, pointed Christmas cards – until last month's exchange at the Hayward.

The long stand-off hadn't been helped by Eve's off-the-cuff remark to a *Village Voice* diarist in the early eighties. There it was, in perpetuity: 'Wanda Wilson's sole talent is for monstrous self-pity.'

If Eve could unsay it, she would. It happened to be true, but it pitted her against the art establishment and was wheeled out far too often in the press, thanks to the Internet, which gave infinite shelf life to casual insults best kept private. It was also, in the public eye, another infuriating link to Wanda. Like atheists obliged by their name to define themselves in relation to a non-existent god, Eve became an 'awilsonist', perpetually twinned with Wanda. In fact, as with the non-believer's deity, Wanda Wilson had no place in Eve's universe. Wanda, though, clearly thought otherwise.

Her annual Christmas cards, addressed at first solely to Kristof and, for the last fifteen years, more irritatingly, to 'Mr and Mrs Kristof Axness', were eloquent. This year's card – no doubt another boastful photograph of one of her shows or an advert for her latest 'immersive art' piece – would be jostling for attention on tonight's bookshelf line-up at Delaunay Gardens.

45

For Eve, Kristof, the gentle Dane who courted her so single-mindedly, was a recessive Viking – the peaceful seafarer as depicted in the Scandinavians' whitewashed version of history. He offered safe sex on demand and he liked her, unlike those angry London punks, spitting with class resentment, or the self-involved pretty boy poets, or the pouting narcissists of Warhol's Factory, tussling with their sexual identities and barely able to tear themselves from the mirror. Unlike Florian Kiš, who never forgave her for defying him and sticking to her creative course, which wasn't *his* course. Kristof walked in just as Aids laid waste to their world, and Eve's quest was over. Domestication, or this bohemian, comparatively well-resourced version of it, came as a relief, with intimacy on tap should she and those hungry hormones require it.

In their early years as a couple, there was still a sexual wildness – a reluctance to accept the conventions of heterosexual pairings. Experimentation was their duty; hasty sex in illicit places, explorations of the outer reaches of fetishism (more comic than erotic, they found). There were affairs too, on both sides. But finally, the needy beast – the monster that demanded instant sexual gratification – seemed to dwindle away. The primacy of work was restored.

Then eight months ago, when most women her age were indulging their grandchildren and packing to go gentle into that good night, the beast was back. He'd been cowering in the shadows all along, lying in wait, and, after two decades, he'd broken free again. But even now, surveying the wreckage, Eve couldn't regret the return of her Lord of Misrule. He arrived just in time, before complacency set in, to shake things up, cast her life in the air and see where it landed. *If* it landed.

5

She looks around the carriage. Another cast change. They're worrying their smartphones or gazing up, unseeing, at the Tube map – lost, like Eve, in reflection. The fallout over the Gerstein show has forced her into a broader retrospective. Yes, if there is any way of measuring her life, her work will have to do.

Fittingly, she started small. For her, so the family story went, it was speedwell: germander speedwell, *Veronica chamaedrys*, bird's eye. Pinpoints of summer sky starring the soft grass beneath her sandalled feet. The child's love of the miniature. She observed it later in her own daughter, though in Nancy's case it wasn't the natural world that entranced her but the artifice of human communities – the doll's house. Nancy would spend hours intervening, rearranging; hers was a Victorian sensibility, drawn to order and propriety.

But it was the secretive, doughty beauty of speedwell that captivated young Eve. The flower was a foreign interloper, from Turkey and the Caucasus, introduced to Britain, she learned later, by those busy collectors of the nineteenth century. *There* was an argument that might

challenge British xenophobes seeking to detach themselves from the wider world in the quest for sovereignty
– look to the English garden, to the cherished flowers of
Albion's cottage beds and borders, and you'll find the case
for diversity and globalisation: roses, peonies, lavender,
hollyhocks, delphiniums – migrants all, making their way
here from Europe, Asia and Africa, enriching the palette
of our pastel Shangri-La.

She sometimes wonders if she was drawn to speedwell in early rebellion; her father, who gardened with
the impersonal zeal of a lab technician, would have been
determined to root out the little flower, which had adapted
so well to English climate and soil that it was reclassified
as a weed, a cerulean stain on the smooth, striped green
Axminster of her father's lawn.

Any drawing she might have done of the flower didn't
survive. She certainly picked it – according to both
parents – and placed it in an eggcup, where she would
have watched it wilt within minutes. A useful life lesson. In
Germany, Florian told her, they call it Männertreu: men's
fidelity. There wasn't, as far as she knew, a Frauertreu,
but if there was, she imagined it would be slow-growing,
lightly rooted, with livid flowers that, once gathered and
placed in a vase, took on the colour of the surrounding
room, all the better to disguise its carnivorous tendencies.

The carriage is filling. Craggy men, Eastern Europeans
and South Asians in dusty clothes stiff as marble drapery,

back from a labourer's late shift; exhausted women, night cleaners, Romanians perhaps, possibly employed in one of Kristof's corporate buildings, gripping plastic supermarket carriers as if they were handbags.

If Nancy were here, she'd make some remark about exploitation and Eve would reply that the migrant workers were making ten times the amount they could make at home and availing themselves of the welfare state while they were at it. London is a city of blow-ins. That's what makes it interesting. Let the English garden flourish. Like thistledown carried on the wind, some fall on fertile ground and thrive, others perish. Nature doesn't discriminate. Why should *she*?

What did her daughter, a gluten-intolerant, humbug-tolerant liberal, want? Her maid, probably an illegal, wasn't paid much more than the minimum wage. Did Nancy want to send them all back? Eve would like to see how she fared without live-in help. These workers voted with their feet. Let them decide.

Eve's aware of her own hypocrisies and is usually untroubled by them. They're part of the texture of her personality, adding tone and depth. Unlike her daughter, she hasn't made a manifesto out of them. But now, roiled by anxiety, the contemplation of personal contradictions seems a calming diversion, like counting sheep. She has a professional interest in preserving the biosphere and a long-standing direct debit to Friends of the Earth, neither of which could ever quite offset the four houses, regular intercontinental travel and the carbon footprint of a small multinational.

Eve sometimes wondered if she could nominate her brother as her private carbon offset scheme. John was a model of anguished virtue, living off-grid in his damp subsistence croft in the West Highlands of Scotland, his quiet asceticism a silent reproach to Eve's clamorous world of abundance and to Nancy's hypocrisy.

Even this post-separation, pre-divorce scaled-down life was pre-revolutionary Versailles to John's anchorite existence. Squinting in candlelight, in his frayed woollens and fingerless gloves, John was always too good for this world. But Nancy? The greedy child became a greedy woman, another proselytising spoiled millennial, an entitled spokeswoman for the wretched of the earth. If that wasn't cultural appropriation, what was?

In her Shoreditch house, a former bookbinder's workshop bought for her by Eve and Kristof, Nancy consumed and expended as diligently as any feckless trust fund kid, the only difference being she favoured Fair Trade labels and small boutiques over big chains, shunned plastic bags and had become an advocate of something called sustainable living. Sustainable, only if your bills were underwritten by parental handouts. She justified her shopping habit by saying it was necessary as research for her work as 'an influencer' and 'lifestyle blogger', for which she put in long hours before a mirror, photographing herself in a succession of indistinguishable outfits.

Plastic bags notwithstanding, Nancy's personal landfill site – taller than any of the Scottish Munros her Uncle John diligently scaled in his northern fastness – would be her legacy. If you seek her monument, look around. Eve acknowledges that, before the separation, she had her own wardrobe full of costly clothes. But she bought selectively and this level of couture qualified as art, referencing or challenging tradition, the product of thought, imagination and skill.

It was, as Florian Kiš taught her, Eve's duty as an artist to treat her body as another medium for aesthetic exploration, to deploy her keen eye in all areas of her life. She had, though she flinches at the term, one of Nancy's favourites, 'a brand' to project. Eve was fortunate enough to have had the means to invest in the pioneering geniuses of the form: the Japanese, Vivienne and Miuccia, the iconic French Houses. There was no equivalence. Nancy was dealing in ephemera and adding to the world's imperishable cargo of tat.

Her dog alone, that ridiculous pug – every pet dog in fact – had a bigger carbon footprint than an SUV. What was the point of it? Unless, as Eve once suggested out of pure mischief, the animal was acquired for what psychologists call 'divisive normalisation' – and less tactful pundits call the 'fat friend factor' – the phenomenon by which people appear more attractive in the company of a less desirable companion. With that bug-eyed midget panting in her arms, even stringy Nancy, with her unfortunate recessive chin, looked like Botticelli's Venus. That was another row that took weeks to get over. After it, Eve began to hold back; it was a waste of breath, this engagement with her daughter. Why speak truth to weakness? Another meltdown would only result in Nancy demanding more sessions with her therapist, and who would pay for that? Now, though, there was no need for candour or discretion. Nancy was blocking her calls. They hadn't spoken in a month. This row was terminal.

The Tube jolts to a halt. Between stations. Always an occasion of anxiety. An accident?

She was old enough to remember the Moorgate crash in the seventies; the driver kept on going, smashing the Tube into the buffers then concertinaing into the terminus wall. More than forty dead. Seventy injured. A school friend's cousin lost both legs in the crash; her colleague died in the seat next to her. Accident or foul play? No one knew. In one account, the usually conscientious driver had suffered some kind of neurological crisis – a catastrophic form of amnesia. The other, more lurid version of the story – favoured, naturally, by the press and stoked by the anguish of the grieving relatives – was that it was a deliberate act of mass murder and suicide, though there was no evidence of motive.

Twelve years later, in 1987, the King's Cross fire seemed personal. She was over from New York with Kristof, who was driving to an evening site meeting in Camden and offered to drop Eve off at the station. She was on her way to Mara's new London place for supper and should have been buying a ticket when the fire, started by a match dropped by a smoker on the wooden escalator, erupted in a flash in the ticket hall, killing thirty and injuring a hundred. What saved Eve that night was her aversion to small children: she had cancelled on Mara, unable to bear the prospect of a conversation dominated by news of potty training and interrupted by infant wails, broadcast over the baby monitor like a tuneless muezzin call to prayer.

Today's risible health and safety culture – Abi, one of Eve's former assistants, was absurdly neurotic about it – at least reduced the likelihood of accidents in public spaces. But these days, accidents weren't the main concern.

Eve looks around the carriage. In this cross section of modern metropolitan diversity, only the super-rich are missing. Everyone is nervously affecting nonchalance in the stillness of the train, while hankering for the safety of the streets above. In such moments of silent urban anxiety, forty metres of compacted chalk and London clay weigh heavily on the Tube traveller.

The carriage rocks into life again and the Tube creeps on to the next stop. Unblown up, Eve's life resumes and she's returned to her thoughts, and to other terrors.

She's made a deadly mess of things. No question. But whatever happens now, whatever horrors lie ahead, her creative legacy is assured. This isn't arrogance; it's fact. What has her daughter done with her life? Reproduction is simple, achieved regularly, without thought or fanfare, by the lowest forms of life. Nematodes – lower than earworms, or those soul-gnawing memory maggots – are adept at it. There's one, at least, born every second. And within three months of the baby's arrival, even Nancy, who anticipated the birth as if it was the Second Coming, with added retail opportunities (that ghastly 'gender-neutral' Baby Shower!), began to seem disenchanted by the project. In that respect, Nancy was her mother's daughter.

For Eve, reproducing the stalked and silent natural world in all its exquisite variations, on paper, vellum, canvas or film, had a stringency, and a controllable outcome, that messy human life could never possess. The earliest of Eve's surviving drawings was of a sprig of cow parsley, *Anthriscus sylvestris* – another weed, though with the paradoxically regal common name of Queen Anne's lace. It was done when she was about twelve, in HB pencil on a sheet of A4 graph paper. The wary toddler had become a self-possessed child, uncomfortable with people, enthralled by nature – particularly plants, whose complications were quietly expressed and knowable – and driven to replicate precisely the natural, non-animal world on the page. Self-sufficient autotrophs, who got their life-sustaining carbon dioxide simply by being, rather than needy heterotrophs, like humans, who had to devour other life to survive – that was the scientific distinction.

She would have been struck initially by the undistinguished presence of cow parsley. Collectively, from a distance, the flower heads were a shimmering haze. Singly, at arm's length, they were barely there, little more than pallidly augmented blades of grass. But Eve always felt impelled to look closer. She admired the complexity of the fern-like leaves, peered into the intricate white constellations on their brittle stems, observed the structural differences between the lacy florets on the outer rim and the minutely delineated flowers at its centre, and marvelled at the hay-scented Milky Way in her hand. You only had to look.

Years later, she was astonished to find that early drawing, folded between the pages of a book – *Down the Garden Path* by Beverley Nichols – when she was clearing the house after her mother died. The discovery was shocking, condemning Eve to replay childhood memories in the unsettling light of this new information: her mother valued her work.

Their relationship was always tense; Eve found her mother's emotional lability mortifying and was enraged by her attempts to persuade her to go to secretarial college rather than to art school. Further education was for boys. John's application to university had their mother's blessing; John always had their mother's blessing. For all the good it did him, it might as well have been her curse – he dropped out of his philosophy course and drifted north to live in a rickety 'peace camp' outside a military base. Eve's later success seemed to baffle rather than please her mother. But she held on to that single childhood drawing, wrapped it in tissue and preserved it in a book on her bedside table. Eve trusted that her mother never knew the other common name for cow parsley – 'mother die'.

Ines Alvaro, the Gerstein curator, fell on this scrap as if it were a lost fragment by da Vinci. Tightly framed in beech, with a cadmium-green mount, it was to be placed in the first room of the exhibition, next to the introductory panel – Eve's life, sanitised and encapsulated in two hundred words of 42pt roman – opposite the wide wall on which her *Underground Florilegium*, borrowed from the Dallas Museum, would hang, and next to the better-preserved watercolour of the crimson-tasselled *Amaranthus caudatus*, love-lies-bleeding, which she completed in her second term at art college.

The museum's explanatory notes would include a rote reference to her as 'muse of Florian Kiš – one of the leading portraitists of the twentieth century', but she had managed to veto use of *Girl with a Flower* anywhere in the show. This would be Eve's retrospective, and also a corrective – she was no mere extra, queuing naked with hundreds of other saps to touch the hem of Florian Kiš's paint-smeared overalls, livid as a butcher's apron. He was a footnote in *her* story.

6

Eve's moment, finally, seemed to have arrived, dovetailing with the fad for ecology among all the social media virtue signallers, her daughter included, who trumpeted their concerns for the planet even as they trashed it. Her work had science on its side, as well as fashionable high-mindedness. Eve outlined the case to the magazine journalist who came to interview her in February.

'One in eight plant species faces extinction while the human population soars,' she said. 'There are new concerns about "plant blindness": as modern humans' view of the world has shrunk to between zero and 15 degrees below eye level, and the anthropocentric focus on the animal world increasingly ignores the importance of vegetal life in the biosphere.'

Though he was diligently taking notes, she could tell she had lost him.

She persevered. 'The human eye seeks movement, conspicuous forms, and unconsciously scans the environment for food, sex – reproductive opportunities – and threat. Static plants, for all their beauty, kaleidoscopic variety and nutritional value, are modest; they aren't cute, they don't require stalking and violence to prepare them for the pot, they don't make great companions and, even in the furthest reaches of human fetishism, they have zero sex appeal.'

The sex appeal line woke him up. He smiled, turned a page in his notebook and continued to write, taking dictation.

'Zoo chauvinism and technophilia have meant that the names of common flowers – bluebell, dandelion – are vanishing from children's dictionaries and making way for words said to reflect contemporary reality – bullet point, voicemail, broadband and blog. How long before the plants themselves vanish from the world?' she said.

'Once the bluebell goes, we all go. After the dandelion, the deluge. Then, as in the wildest dreams of psychopathic loners and murderous ideologues, the whole thing will blow up. We'll be doing their job for them, packing the dynamite, lighting the blue touchpaper and standing back to watch a planetary version of that exploded shed in the Tate. Except we won't be standing back and watching. We'll go up with it.'

Eve always scorned the limitations of the eye-level gaze: she liked to look down, the full 90 degrees, to seek out the discreet and the hidden. In the eyes of her recent champions, her art is a passionate propaganda tool. She doesn't see it like that. Her purpose has always been simply to look, and to reflect, as accurately as she can, in tranquillity. For this she has endured years in the wilderness, been dismissed by critics as 'the Laura Ashley of the art world', and compared to Cicely Mary Barker, spinster illustrator of the saccharine 'Flower Fairies' children's stories. Meanwhile, Wanda Wilson and her cohorts were elevated by those same critics. Not just 'plant blind' but 'art blind'. This is Eve's moment, at last. She'll take it, and they can interpret her intentions whatever way they wish.

Still, the comparisons with Georgia O'Keeffe, as well as Mapplethorpe and Matson, grate, and she can never escape Florian's portrait. Every feature about Kristof, each review and press mention of her own work (including that recent colour supplement interview), is an excuse to reproduce *Girl with a Flower*. It's like being chained to the naked corpse of her dumb teenaged self. Luka had laughed when he pointed out a reference to Eve as 'the flower lady' in a tabloid story about a TV soap star who turned up at the Sigmoid party. Eve was furious. It made her sound like some cockney street seller of posies, an Eliza Doolittle cheerfully offering bunches of violets to passing punters. One of their first rows. Not their last. These passionate storms became more frequent, more intense. But, she tells herself, they were preferable to the temperate civility of her marriage.

The Tube has stopped at Earls Court – marked in her *Underground Florilegium* by a crimson waratah, *Telopea speciosissima*, in acknowledgement of the number of Australians who lived in the area in the seventies.

60

Two labourers wearily get to their feet and leave. Their seats are taken by a middle-aged couple, man and woman. Middle-aged and middle class. They're probably tourists – both wear the parodic British costume of beige raincoats (Burberry knock-offs), deerstalkers and tartan scarves, and they are carrying Madame Tussauds jute bags. What self-respecting Londoner goes to Madame Tussauds? If it weren't for their identical outfits and souvenir bags, you wouldn't guess they were actually together. They scrutinise their phones in silence. At some point, like Eve and Kristof in their early days, they must have been unable to take their hands off each other. What keeps them together now? Children? Grandchildren? Inertia? A shared interest in heritage tourism? The ecology of relationships is always unknowable. The life cycle too, though there's only one outcome. It's doomed, one way or another. Death for those with staying power. Divorce for the fainter of heart, or the courageous, *then* death.

Eve's affair wasn't exactly a *coup de foudre*. She barely noticed Luka when they first met. Perhaps she took in the pleasing symmetry of his face and the self-conscious bohemianism of his style – the tattoo and the utilitarian workwear, livery of all the postgrads and tyro artists who vied for a position at the studio. His apparent shyness was a welcome contrast to the noisy assertiveness of the other assistants; they were always either fighting at work or fucking off duty. Luka just quietly got on with the job

– stretching and sizing canvases, priming them, leaning them against the wall ready for Eve's attention, arranging specimens, mixing paints, cleaning brushes, angling cameras – a silent, muscled paragon of diligence.

Gradually, he made himself indispensable. Eve, who saw herself as uniquely self-reliant, was perplexed and a little thrilled by this new sensation of dependency. The other assistants had, whatever gloss they might put on it, always been labourers – personally demanding and irksome, but necessary for the heavy-lifting required to complete her work. She sometimes enjoyed playing them off against each other, beaming the searchlight of her attention on this one for a day, casting him or her into outer darkness the next.

Some almost became her friends: lanky Glynn, with his paint-stippled overalls and his George V beard; Josette, the quirky drama queen – Billie Holiday with pink hair, a bubbling laugh, and a weight problem. They'd both once had ambitions to be artists themselves, and in her early twenties, Josette featured in the *Observer* colour supplement as one of the promising 'New Generation Minority Artists'. Her silhouette cut-outs with gritty themes – crack addicts in urban wastelands, street violence, non-binary zombies – were compared to the work of the American artist Kara Walker.

Walker was now globally renowned – almost as renowned as Wanda Wilson. But Josette D'Arblay abandoned her own work to become a handmaiden to another artist. Eve never asked about the crisis of confidence that must have been behind Josette's decision to walk away. Was she still working on her paper crafts, thanklessly snipping away in her tiny flat in south-east London? Eve meant to ask, but it always slipped her mind. Glynn was open about his failed career as a sculptor. 'I was crap,' he volunteered to Eve. '*This* is what I'm good at, what gives me pleasure – making order out of chaos. Getting to watch a *real* artist at work and help her achieve her vision.'

They were both devoted to Eve but they bickered – they were gay so at least fucking wasn't an option – and they jostled for her approval. She once took them to Paris for the weekend, for the opening of her exhibition in Rue Casimir Delavigne, and they'd fought like wolverines.

Luka, the quiet boy in the shadows, crept up on Eve. His silence began to intrigue her. He had the face of a young poet – the heroic jaw and tousled hair of Rupert Brooke, the haunted eyes of Rimbaud. He looked sensitive and damaged, running for cover from a world of extroverts, and she felt a curious kinship with him. Even odder, for a woman who openly admitted to scant nurturing urges, she found herself wanting to make things better for him. She silenced the others to give him space to speak, sought him out and gave him interesting tasks, all of which he performed with exemplary rigour. Glynn and Josette, she noticed, began to give him a hard time and soon the boy was the studio pariah, taking lunch on his own outside at one of the canalside benches, a cordon sanitaire cleared around him. Those stupid kids. You'd think they would have worked it out, that she, the artist, a perpetual outsider, would be drawn to the pariah. And now she was one herself.

The night before her Sigmoid *vernissage* in April, Hans arranged a party in the studio to thank the assistants, who'd worked through the previous night to get everything ready in time. Kristof refused to come. 'You don't need me there. The real party's tomorrow night.' For a moment, she considered listing the innumerable dreary work events she'd attended on her husband's behalf, but she had no time for a row. She would go to the studio, raise a glass and smile at the assistants, make her excuses and leave them to get as drunk as they liked at her expense.

The weather was exceptionally warm and the glass doors were open onto the canal. Someone had strung up coloured lanterns round the studio, the sound system was ramped up, a vegan catering company had prepared a spread of salads, and there was a vat of punch, which Josette, wearing a joke-shop tiara, ladled into plastic cups. In the early-spring heatwave, it felt like high summer. Everyone was already a little drunk – Eve knocked back another cup to fortify herself against the evening's social duties.

The noise level was almost intolerable. She watched the boy silently skirting the room. He caught her glance and held it. There seemed to be a question in his returning

gaze. Turning her back on Glynn, who wanted to intro-
duce her to his new boyfriend, Eve walked over to Luka.
She had an urge to put this gauche kid at ease. They
moved together towards the open doors, where it was
quieter, and looked out at the moon reflected in the waxy
sheen of the canal. She asked him where he lived, about
his studies, his work: perfunctory enquiries masking the
big questions – Who are you? What's going on in that
pretty head of yours?

He told her he shared a flat with his sister in Archway.
After a foundation course in Canterbury he'd gone to
Eve's old art college, now part of a new corporate university which makes its money charging exorbitant fees to
overseas students.

'I scraped through then did my dissertation at the
Royal College.'

For the past five years he'd been earning a living
copying Old Masters and Impressionists to order for an
American website.

'The money isn't bad.'

Then he parried with some questions of his own. He
wanted to hear about her time at art college, about New
York in the late seventies and early eighties.

'It's all so tame now,' he said. 'It must have been
amazing to be there then.'

She scanned his face and took in, for the first time, the
full extent of his beauty. How had she missed it? With his
dark curls, pale unblemished skin and cobalt eyes he was

an exquisite St Sebastian. What arrows had pierced that perfect torso?

'And Florian Kiš? One of the greats,' he continued. 'What was he really like?'

She tensed. Her assistants, all her circle, knew better than to mention Kiš's name. Normally, when it came up, she would walk away. But her inquisitor was an innocent so she smiled, ignored his question and asked him the subject of his dissertation – she might have been interviewing him for a job. He hesitated, drained his drink and lowered his eyes, modest as a Pre-Raphaelite maiden. She pressed him and he sighed, lifted his chin and looked at her, full-on, before giving his answer.

'You,' he said.

Someone turned up the volume on the sound system and there were ragged outbreaks of dancing. Josette came around with more drinks and shot a hostile glance at Luka. Hans had already said his goodbyes and left. Normally, this would be the cue for Eve to head slyly for the exit and get a taxi back to Delaunay Gardens. Instead, she heard herself asking: 'Aren't you going to dance?'

'I hate dancing,' he said.

'Me too.'

She grabbed his hand and led him through the crowd to the centre of the studio. There, lost in the throng, they embraced, and it pleased her to see him laugh as they swayed satirically to cheesy Europop. Someone passed him a joint. As he inhaled, a slow smile spread across his face. He held his breath for twenty seconds then blew out the smoke and passed the joint to her. She drew on it deeply – she hadn't smoked cannabis in two decades but to refuse would have been prissy. She sensed some amused glances around them. To hell with propriety.

The music changed. Some awful hip hop. They disengaged. How were you meant to dance to this? She tried to mirror his moves, simple side steps, swaying hips, pumping arms, following the pulse of the bass. For two non-dancers, they weren't bad. The cannabis – bred for potency these days – may have had something to do with it. She and Luka were in perfect sync. They looked at each other and laughed again. Swirling strings announced a slow ballad – who chose this music? – and they were in each other's arms again. His tensile warmth was a current coursing through her body. He held her gently at the hips. Did she imagine the extra pressure – the ghost of a grope? Time expanded, then folded in on itself. The music speeded up, the party raged on. But for Eve, it seemed that she and Luka were alone, vacuum-sealed, two cosmonauts spinning through uncharted space.

Sometime later, she sensed the room was emptying; there were shouted goodbyes, outbursts of laughter trailing off into the distance, the door opened, casting a rhombus of light across the floor, then closed, and finally the music stopped. When she and Luka disengaged, they were alone and the sun was beginning to rise, casting a brassy glaze over the canal.

They hurriedly left the studio in its post-party disarray and locked up, barely able to look at each other. Josette and Glynn would be back to deal with the mess later. Eve called a cab to take her home and Luka turned away and walked towards the bus stop. Their farewell was awkward and hasty. They didn't even kiss, though she was usually adept at the affection-free social embrace. In the dawn light, the night's mystery evaporated. She was the employer, a woman of means and status, and he was her employee. Only in his youth did he have the advantage. On that scale, he was a feudal lord in silks and lace, surveying the pleasures of his vast estate, and she was a serf, toiling in rags on her diminishing smallholding.

7

The Tube has stalled again, the lights flicker, and a noisy crowd of young people stumble through the connecting door into her carriage. Three of them are wearing red caps trimmed with white fur – Santa hats. Drunk or stoned, or both, they look around, laughing, assuming their hilarity is shared. These days, not everyone observes the rules of Tube etiquette; silence, eyes averted, and in the press of rush hour, body against body, the shared pretence that boundaries remain intact and you are in this alone.

Eye contact with the grinning boobies must be avoided. Eve opens her bag and takes out a book as cover – Wanda's book, with its taunting inscription, unopened since last month's exhibition. There are other young people in the carriage, gazing at their phones or staring ahead, pretending to be absorbed in their thoughts. Let the revellers draw *them* in. Who would want to engage with an unremarkable woman on the brink of old age, swathed in soft-hued winter clothing, staring at a book, lost in her past?

Wanda – now here's an occasion for bitter laughter. There she is, in a collage of photographs, in various states of phoney self-abasement, on the subject of love:

'In the absence of the love object, I cut myself to reinforce and sanctify the pain of loss …'

'I shave my head in a ritual akin to that undertaken by those seeking admission to holy orders, a postulant nun, dedicating her life to art, transcending the limited possibilities of womanhood; love object, whore, mother, crone. My physical renunciation begins …'

'With fire – branding – and water – submersion – the transition is final and I move away from the earthly and on to the spiritual plain …'

Hogwash. It was a toxic combination – masochism and grandiosity. The plain fact was that men, even the sadists, could never stand Wanda and her neuroses for long. It wasn't simply Eve's talent that rankled with Wanda but her success with men. Was it Eve's fault that she had romped, feted and unscathed, through the carnival and that, when the music finally stopped and the party was over, she left the scene on the arm of a handsome Dane who was destined for success?

Unlike Wanda, Eve never 'got off', as the phrase went, on pain. Wisely, at a time when wisdom wasn't at a premium, Eve intuited that there would be enough agony down the line, not necessarily physical and not all of it connected to love. After the bracing interlude with Florian, pleasure became Eve's guiding principle. Work and pleasure. Only now did she see that while she stayed true to the work, even as family life conspired to divert her from it, the pleasure principle was forgotten. It had taken the boy, and the ensuing cataclysm, to return her to herself.

By the time she got home after the studio party, the sun was above the trees in Delaunay Gardens. She slipped into bed alongside her gently snoring husband and lay awake, exultant, keenly alert, thinking of the evening, and of Luka, the lightning strike of that first glance, then the embrace that seemed to promise more, thinking of how the evening might have ended if she'd been bolder. It was thrilling and preposterous. To those young people whooping and smirking opposite her on the Tube tonight, it would be grotesque. She was a sixty-year-old woman. A grandmother. He was thirty. She had made a complete fool of herself. Had her drink been spiked? They were a druggy lot, some of her assistants.

The Tube train Santas and their friends have quietened down, chastened by the silence of the other passengers. She puts Wanda's wretched book away. She no longer needs a prop.

Eve tries to remember the last time she'd felt that physical need. By her mid-fifties, it seemed that her recently fitful inner fire had finally died and, after a period of mourning, she came to see it as liberation rather than loss. Let work at last be her sole passion. Yet there she was, eight months ago, lying in her marital bed feeling the old hunger, crazily consumed by it, touching herself at the thought of a boy who was younger than her daughter.

Perhaps the cold hearth was Kristof's all along. Sexual indifference seemed mutual. She thought of a sign she once saw outside a village hall in Wales: 'Ukulele classes – Discontinued due to lack of interest.'

At first, they sought medical advice: unguents for her, small blue pills – Viagra – for him. It worked, for a while. Then, as with shared undertakings to new exercise regimes – biweekly Pilates, high-intensity training – their resolve fell away.

She remembers listening to a radio programme in which a woman in her nineties described a conversation she'd overheard as a girl. Her mother and her aunt, in their forties, were talking about a mutual friend of their own age.

'She doesn't go to parties any more. She's given up dancing,' the mother said.

In the pomp of girlhood, the eavesdropper shuddered and thought: 'If I ever give up dancing, kill me, because I might as well be dead.'

And now, sitting immobile in her retirement home – her walking days, as well as her dancing days, long behind her – the old woman reflected that, in the end, it hadn't been so difficult to give up youthful pleasures. 'Nature can be kind,' she said, 'and it reconciles us to loss.' When creaky hips and knees banish us from the dance floor, we look on as wallflowers and find the hectic capering faintly absurd. So it was with Eve and sex. Then she met Luka.

That morning, Kristof began to stir from sleep. He stretched his long limbs, grey and slack as a corpse in a Cranach pietà, softly grunted and, as usual, left the bed without checking whether she was awake. If he'd bothered, he would have been surprised by her sudden need. When was the last time? As he closed the bathroom door, she shrugged herself further under the duvet and closed her eyes, her consoling hand still between her thighs. Then she slept. By the time she finally woke, her husband had left for work.

They were to reconvene as a family at the opening of her Sigmoid show that night. Nancy was coming with her husband, Norbert, an earnest, woolly-bearded entrepreneur from the Netherlands who ran a technology start-up, 'providing integration points for platform-enabled websites', the purpose of which, even after three years, Eve had never quite discerned. When does a start-up cease to be a start-up? At what point, she had resisted asking her son-in-law, would it be sufficiently self-financing to enable her and Kristof to end their subsidy? Would Norbert's company then become a carry-on? And if it failed, what would they call it?

Nancy and Norbert were leaving the baby at home with the couple's 'help', their term for the low-paid

Sri Lankan woman who cooked, cleaned and 'walked' the pug – insofar as the hideous creature ever waddled anywhere – and looked after little Jarleth for them. Since her teens, Nancy had reproached her mother for the crime of neglect, largely because Eve had availed herself of regular childcare. By this calculation, Nancy and Norbert were arch-criminals too.

At least Eve had delegated the child to concentrate on work. Nancy saw herself as a countercultural warrior but chose to live like a fifties suburban housewife, abandoning her fledgling career in magazine journalism for married life, motherhood, homemaking and – the twenty-first-century twist – blogging. What else would Nancy have to write about in her blog but married life, motherhood and homemaking, particularly if it involved shopping? Online, Nancy was silent on the subject of her other occupation – full-time victim with a borderline eating disorder, engaged in weekly therapy (paid for by Eve and Kristof), and hooked on antidepressants. Offline, in the company of her parents, Nancy talked about little else.

Her recent, definitive sulk was, in many ways, a blessing. How seductive was the narrative of the perpetual injured party. 'Look how I suffer!' 'Someone did this to me!' Political movements, entire national narratives, were built on this premise. Nancy's bespoke version had a narrower focus. Eve tried talking to her, when they were still talking: We are given the materials to make an artwork of our lives. What we do with them is up to us – a

Goya masterpiece of light and shade? a Dürer engraving of fabulous complexity? or some lightly incised graffiti on a lavatory wall? You choose. She might as well have been talking to Nancy's pug.

Eve's opening at the Sigmoid that night should have felt like a triumph. Instead, it was a distraction: the dressing-up, the limo, the champagne, the throng of cultural dignitaries, the press. There was some satisfaction in the social reversal. Once, these titans of the art world would have looked over her shoulder to seek out Kristof. Now they queued to shake her hand, while she looked over their shoulders for a glimpse of the boy.

Kristof knew them all and glided through the crowd, drink in hand, smiling and nodding, a sharp-suited, vulpine version of a plastic dashboard dog. This was his medium, not hers. He greeted them – arts bureaucrats, sponsors, journalists, artists, architects, finance types, actors, models and pop stars with intellectual aspirations – as if they were old friends coming to lend personal support to the exhibition. As if, in fact, this was *his* exhibition.

She was under no illusion. They came not to celebrate *Foundlings – an Urban Florilegium*, the culmination of a two-year exploration of London's wayside and wasteland plants, and her recent giant hippeastrum canvas. Nor were they there to laud, in her sixty-first year, her lifetime's labours. They turned up because there were worse ways to spend an exceptionally warm spring evening than drinking icy champagne at a fashionable party in Hyde Park. Behind the public congratulations was private scepticism – the dagger concealed in the firmest handshakes. 'How does she get away with it?' It was a question Eve often asked of herself. Her confidence wasn't boosted by the fact that the venue for her exhibition was offered after Kristof agreed to design a satellite gallery for the Sigmoid in Shanghai.

As a young woman, Eve had the edge on talent and on sexual attractiveness, but in creative self-belief Wanda always took the prize, even as a student. The galleries, duped by Wanda's arrogance, competed for the chance to host her travesties. It had been one long round of awards and honours for her ever since. Where did it come from – Wanda's effrontery and Eve's self-doubt? Nature or nurture? Florian's scepticism about Eve's work had undermined a confidence that was always fragile. She feared the public exposure craved by Wanda. While Eve wanted recognition – what artist doesn't? – she hated scrutiny. This show was said to be the pinnacle of her career – *her* night, as everyone kept telling her. Others in her position would have preened. But she'd always been ill at ease at these events. She walked the room, running the gauntlet of goodwill, deflecting plaudits, yearning for the real thing. For connection. Where was Luka?

At last, she glimpsed him in the corner of the gallery by the drinks table and made her way towards him. Nancy intercepted her.

'Congratulations, Mama!' She kissed Eve on the cheek and reached for her hand. 'You've really done it!'

Nancy's hand was cold and her nails were lacquered a sickly stone grey. What was she wearing? Yellow had never suited her – it gave her a jaundiced cast.

'Thanks, darling.'

Eve slipped from her daughter's grasp. By the time she reached the drinks table, Luka had vanished.

Hans appeared and together they posed for a press photographer. At least her dealer didn't gush.

'Solokoff is here.' He pointed towards the Russian energy magnate, a bluff, bearish figure known for his contemporary art collection and his taste for young lingerie models. 'You must meet him.'

'Must I?'

The Russian gripped her hand and smiled, flashing a set of iridescent veneers.

'Very nice,' he said, indicating, with a tilt of his chin, her oil painting of four stems of shaggy golden *Taraxacum* – dandelions – hovering next to the ghostly globes of their seed heads.

He was with two lanky girls, anorexic by the look of them, barely out of their teens, skinny calves taut in heels that seemed longer than their skirts.

Eve thanked him and walked away, leaving Hans to talk to him. All she wanted was a sight of the boy. The noise of the crowd was oppressive. No one was looking at the pictures, and the video booth, whose set-up had involved days of tantrums from Glynn and Josette, was empty. The life cycle of *Chamaenerion angustifolium*, rosebay willowherb, from wind-borne seed to flowering spire, was playing, unobserved, on repeat.

Glynn and Josette rushed over to greet Eve with an overfamiliarity which suggested they were all in on some shared joke, or, worse, that *she* was the shared joke. They would have seen her dancing with Luka the previous night and must have found the spectacle ridiculous.

Glynn was a roving Jackson Pollock in his paint-spattered overalls while Josette was wearing can-do denim dungarees and a Rosie the Riveter turban. 'We are workers in the service of art,' their costumes declared.

Eve dismissed them with a remark about an unsatisfactory juxtaposition in the hanging. 'Buddleia next to lilac? I thought I said that was a no-no?'

They hurried away to deal with it.

Then she saw him, talking to a waiter by the door. Ignoring greetings on all sides, she pressed on through the crowd. Luka turned to her and smiled. He seemed limned in gold, dazzling among the dull, homogenous crowd. A Greek icon set in a Lowry street scene.

'Fantastic!' he said. His eyes reflected the light of the setting sun streaming through the windows.

'You like it?'

'Amazing!'

Hans was back, grabbing her arm, trying to pull her away. She shrugged him off.

'Later …' she said, keeping her eyes fixed on Luka.

He was wearing a faded tuxedo with a pristine white collarless shirt – a Singer Sargent Endymion in Converse sneakers. She was touched that he'd made an effort to dress up for the evening, unlike Glynn and Josette. His tuxedo – probably a charity-shop find – was slightly too big and gave him a louche vulnerability.

'What do you like best?' she asked him.

'All of it,' he said.

She needed to keep him there, to keep him talking so she could feast on him. A waitress came between them with a tray of canapés. Eve shook her head impatiently and the girl shrank away.

'Did you get back okay last night?' asked Eve.

A stupid question. He'd clearly got back all right.

'Yes. Kind of. There were no buses so I walked most of the way. Is that Richard Rogers? Talking to Nick Serota and Timor Heschel from the Alt Gallerie?'

She sensed his awkwardness. He was out of his depth.

There was a tap on her shoulder. It was Ines Alvaro from the Gerstein, her small face tight and beseeching.

'Eve! I'd really like for you to meet some of our most important patrons. This is Mr and Mrs Wennacker …'

'Not now, Ines,' said Eve. She turned back to Luka. She wanted to stay on the subject of last night. 'It was so late, wasn't it?'

He smiled. 'Yeah. I didn't realise the time until we left the studio. Amazing party.'

Then Hans and Kristof were upon her – a pincer move-ment – and guided her away.

'You must meet the mayor,' said Kristof. 'He's just about to leave.'

She looked back towards Luka, who smiled and nodded a farewell. Then he was gone.

8

The young man sitting diagonally opposite her on the Tube is dark-eyed and tawny-skinned, with the black beard and erect bearing of a Velázquez knight. He has planted a large rucksack between his trainer-shod feet. Her pulse falters. In her youth, such a sight would have had no meaning for her, and at a time when pubs and department stores, as well as Tube stations, were targets for bombers, it was the Irish who were in the frame; an innocent bystander with a telling accent, the wrong religious affiliation and a Hibernian name could be arrested, tortured and handed a life sentence. Terrorism makes racists of us all. Racists and juvenophobes.

She stares at the sinister bulk of the rucksack. The worst outcome – blinding flash then annihilation – would have the advantage of being quick. Survival with 'life-changing' injuries, that dreadful circumlocution, would be insupportable. She talks herself down. He's probably a student doctor, carrying his textbooks. She's no racist, Eve assures herself – whatever Nancy might say – and she doesn't share the automatic hostility of the old towards the young. It might have been better for her if she did.

She thinks again of another young man, pale-skinned, equally beautiful, lying waiting for her tonight, fifteen miles across town.

There was a thrilling inevitability about it. She didn't so much stumble towards the precipice as run at it and hurl herself over. After the Sigmoid show opened, the freelance assistants were no longer needed. Only her permanent staff, Josette and Glynn, remained.

But Eve told them that she wanted to keep Luka on – 'the tall, quiet boy' – for a while.

'He's a good worker. No trouble,' she said.

Then she arranged to send Josette and Glynn to New York to liaise with Ines Alvaro.

They resisted: 'How will you manage without us?'

How indeed. But the lure of an all-expenses-paid trip trumped their sense of duty and she was left alone in the studio with Luka.

For two days, over the May bank holiday weekend, she worked with him on an oil commissioned by Solokoff – a spray of camomile, national flower of Russia, suspended against an azure background. She resented the work and resented Hans for persuading her to take it on, as a project to tide her over once her exhibition opened. It seemed like treading water, and she was glad that this empty, formal study was going to disappear into a private collection.

The work was of no interest, but her assistant was. Luka referred to the painting as 'the daisy work', and she didn't contradict him. As she delineated the petals with zinc white and stippled the feathery leaves in phthalo green, he worked beside her diligently, deepening the blue background with intense cobalt at the edges of the canvas. His hand was steady and his brushstrokes were swift and efficient – his time spent turning out copies of Old Masters had not been wasted.

They talked only rarely as they worked and the silence between them echoed in the empty studio. Sometimes, she found it unbearable. Her centre of gravity seemed to have shifted to her groin and she could think of nothing but that ache of need. She wanted to put down her brush, give up this pretence of work and ask him to retreat with her – now! – to the bedroom. Only the fear of his refusal, of making herself look ridiculous, stopped her. Then she would put on music, jazz or baroque, at full volume to distract herself. Their late-evening farewells were constrained as he headed towards north London and she to Delaunay Gardens. It was as if that night of playful wonder on the eve of the Sigmoid opening had never happened.

The third night – after their last day alone – they worked until eleven, when she arranged a delivery from a local Indian restaurant. She found a bottle of good red, left by Hans more than a year ago, dimmed the studio lights and lit a couple of candles. In the wavering flames, Luka was a brooding, chiaroscuro Caravaggio, poised over the glinting foil cartons.

They forked curry desultorily (too oily, too spicy, they weren't hungry anyway) and talked on in the half-light. She asked the questions and he answered.

The flat he shared with his younger sister, Belle, in Archway was a rented basement.

'It's too small. It's all we can afford. We're driving each other crazy.'

Belle, another fine arts graduate, had won a prestigious scholarship to study in the States last year.

'She's just back, doing a temporary job in promotion and arts marketing, and she's impatient with my lack of focus,' he said.

Eve had no interest in his sister's career plans but she was happy to let Luka talk. This confiding mood might be a prelude to a more profound unburdening.

'She's driven,' he told her. 'Ambitious. A born networker. She'll end up marrying some rich old bloke to subsidise her art and keep her in style. But I don't want that kind of life. Trouble is, five years on from leaving college, I still don't know what kind of life I *do* want. The copying job brings in enough money to keep me going. So, I'm Matisse one week, Constable the next. I finished another *Haywain* at the weekend!' He laughed. The wine was making him expansive. 'Once, I thought I'd be an artist myself but now I know I don't have the talent to make it. Technique isn't enough. You need ideas.'

She poured another glass for him. 'What do you *really* want? What gives you pleasure?'

'I guess I'm just happy hanging around, waiting for inspiration.'

'What about a more permanent position in the studio? Would that inspire you?'

He put down his fork.

'What? Here?'

She nodded.

'With you? Sure!' He grinned.

'Only,' Eve said, meeting his smile with her own, 'I'm in a state of flux myself. I've got to make some changes round here.'

She'd set it all up but it had to be initiated by him; she needed that small corner of self-respect. How could she know that her self-respect would be making its farewell appearance that evening? They clinked glasses, sealing the deal, drained the last of the wine and fell silent. Then he reached across for her hand. That was the only cue she needed. Within minutes they were making their way towards bed.

That morning, while he'd worked at the canvas, she had rearranged the bedroom with the attention of a set designer: fresh linen, flowers – a jar of blowsy peonies – a tuberose candle. She'd prepared herself too – the extra shower, the buttressed silk underwear from the French atelier, the scent – anxious about presenting her sixty-year-old body to this beautiful boy. Even as she hurried like a housemaid to get everything ready, she knew she must steel herself for humiliation.

Over the years, she had worked to keep herself in shape. The studio gym was part of her daily programme. An hour alone on the machines cleared her head. It also, with regular bouts of fasting, slowed the spread and droop of flesh. Slowed, but didn't halt. Her hair was dyed every six weeks at a Belgravia salon – her daughter had more grey hairs than she did – and each morning and evening she massaged some expensive cream, derived from crushed slugs, into her face. But nothing could convincingly smooth and reinflate ageing skin, elevate breasts and butt, erase veins livid as a drunk tattooist's scrawl and eliminate the mutilating snail-trail scar of a C-section.

Cosmetic surgery inflicted its own disfigurements. Several acquaintances had submitted, with mixed results. Mireille Porte had changed her name to Orlan and turned her surgical addiction into performance art. Wanda had signed up too, as evidenced by the photos. Eve wasn't impressed. They all looked related, these plastic surgery addicts – like close family members who'd suffered burns in a house fire and undergone reconstructive surgery at the hands of the same bungling amateur. Now Wanda, after all that expense and pain, simply looked like a fat burns victim. An old, fat burns victim.

Eve was an artist. She knew how tricky it was to get the line right, how once you'd committed to paint, erasure was more difficult; how much harder it would be to correct mistakes – a clumsy slip, a miscalculation – when your medium was flesh. Why would she place her delicate physical carapace in the care of the surgical equivalent of a cack-handed Sunday painter? If Michelangelo were to open a Harley Street consultancy she might reconsider. Until then, lighting would be her cosmetician. Lighting, and good red wine, for subject as well as spectator.

All this anxiety, she realised, was an amplified echo, resounding down the decades, of that tremor of insecurity she always felt, despite her sexual confidence, before she went to bed with a lover for the first time. Then, the final tumble into bed, after whatever complex preliminaries and spasms of self-doubt, was inevitable. Now, it was far from a foregone conclusion. Only the self-doubt was certain.

A sudden flurry of pale pink in her peripheral vision draws her attention down the carriage. It's that old-fashioned, self-important gesture of newspaper page-turning. Big broadsheet pages, unwieldy as a duvet cover. The *Financial Times*. Its rosy hue, these straitened days, could be a guilty blush.

He's the only passenger in the carriage reading a paper. He must be a City worker or, as they call it now, a financial services employee. Fifty years ago, his counterpart would have worn a pinstriped suit and a bowler hat. This one has a tattooed dragon snaking above the collar of his loden coat.

They are all tattooed now. The hand that took hers that first night had the inky outline of a small grinning skull, a Mexican Day of the Dead calavera, with a tiny stylised flower between the eye sockets, etched between his thumb and forefinger. Luka pulled her towards him, leaned in and kissed her. Only then was she free to lead him across the studio into the bedroom. There was no haste, but there was no hesitation either.

The lights were on their lowest, warmest setting and she didn't look at him as she undressed, hoping he would return the favour. She pulled back the duvet, slipped beneath it and quickly drew it up to her neck, as if she was cold. He was seconds behind her. They laughed uneasily.

She closed her eyes as, with trembling fingers, they tentatively explored unfamiliar flesh. Gradually mutual self-consciousness yielded to a rapt awareness of the other. His skin was a marvel of warmth and softness, taut yet yielding over the swell of muscle. The hunger was back and only he could sate it. It had been so long yet it was all so familiar – the sweet agony of need and the sublime relief of surrender.

The following morning, they showered together, all inhibitions gone, and as the hot stream beat down on them, he knelt and kissed her scar.

Glynn and Josette, fresh off the plane and full of vicarious New York energy, were already at work, stretching a canvas. Eve felt a pulse of warmth towards them. If they knew what was going on when Eve and Luka emerged from the studio living quarters, they were circumspect. After their presumptuousness at the Sigmoid party, the shutters had come down again. No further reference was made to the wild night at the studio. Their practised cool had its advantages.

They all worked well together that day although, as the hours passed, jet lag set in for Josette and Glynn and they became unusually quiet. Glynn put some John Cage on the sound system – a piano solo, 'In a Landscape' – and its tidal reflectiveness, waves of notes tumbling and receding, seemed apt, a series of beautiful questions posed and almost answered, again and again.

While Eve stippled cadmium yellow at the centre of Solokoff's camomile, Josette and Glynn imposed some order in the studio and Luka unpacked new deliveries from Latin America – flesh-eating cobra lilies, their curled leaves rising like snakes poised to strike their prey. At Ines Alvaro's suggestion, Eve was preparing a multi-media addendum to her early New York carnivorous work for the Gerstein show. She was through with damned daisies.

She watched Luka surreptitiously as he stacked the plants in the fridge. That beautiful body, flexing and stretching, had flexed and stretched for her. Those hands, tearing at packaging then gently cradling the bloated flower heads, moved so decisively and tenderly over her and would do so again. In the studio over the next week Glynn would dissect the lilies, she would paint their parts, Josette would film the process, and Luka would be there, her ministering angel, bestowing grace and light on the whole project. A new project for a new life.

But how would it work, this new life? There was the inconvenient matter of the old one. Easier to postpone difficult questions and respond to the call of the body. She and Luka exchanged furtive glances weighted with longing, but they had no time alone together during this first day. As evening fell, Josette and Glynn packed up to go and Eve looked across at Luka expectantly – how would they arrange this? He smiled back and she watched, with a sudden billowing confusion, as he began to gather his own belongings and walk towards the door. He was leaving too. There was no time or privacy for an explanation. She couldn't put Glynn and Josette's discretion to the test by asking him directly. What was he doing? Where he was going? Why?

At the door, standing with his colleagues, he answered one of her unspoken questions: he was going back to Archway, he said, in a voice that seemed a little too loud to be casual. The cruel message was as much for his colleagues' ears as for Eve's.

She watched him leave and her desolation was total. She felt like weeping. Like screaming. Instead she went to the kitchen and poured herself a glass of wine. She couldn't bear to go into the bedroom, to look at the scene of last night's bliss-filled abandonment, transformed to a seedy site of betrayal. She'd been deluded and she hated herself for it. The boy had been playing with her, idling away the time, of which he had an abundance. It meant nothing to him. She threw the wine down the sink, called a cab, put out the studio lights and returned to Delaunay Gardens.

9

The Tube slows to a halt – between stations, again – and again the lights flicker. We're always seconds, inches, away from total breakdown but if we dwelt on it we'd never get out of bed: why bother with that strenuous interlude – the demanding middleman – between birth and death?

A swaying figure looms in her peripheral vision then sits down heavily next to her; another breach of etiquette on a comparatively uncrowded train. There are three empty seats further down the carriage. Why couldn't he sit there? He's about her age, with the profile of a dissipated Roman noble, shabbily dressed in a frayed moleskin jacket and stained slacks. Once he might have been handsome but tonight he's a ruin of a man. He smells strongly of drink – whisky, she guesses – and he gazes, abject, at his feet in their battered brogues. The evil imps of age and alcohol have done their work. Suddenly he slumps sideways, resting his head on her shoulder and, for a second, they are a Gillray caricature of companionable dereliction. She jumps up, horrified, and moves further along to one of the empty seats.

She looks back down the carriage and sees he's now sunk further in his stupor and hasn't noticed her leaving. What misery is he anaesthetising himself against? The lost jobs, failed marriages, estranged children, vanished dignity. She should feel some kinship but she's repelled.

Even in the more rule-bound days of her youth, she has to acknowledge, there were daily transgressors. The old are prone to golden-age delusions and the tendency needs to be watched. It's another trick of the light – those days were gilded by nothing more than the reminiscer's youth. In the sixties and seventies, in rush-hour carriages murky with tobacco smoke, few women Tube travellers under thirty could escape a journey without some stranger slyly squeezing their buttocks or cupping their breasts. Today, faced with the same opportunist gropers, Nancy's lot would be calling their lawyers, venting on social media and embarking on ten years of therapy.

Eve's gaze falls on the elderly couple opposite. She has to watch that designation – elderly – too. One person's old age is another's prime. They're probably in their mid-seventies, a mere fifteen years older than her – half the age gap between her and Luka. They smile at her sympathetically; they must have witnessed the scene with the drunk. Dressed in hikers' fluorescent waterproofs and orthopaedic shoes, they're holding programmes, large and garish as pizza menus, for a West End musical. There was another thing Eve and Kristof had in common – they couldn't bear musicals.

The couple weave swollen-knuckled fingers to link hands. They've made it through; their marriage a steady ship chugging through calm waters. These ancient mariners never dared the high seas. But what does she know?

Hers wasn't a bad marriage. She and Kristof had what was known as a 'strong' union. They weathered standard difficulties and indiscretions over the years. Kristof was a child of the sixties, able to recall marijuana-infused days in a Venice Beach bungalow with Tibetan mandalas on the wall, Hindu prayer mats on the floor, and the Doors' portentous anthems booming from the hi-fi. Eve came of age in the seventies, when interior design and music took a more dystopian turn. But for both of them in their youth, in their different countercultural circles, the slogan 'property is theft' had currency. 'Property' included any claim on another person: loyalty, honesty, even the expectation that they might turn up at an agreed time and place. Stephen Stills' lyric, 'If you can't be with the one you love, love the one you're with', was the soundtrack to many light liaisons, before and after marriage.

When property ceased to be theft – Kristof turned out to have a genius for acquiring, designing, renovating and reselling it at profit – sex was, at least in their first torrid decade together, still up for grabs, however constrained by new precautions in those plague-ridden days. It was rarely about the other, this wild reel with interchangeable partners; more an interior journey and a means of self-discovery – a high-intensity programme of masturbation in company.

As a couple, they reconciled themselves calmly to material acquisition but they held out on formal marriage. Then one afternoon, ten years after they first met, following too many drinks at a West Village restaurant, a mad impulse saw them paying a few dollars for a wedding licence. The next day, animated by a sense of irony, they were married at City Hall.

Kristof's affairs were more numerous than hers, which from this distance seemed retaliatory workouts – effortful, sweaty and repetitive – bringing little satisfaction in the way of vengeance. Back in London, she was thrown by his fling with Mara. Eve arrived home in Delaunay Gardens a day early from the Venice Biennale and surprised the pair in the marital bed. She left the house without saying a word, returning in the evening once Mara had gone. After a spell of tight-lipped 'mature discussion', some manoeuvring, and an excruciating tit-for-tat weekend in Rome with Mara's then husband, a garrulous, good-looking 'society naturopath' who couldn't believe his luck, Eve managed to keep her poise and preserve her marriage, as well as her relationship with Mara, whose own marriage didn't survive the fallout. Eve felt a degree of schadenfreude when her friend came weeping with news of the naturopath's defection. But really, Eve had done her a favour so it hardly counted as retribution. More satisfyingly, three years later, on the best-eaten-cold principle, she exacted exquisite revenge, deploying a long-range guided missile on the complacency of her treacherous friend. Now, finally, they were even.

Kristof's interludes were mostly with low-status young women from the office – easy come, easy go – though it was a dalliance with an au pair that nearly broke their marriage for good. Once it was out in the open, it was clear that Elena could no longer work at the house. Kristof was obsessed with her: striking and sinewy with dark corkscrew curls and lapis lazuli eyes. He wouldn't give her up. Kristof even invoked the sixties by proposing a threesome.

'We don't have to be bound by the old rules,' he said. 'Why can't it work? I love her ... I love you ... You love me ...'

'Don't count on it,' Eve replied.

A job was found for the girl in a local nursery and Kristof paid the deposit on a rented flat near the park. For a month, he operated by his self-devised new rules, shuttling between two women. At Delaunay Gardens, Eve, quietly simmering, insisted that he sleep in the attic guest room. In silence, she took stock. She loathed hapless Elena, she loathed Kristof, and she entertained murderous fantasies – she would let herself into the flat with a stolen key and lay slow and methodical waste to them both with a scalpel. She'd start with that Medusa hair and go on from there, setting them out like two plants on her dissecting table, stripping them down to stalk and pith.

She did nothing, said nothing and sat it out. There was always the nagging sense that her fury was just a touch bourgeois. Couldn't she be more French about it? If she wanted to keep her marriage, and her life, wasn't this how it had to be? It was, though, a close-run thing and she confided in Mara, seeking a recommendation for a divorce lawyer. Mara, of all people, knew the score – she'd done rather well out of her own divorce from the numbskull naturopath – and it was pleasing to see her beginning to run to fat, miserably alone and puffed up with jealous indignation at the news that this lightweight girl had captivated Kristof, the former lover who'd discarded her so lightly.

Eve finally booked an appointment with a solicitor in Lincoln's Inn. But then Elena undid the affair all by herself by turning up at Delaunay Gardens after midnight, hammering on the door, pleading and railing. Kristof's new rules weren't working out for her either. She'd missed the sixties by several decades and was too young for 'mature discussion'. Kristof was her man, her property, and she'd come to claim him. She matched and magnified Kristof's sexual obsession, venting the fury of a *bambina viziata*, unable to accept that she couldn't have her way. Neighbours were woken, the police were called. Kristof, horrified, bought her a one-way ticket back to Bologna. She was never spoken of again. Only Nancy missed her. Given Elena's pathological immaturity, it was hardly surprising she'd been so adept at childcare.

What doesn't kill us makes us stronger — one of the insufferable platitudes Mara used to invoke. The affair with Elena certainly stiffened the heart. But Eve's marriage was more than a fragile fortress constructed from error piled on forgiveness, or forgetfulness, piled on error. It wasn't simply an alliance of convenience. The little lies, honed during those affairs, were grace notes – disgrace notes – ornamenting the simple melody of their union. They got on, Eve and Kristof. They were alike. They shared a love of order and disdain for mess – emotional and otherwise. Their interests overlapped: art, naturally; mid-century design; jazz; opera. They had that querulous daughter, with her constant needs, in common too. Then there were the friends, the houses, the paintings and sculptures, the holidays. How could you even begin to unpick all that?

It proved to be easier than Eve could ever have imagined: she tugged at one thread and the whole tapestry unravelled.

But, eight months ago, on the cab ride home to Delaunay Gardens, tortured by the thought that Luka had walked out on her after one miraculous night, she counted up the virtues of her marriage like an old nun telling her rosary beads.

She couldn't give up the boy. But he had given up on her. And so soon. She had thought the night's pleasures were reciprocal. The morning kiss in the shower seemed to seal it. He didn't have to do that. If he was dissembling, he was a master of deception. But then, how could she be so foolish as to believe that a beautiful boy – from her perspective, he was still, at thirty, a boy – should feel desire for a woman of her age? His arousal, though – he couldn't have faked that. She felt feverish, oscillating between rapt memories of the night and the racking certainty that Luka had gone from her life as suddenly as he'd arrived. It was as if she'd stumbled across a remarkable new pigment, not a blend of old familiar hues but a unique and blinding primary glow that suffused the world, illuminating its darkest corners. And now, a switch had been flipped, every colour had drained away and, like an old movie, life would have to spool on in black and white.

The cab pulled up in Delaunay Gardens. She hesitated before pushing open the gate and walking to the front door. She turned her key in the lock and braced herself to step into that familiar place knowing that everything had changed. She had changed. Nothing could be the same.

Kristof was smiling when she walked in: 'Eve! Good news!'

He kissed her on the cheek and slipped his arm round her waist, leading her down into the basement kitchen. He was celebrating. He'd won the contract for the Imperial Straits Bank headquarters in Singapore and tonight he would cook dinner – fish and samphire, bought by his personal assistant from Billingsgate market. He opened a bottle of Sancerre, talking breathlessly of his success and the politicking necessary to achieve it.

He didn't notice his wife's altered state. Eve felt so transformed, so different from the cool, controlled woman whose last exchange with her husband was over the coffee machine yesterday morning – procedural groundwork for the little lie necessary to explain in advance last night's absence – that she might as well have had a tattoo across her forehead. A tattoo of Luka's name. In the space of twenty hours she'd experienced rapture and humiliation, climbed Everest and plumbed the Krubera Cave. How could she be the same?

Yet, against the odds, she went on to enjoy the evening. Her appetite was good, an echo of that other reawakened hunger, and if at times she was bored by Kristof's boasts of business prowess, didn't fully follow his narrative and couldn't take in the cast list – numerous warring board members, conniving marketing people, rival firms – his monologue gave her permission to mentally retreat, nurse memories of rapture and try to protect herself against despair.

Her husband talked on then got up to fetch another bottle of wine from the cellar.

'This will amuse you,' he called over his shoulder. 'The office has had an enquiry from Wanda Wilson. She wants me to pitch for a commission for a new $42 million immersive performance space on her Art Ranch in Connecticut.'

'Wanda?'

'Yes. There are two others in the frame – a new Japanese architect and Bertoli, the Italian firm. I think we could really do something there, though. That's if it's not a problem for you.'

Why should it be a problem for her? That stuff with Wanda was so long ago – nearly forty years. She'd moved on. It seemed Wanda had moved on too – her approach to Kristof was proof of it – and the bunkum business was clearly booming. If Eve was really looking for problems she wouldn't have to go far. She smiled and nodded at Kristof, and tried out a sad scenario on herself; yes, Luka had gone. For him, their night was an act of wild folly. His admiration for her art – a sweet youthful hero worship – had, under the influence of wine and her attention, mutated into a kind of lust; the star-struck boy had wanted to pleasure his heroine and, in the process, had a reasonably good time himself. But, after that night, out of bed and dressed, with the pitiless morning light flooding the studio windows, reality had set in. In her paint-stained overalls, strands of hair unravelling from a hastily pinned bun, Eve was a tired old woman doing her best, engaged in the futile struggle to outrun the clock. How could he desire her?

'Are you okay?' Kristof asked.

'Yes. Go on …'

Luka had gone. But her memories of that one night would be a comforting keepsake, a talisman to see her through the sterile years ahead.

Later that night, in bed with Kristof, she reconciled herself to the status quo. The ageing warrior was still full of boardroom battles but those of the bedroom were behind him. Their marriage was mostly comfortable. That, at this end of life, with the grave yawning at her feet, may be the best one can hope for. There would be no more imperilling spikes in blood pressure or lurching accelerations in heart rate. She fell asleep finally, resigned to unthrilling contentment.

Just after dawn, she woke with a start, and in the grey light, lying next to her sleeping husband, she reckoned it all up again and knew that the accumulation of years, the shared experiences and entanglements, the weight of jointly acquired stuff, could never stack up against that one night of pure feeling. But it would have to do.

10

They've reached Notting Hill.

'Change here for the Central Line and trains to Ealing Broadway and Epping.'

The recorded female voice is low, with a chummy Estuary twang. Once the announcer would have been male, and his accent patrician BBC – the clipped voice of authority to Eve and her art school crowd, who were intent on shaking things up and breaking down barriers: class, sexual mores, gender roles. That project didn't go so well either. She stands up, as do most of the passengers in the carriage. They are all changing here. She inserts herself in the crowd, moving along narrow, low-ceilinged corridors – static tubes – up an escalator then down, to the eastbound Central Line platform. She has just missed a train. She sits on a bench to wait for the next.

After her night with Luka, as she lay awake next to her sleeping husband in Delaunay Gardens, Eve knew it was futile to count her losses. She'd chosen ease over passion when she married and this was where it got her. Too late to change now. Let sufficiency be her succour.

For exaltation, she would look to work. Home offered composure. And composure was not nothing.

But later that same morning, it all changed again in an instant when she walked towards the studio and saw Luka, standing there waiting for her with a backpack slung over his shoulder.

'I went back to Archway to get some things,' he said.

She hesitated, taking in his words. Was he saying what she thought he was saying?

He frowned: 'You did mean it? About the job? That you wanted me here? That's still on? Right?'

There was a note of panic in his voice. Now *he* was anxious and she had the power. He didn't just want to work in the studio, he wanted to move in. He was one step ahead of her. Was she ready for this? So soon? She hesitated. Let him feel the desolation that wrecked her sleep last night. Just for a moment. She didn't say a word, turned the key in the lock and they walked into the empty studio. She couldn't hold out for long. She answered his questions with a lingering kiss.

They only had an hour alone together before Josette and Glynn were due to arrive, but in that time Luka made his commitment clear. Her resignation to a half-life at Delaunay Gardens and unconvincing resolutions about strength in solitude – who was she kidding? – vanished.

The Tube indicator board flashes then goes blank. She winces at the screech of a tannoy. Everyone looks up expectantly, as a male voice (live, not recorded, and not patrician BBC) announces: 'Due to a person on the line, Central Line services have been suspended. Passengers are advised to find an alternative route.'

She sighs at the grim euphemism. Person on the line. That makes two of us. She gets to her feet and joins the exodus. What else would we do? Sit and wait until the police and paramedics have done their work and hosed away the last gout and smear? It would be hours.

She joins the human tide surging up the escalators to the exit. A taxi would be the simplest, quickest option, but she baulks at the idea. She is in no hurry to get back. Though it's a cold night, it's dry at the moment, her coat is warm and waterproof and she has her umbrella in case the weather turns again. The walk will do her good. She has a weakness for expensive high heels, but when she travels around London she is always what her mother would call 'sensibly shod'. It's a legacy from her Doc Marten student years; she likes to be equipped for flight. You can't run in heels.

She leaves the station and sets out towards Bayswater. She has some of her best ideas while out walking. Some of her worst, too. Walking and thinking – the beat of her feet underscoring the mind's melody, or drumming up discords.

In early May, the gardeners' time of growth and renewal, the idea for her new creative engagement with the natural world seemed to come to her intact and vivid as a dream. But as a synthesis of her personal and professional preoccupations, the seed for the new *Florilegium* was sown long ago —twenty years at least, during her inspirational week in Paris. A trip to Ticino, where she'd gone last spring as the eternal Plus One, had been a further unconscious spur.

This new work was to be an act of restitution for the invisible women of botany and art; for the unacknowledged legion of female painters of medieval herbals and florilegia, who patiently coloured the monochrome drawings of their credited male counterparts; for Fede Galizia and Orsola Maddalena Caccia, the Italian Renaissance painters of still lifes, and their later Dutch counterparts, Clara Peeters and Maria van Oosterwijk, whose haunting mimesis was dismissed as mere mimicry; for Jeanne Baret, the eighteenth-century French naturalist who circumnavigated the globe disguised as a man on a plant-collecting voyage with her lover, Philibert Commerson, who received the credit, two years before Joseph Banks followed their route and laid claim with his own *Florilegium*; for the brilliant Victorian maids and matrons who spent years gathering, rigorously identifying and drawing flowers in the face of hostility from critics who thought taxonomy, with its classification of the sexual parts of plants, an unseemly pastime for women and excluded them from scientific circles.

As she walks on through late-night London, she redoes the calculations – it really was two decades ago when she took Theo, her teenaged godson, to Paris as a birthday treat. Another soul worm. How many boys of that age would have forgone the Eiffel Tower, a tour of the Pompidou Centre and a boat trip on the Seine to pound narrow cobbled streets alongside a forty-year-old woman in pursuit of eclectic intellectual passions? Theo was an appreciative companion on many thought-rich walks, eager to learn, impressed by her rusty schoolgirl French, bewitched by the Musée de Cluny and *The Lady and the Unicorn* in her *mille-fleur* field of stars, and sweetly delighted by the motto emblazoned on the Lady's richly embroidered tent – '*À mon seul désir*'.

On their last day, Eve thought she was pushing her luck when, instead of taking him to the Catacombs, as promised, she dragged him off to the herbarium at the Muséum National d'Histoire Naturelle to look at the bound herbaria and florilegia collected and compiled by Baret and Commerson. But no, Theo was as excited as she was. Perhaps too excited – he bombarded the obliging curator with so many questions that Eve finally told him to shut up.

'You're a tourist,' she told her godson. 'I'm working.'

In Ticino last spring, while Kristof spent the days discussing new vertical cities and urban infrastructure at an architecture conference, Eve hiked alone in the high pastures, marvelling at the wild flowers, a polychromatic cosmos scattered across miles of emerald turf that made her think again of the medieval tapestries in the Cluny, of

Galizia and Caccia, and of the uncelebrated work of Baret, and all those botanising women of the nineteenth century.

Two weeks after the Sigmoid show opened, she was casting around for a new project. She'd dispatched the Solokoff camomile and was finishing the revisited carnivorous sequence for the Gerstein. Her meticulous botanical investigations were usually of individual specimens and these recent pieces had been mere five-finger exercises. She needed a challenge, a project that would fully engage her technically and intellectually and extend her range as an artist.

Then it came to her — she would address her own *mille-fleur* study and subvert the form, take it away from wholesome wild-flower meadows and formal imagery of feminine abundance. Her field of stars would be scattered with vivid representations of the most venomous flowers in the ecosphere.

When she told Luka about her plans for the *Poison Florilegium*, his response was encouraging.

'Fantastic! So ambitious! So different from your previous work.'

If this was veiled criticism, she didn't pick it up. His eager approval was a gift. She wasn't used to it. Real excitement hadn't been part of her emotional palette for years. Kristof always expressed the sort of irksome, empty effusiveness displayed by Mara, three decades ago, when presented with a clumsy drawing by one of her small children: 'Marvellous, darling. What is it? Now, here's more paper – do another.' Eve, for all her flaws as a mother, always credited her own daughter with a degree of sophistication and refused to pander to her. If Nancy's drawing was crude or indecipherable, if the colours were muddy, Eve would say so. This tougher, more honest school served Nancy well. She soon realised art of any sort was not for her.

Whenever Eve discussed new work with Hans, he listened with grave attention but she could never banish the suspicion that he was calculating his percentage. The muted response resonated. Eve always questioned what she was doing, wondered if it amounted to much, or anything at all. Was it Freud who described art as dung daubed on the portals of civilisation? By this account, she'd been permanently on 'dirty protest', like those Irish prisoners in the seventies; in her case, painstakingly inscribing flowering plants in ordure.

Just before the Sigmoid show, she had been surprised and encouraged by support from the notoriously acid reviewer Ellery Quinn, chief critic of the influential *Art Market* journal. He had, for most of her career, when he mentioned her at all, made slighting references to her and her work ('an ape of nature', those Cicely Mary Barker and furnishing allusions). Then, in his preview of her show, he seemed to have come round to her, calling her 'one of the most interesting, and unsung, practitioners on the circuit today'. After the opening, his review was rapturous.

She pauses by a doorway — a money-changing shop offering loans, still open for those in urgent need of credit at punishing interest rates — and pulls out her phone. She scrolls through the good reviews she keeps in her notes: her prayers and invocations in times of need. To passers-by, she might be consulting a map.

Here it is. 'By scrupulous observation and consummate skill, Eve Laing bestows on us the gift of sight, allowing us to see the natural world as if for the first time. Her botanical reflections engage the entire sensorium, a glorious, vividly hued tribute to Nature in all its intricate, infinite variety. This isn't art imitating life, but life itself.' The fact that Quinn was said to have lately bedded Eve's dealer didn't spoil her pleasure in the review. She walks on, recharged.

It was partly about legacy. Wasn't that the root of all ambition? What mark would she leave on the world? A child — that spoiled and brittle daughter who didn't even like her — was not enough. Here was the hard unspoken truth: most children were disappointments. Whether their parents were honest enough to admit it was another matter.

As a child, Nancy was a prodigious fancy-dresser. They gave her a trunk of costumes, some of them Eve's discarded designer clothes and shoes. The child was always mincing around the house like a tiny drag queen in feather boas, wide-brimmed hats that slipped over her face, and perilous gargantuan heels. It was sometimes difficult to dissuade her from wearing her costumes to school.

Eve and Kristof hoped this appetite for display suggested a future in theatre – design or even performance – and signed her up for drama classes. But Nancy proved a poor actress – flat enunciation, off-key timing, no presence – and showed little aptitude for stagecraft. Her talent for drama was confined to the domestic sphere. But a childhood spent flouncing about in other people's clothes was a perfect apprenticeship for her adult métier as a blogger, a chirpy tweeter and ceaseless Instagrammer whose only undocumented corners of life took place in the lavatory and on the therapist's couch, and whose highest aspiration was a sponsorship deal with a high street chain store, albeit one that claimed to pay a living wage to employees in its Third World factories. Of all the curses that might be visited on one's children, the cruellest was mediocrity.

Look at Mara. Did she honestly rejoice when Esme, a doggedly unambitious IT consultant, announced that she was on a regime of hormones prior to gender reassignment and was from now on to be known as Emmet? Mara went through the motions and even held a small party to celebrate Esme's announcement. But would a health food purist who never knowingly let sugar or additives pass the lips of her children, a science sceptic and conspiracy theorist who believed all doctors were butchers and poisoners in the pay of Big Pharma, seriously delight in the news that her daughter – or rather her son – would be taking daily medication and had signed up for major surgical intervention? Perhaps if there were a homeopathic remedy – a handful of sugar pills and a herbal cream you could rub on the offending parts – that would transform unhappy Esme into fully realised Emmet, Eve would have believed in Mara's smile when she first imparted the news.

And, before that news, there was the job. Would anyone truly wish on their child a future spent tinkering with the computers of the technically illiterate? Mara's second child wasn't a source of unalloyed pleasure, either. Having enjoyed Esme's early years so much, and displayed such prodigious patience for finger painting, plasticine modelling and nursery songs, Mara went on to adopt a toddler from a benighted corner of North Africa. Theo, the glimmering boy. Eve, with an atheist's misgivings, agreed to be his godmother. It was a reciprocal deal; Mara took on mentoring duties with Nancy. At first, Eve got the better half of the bargain. Theo was a gifted musician and mathematical prodigy with a winning nature and the dreamy-eyed looks of a Giorgione pageboy.

He could have done anything with his life but that sweet, accomplished teenaged companion in Paris – so eager to learn, so responsive – subsequently soured. He fell in with a bad crowd and abandoned his studies. In the old days, at art school and in New York, Mara and Eve had flirted with bad crowds themselves – some said *they* were the bad crowd – but they remained engaged and productive. Theo didn't have the backbone. He drifted, funded by Mara and later, when he needed rehab after a spell of drug-induced psychosis, by Eve. He went back to Paris for a while, said he wanted to make his way as a DJ – it still mystifies Eve how anyone could make a career out of putting on records. He even flunked that. Now a seedy, marginal figure in his mid-thirties, he was running a beach bar in Thailand. The last time she heard from him was a phone call from Phuket more than eight months ago. He wanted more money, it seemed.

Mara never complained and went on to rebuild her life, up to a point. She's living with a new lover, Dot, an older woman, a former social worker. With her new stepchildren, clever Dot took on a challenging caseload to occupy her in retirement. Mara abandoned sculpture – she was never much good anyway (her real medium was plasticine) – and retrained as a psychotherapist. A pity she didn't try her hand with Nancy and give her a friends-and-family discount. Mara's own wounds, caused by anguish over her children, must be deep. Psychotherapist, heal thyself.

In that last phone call, Theo asked Eve about her work and wistfully expressed interest in the Sigmoid show.

'I'm stranded,' he said, 'I wish I could be there but I'm completely broke.'

He was angling for the fare home, trying to please her with references to that trip to Paris, so long ago.

'*À mon seul désir* ... Remember?' he said.

He had caught her at the wrong moment, with much to do in the studio and the Sigmoid opening only days away.

'Since we're talking about money,' she said, 'how about getting a real job and repaying me some of the thousands I've spent bailing you out?'

The line went dead. Perhaps she'd been too harsh. That was the last she heard from him.

11

'Any spare change?' The voice by her feet breaks her thoughts. A young man sits cross-legged in the filthy doorway of a souvenir shop. Displayed in the window, framed by strings of Christmas lights, are Union Jack mugs, Beefeater teddy bears, and teacups marking the Queen's ninetieth birthday and recent royal weddings. There are also miniature replicas of Routemaster double-decker buses and red telephone boxes – both unremarkable, everyday features of Eve's London youth, now exalted to the status of historical artefacts. Which must make her a historical artefact.

'Merry Christmas, missus.' The voice by her feet is trying another tack.

Her gaze remains fixed on the window and she winces as she recognises, on a rack of postcards of Big Ben and Tower Bridge, a fragment of her own work – a postcard-sized print of the central section of the *Underground Florilegium*. Who sends postcards these days?

'Please. If you can spare anything for a cup of tea?'

She looks down at him and he extends a hopeful grimy hand. His soft, girlish face is so far unmarked by degradation – he could be the model for Guido Reni's pretty St Michael, whose ornately sandalled feet trample the head of Satan. But Satan seems to have got the better of this St Michael. Someone else's lost child. She walks on.

It was a cycle. She was a disappointment to her own parents. Though they lived long enough to see and admire her material success, they always regarded her as an unnatural daughter, too wilful and wayward to be properly feminine. On this, through disputatious marriage and poisonous divorce, they agreed. They were appalled by the publicity over her affair with Florian Kiš – 'he's older than your father', her mother said. 'Couldn't you have put some clothes on?' was her father's pained response to *Girl with a Flower*. Now she wishes she had. After New York and the years of estrangement, they thought she'd become too grand, as the wife of an internationally successful architect, to be bothered with them. They had a point.

Parents start out as household emperors and end their days as barely tolerated buffoons; the only difference being the speed and gradient of descent. She couldn't remember the time when her parents bestrode her world, though they must have done, once. Let-down set in early for Eve. Forget love or grief. Disappointment – dashed hopes and humbled dreams – is the intractable human condition.

Progeny couldn't cut it. She never wanted a child – least of all with Florian, who was said by the end of his life to have sired some thirty offspring with a succession of daft girls who, their brains addled by romantic fiction, thought the role of muse was the highest calling. Eve was grateful for his parting gift – £100 cash for an abortion, posted through her Hackney letter box by the same henchmen who once delivered regular summonses to his bed. Two months later, when the money started coming in from the *Underground Florilegium*, she returned his £100 along with a single pressed pansy.

Ten years later, pregnant again, she let Kristof talk her out of a second termination. After Nancy's birth, Eve, in a retrospective rage, insisted Kristof have a vasectomy. Never again. From now on, she said, she would focus on work. Time was running out, she declared, at what she thought of then as the advanced age of thirty. Today she's twice that, her own distracting experiment with romantic love seems to be over and all that is left is work. No wonder she's been going at it in a frenzy.

It always came down to the work. She didn't make it easy for herself. The field was crowded, with mediocre successes as well as brilliant failures. Wanda Wilson – one of the Three Msketeers, as Mike Arrigo called them, referencing the honorific then favoured by second wave feminists – could barely draw a straight line with a sharpie and became a titan of the New York conceptual and performance art scene. Mike could reproduce a da

Vinci sketch with his eyes closed but ended up, before his health gave out altogether, feeding his drug habit by churning out bad abstract oils for a budget hotel chain.

And then there were the giants. Who could compete with a body of work like Van Gogh's, achieve perfection of line like Botticelli, or make pigment ring with the commanding clarity of country church bells like Matisse? Deconstruction was over – from cheeky, one-joke Duchamp to the po-faced ninnies of Fluxus and those self-mutilating clowns, the Viennese Actionists. They'd thumbed their noses and swung their wrecking balls through the academy. Demolition complete, where could they go from there? For Wanda, it seemed the only way was down. She was now deploying industrial excavators to dig her barren furrow. Soon she'd strike the earth's core and invite the public to watch her – or one of the hapless victims of her new 'relational art' – bathe, howling, in molten magma.

Eve took a less fashionable approach, relying on a degree of patience, skill and hard work that would have been familiar to Renaissance masters. She went on to make a decent living and finally achieved a six-figure sum at auction for her *Rose/Thorn* series. But that wasn't enough to lift her above the herd. Purity of purpose was the artist's aim, Florian said. 'Paint and a passion' was all you needed. One pure work was all she ever hoped for or, failing that, one pure colour, like Yves Klein, who gazed at a cloudless French summer sky and dreamed up a hue so brilliant and so obvious that it was a miracle no one came up with it before: Yves Klein Blue.

Tonight, as she walks through the city towards her studio where the paint is drying on the final canvas of her *Poison Florilegium*, she knows this will be her master-work. But recognition – that arbitrary trick of the light – is not guaranteed. She knows this too. Look at Vermeer, whose genius wasn't acknowledged until almost two hundred years after his death. Or poor Van Gogh, who died leaving nearly a thousand paintings unsold. Yes, one pure, perfect, piercingly authentic colour of her own – Eve would settle for that.

Kristof has never been troubled by self-doubt. His legacy is assured. He isn't daubing the portals, he's building them. It would be hard to find a major city in the Western world, the Far East or plutocratic corners of Arabia which doesn't have a distinctive Kristof Axness high-rise, a vaunting monument to technology, capitalism and human audacity. He's always looking upwards, squinting against the sun at giant cranes swinging their loads, mechanical beasts doing his bidding and assembling his dream. By night, illuminated, his work defines the skyline and defies the stars. What chance did she ever have?

Her work was, in comparison, domestic and small-scale, a sprig of speedwell hidden in moss beneath his mighty redwoods. It wasn't surprising that details of her projects rarely registered with him. But it irked her. 'Excellent, darling. You're in your prime,' he'd always say.

She'd been in her prime for twenty years by his reckoning. It cut both ways, though. What did she know – or care – about his new buildings, the Manila Tower and the Singapore Spire, or his proposal for Wanda's ludicrous Art Ranch?

Her pace slows as she skirts Hyde Park, where the Sigmoid Gallery is now showing the work of an artist whose medium is seaweed. Something skilful could be done with marine algae, Eve supposes. But this isn't it. She has seen the posters and concluded that more craft, creativity and meaning is in evidence among juvenile sandcastle builders on an average bank holiday beach.

In those moments when she's had a good day in the studio, when she considers the abysmal efforts currently lauded as great art, she can banish self-doubt, look around and ask, 'How do *they* get away with it?' Then she knows it is her misfortune to be the real thing in a world of mountebanks.

In most areas of creative endeavour, there is some kind of measurable standard. Writers, mostly, need a grasp of the rudiments of language. Musicians don't get far if they can't actually play their instruments. Only in the visual arts can you set yourself up as a practitioner without a single baseline skill, though acting comes a close second as a forum of opportunity for the inept. How can you trust the judgement of someone who thinks Wanda Wilson has a scrap of talent or anything interesting to say?

Eve distrusts all responses to her work. She has spent too long parsing the nuances of polite indifference. But Luka's excitement was new. It was all new: this directness, honesty, passion – in the studio as well as the bedroom.

Her new project would be a departure, she explained, telling him about the anonymous medieval women colour artists, about the Italian and Dutch women painters, geniuses of the still-life genre, who were ignored by art historians, and the Victorian women botanists excluded from the Royal Society and the Linnean Society on account of their sex. She showed him photographs of the flower-starred pastures of Ticino and the tapestries in the Cluny – omitting details about her young companion at the museum two decades before – and she suggested he read a biography of Jeanne Baret, whose lover and botanical partner gave his name to seventy species while she was written out of history entirely.

Luka made a note of the book's title on his phone. 'Sounds amazing,' he said.

His next question, though, was dismayingly crass: 'Does your new *Florilegium* have anything to do with those Russians poisoned in the West Country last month?'

'No it does not,' she said firmly. 'Because then it would be journalism, not art.'

He wouldn't make that foolish connection again. She forgave him and continued to outline her plans. Monumental in scale, intimate in focus, the *Poison Florilegium* would be a seven-panel full-scale interpretation in oils of those Swiss meadows. Alpine flowers, sweet and bright as candy, would be exchanged for the deadliest plants, lovely as their innocent sisters, venomous as snakes – nature's most vicious prank. Each 8ft by 15ft green 'field' would be devoted to sixty-seven repeated representations of a single flower, one for every year of Baret's life, its colour chosen to depict an element of the Newtonian rainbow. Seven canvases for seven colours, scattered across their parcel of green ground.

This would be an exercise in science and craft as well as art. The oils would be mixed in the studio from pure powdered pigments, plants would be dissected and photographed, and complementing the large canvases would be smaller botanical watercolours on vellum of each flower, alongside which would be printed accounts of their properties, uses and place in folklore. Specimens of the flowers, dissected and whole, representing their entire life cycle, provided by specialist nurseries in South Africa and Latin America, would be suspended in preserving fluid in seven under-lit glass-and-steel display cabinets, creating a floral aquarium, or floating herbarium. Alongside the canvas panels, the works on paper, the photographs and the herbaria, would run a time-lapse film of the life cycle of each species – the footage provided by a US government-funded ecology institute, itself facing extinction under the current bio-sceptical administration – opening with the first tentative thrust through soil and grass, through the hopeful unfurling, to full bloom and the gaudy moment in the sun, before the shrivelling and obliteration of decay.

'You should film it, too,' said Luka. 'You at work!'

She resented his interruption. 'It *will* be filmed. Josette always videos the process.'

'You need more than that. Proper documentation, start to finish, with interviews, commentary.'

Her assistants usually knew better than to offer suggestions about work in progress. This was her work, not theirs. But there was something in his idea. She could screen the life-cycle sequence in parallel with studio footage, in which she would talk through the inspiration for the project, telling the story of Jeanne Baret and the forgotten women painters, naturalists and botanical artists, and explaining the studio process, from the drawing and watercolour stage, to the last colour-laden brushstroke on the final oil canvas.

She outlined her plans to Hans who nodded and murmured mildly but expressed no view. She wasn't discouraged. He received his 20 per cent for selling her work, not for his aesthetic judgement. He did, though, go on to discuss this proposed new work with some select clients – major galleries in America, including the Gerstein, private collectors in the Middle East and Russia, as well as a new corporate player in Shanghai. There was, he reported later, with the faintest hint of enthusiasm in his voice – a slight rise in pitch and warming of timbre – already some interest and keen competitive bidding.

There was much to be done and, in the unprecedented spring heatwave, as London impersonated Southern Europe in high summer – thronging street cafes, supine sunbathers on every parched patch of grass – Eve felt a vigour and urgency she hadn't experienced in a long time. Not since art school. It can't all have been down to Luka.

Glynn and Josette began to prepare the canvases, stretching them, sizing them with rabbit-skin glue and applying gesso primer. They ordered the powdered pigment, funnelled it into reagent jars sealed with glass stoppers and stacked the jars on shelves built for the purpose. That corner of the studio began to look like an old apothecary shop.

Vats of glue and primer, sealed jerry cans of formalin for the floating herbarium, and fresh supplies of turpentine and oil began to arrive. Josette and Glynn brought in two rock roadies in denim and bandanas to set out the chemicals, help with the canvases, lean them against the wall at just the right angle – 'this is about precision. No Pollock drips here,' Josette warned them – and assemble the display cases for the floating herbaria. It turned out that these two musclemen, Hugo and Matt, were well-brought-up ex-public schoolboys with an interest in art. As the most recent recruits to the studio, they were also responsible for coffee-making and fetching lunch from the nearby deli, tasks which they undertook grudgingly.

'It's as if handing out sandwiches is an assault on your masculinity,' Josette scolded.

In contrast, Luka, primarily in charge of specimens and dissection, volunteered for every chore and offered to help Josette with filming. Another addition to the team was Abi Fulton, a recent Slade graduate who dressed like an Amish matron, her geeky look heightened by a white lab coat, gloves, mask and protective goggles. She supervised the pigments and still photography and in her self-appointed role as health and safety representative, insisted on ordering protective equipment for everyone in the studio – 'standard practice these days', she said. The other assistants, who preferred their own customised utility wear, were sceptical.

'We're dealing with toxins, heavy metals,' Abi protested.

'You look like a beekeeper,' Luka told her.

Eve had her own studio uniform – in the laundry room she kept a rail of identical navy sailcloth boiler suits, made for her in Suffolk – and she had no intention of wearing one of Abi's cheap white coats. But she was determined to ignore any messy personal undercurrents from the team and shelled out for the safety gear. Let them sort it out. Nothing was going to divert her. She had a vision and she was intent on pursuing it.

She started on the violet sequence. She was done with the eponymous sweet violet, 'half hidden from the eye', of the *Underground Florilegium*. Sweet anything was over for this new work, and so was reticence. This was about toxic beauty – the flower that entices then destroys. No one could confuse this project with flower fairies; scale alone propelled it beyond the tame domestic sphere. These canvases would only find a home in big institutional spaces. And the plants themselves, our subtle, seductive enemies, would pre-empt the most hostile critic's sneering reference to sprigged furnishing fabrics.

Monkshood was to be her first subject. She chose a single specimen, an intact cluster of cowled petals flaring from a tapering stem, and started sketching for the small watercolour.

'It's kind of creepy, this one,' said Luka, bent over the dissection tray, scalpel flashing, carefully dismembering the flower, wearing the gloves Abi had insisted on. 'It *looks* poisonous.'

'*Aconitum napellus*,' said Eve, reading from a herbal manual. 'Monkshood. Devil's helmet. Wolf's bane is another name. They used to smear arrowheads with it.'

He looked up. 'Should I be doing this?'

Abi, fully robed, masked and gloved at the grinding slab, gave a snorting laugh.

'*Now* you're worried!' she said.

'Relax,' Eve said. 'It won't hurt you. Just avoid eating it, okay?'

125

'What happens if you do?' Luka asked.

Eve consulted the herbal. This information would be typed in for the printed panel that would hang alongside the watercolour.

'Mmm … "Death can be instantaneous,"' she read. '"Or at least within the hour. Gastrointestinal crises, sweating, headache, confusion and –"'

'Sounds like a bad hangover,' one of the muscle boys said.

His friend sniggered into the awkward silence. These two hadn't grasped the first unspoken rule of the studio; no one – least of all rude mechanicals – interrupted Eve.

'And?' Josette asked, overriding the interruption and prompting Eve to finish her sentence.

'"Paralysis of limbs followed by paralysis of the heart,"' Eve read out. She closed the book with a dramatic snap and resumed her sketching.

Glynn whistled. 'You won't get far with a paralysed heart.'

'And the name? Monkshood?' Luka asked, marvelling at the beautiful weapon of mass destruction in his hand. 'What's that about?'

'Look at it,' Eve said, getting up and walking over to him, conscious of a throb of heat passing between them. She pointed. 'The answer's in your hand. Those flowers, half hidden by their mantles … like the faces of medieval monks shrouded by sinister drapery.'

'Wow. Yes. I see it.'

He saw it. That was the great thing about Luka. He saw her work and he understood its value. He saw her too.

While Eve finished her preliminary sketch for the watercolour, Glynn and Josette measured out the powdered pigment – phthalocyanine green with cadmium, two parts to one – for the meadow base on the large canvas. Bickering like tetchy sous chefs, they took turns to use the glass pestle – the muller – mixing the heaps of powder with linseed oil and turps on the grinding slab, checking the density of the finished colour with Eve. Then they carried their trays of paint up ladders onto a wheeled platform, loaded the big hog-bristle brushes and began work on the first canvas, laying out the flat green field over which Eve was to scatter sixty-seven spikes of monkshood, rendered in manganese violet, dioxazine mauve and carbazole purple, their grassy stems and palmate leaves picked out with viridian and gamboge yellow, highlighted by zinc white.

At the small easel, she began to fill in her pencil sketch with limpid watercolour. She felt Luka's presence across the studio as a voltaic charge. It was hard to resist looking at him. When she was confident she was unobserved, she watched him for minutes at a time – his beautiful face sombre with concentration, his long pale fingers using the scalpel to strip the sepals then the petals, splitting the ovum and setting out the parts on vellum for Abi to photograph later. His subtlety and precision was a personal tribute to Eve, an act of love, and turning back to sketch the flower, she felt a mad, transgressive glee, recalling those delicate hands playing over her body.

That month, with perfect timing, Kristof went to Singapore to work on the Imperial Straits Bank commission, leaving her free to move into the studio and devote herself exclusively to her own project, and to Luka.

Their night-time routine would begin at 8 p.m., as the others prepared to leave. Luka would make a show of departure, pack his bag and head for the door with them. Once outside, he lingered a little and then, when everyone had dispersed, he doubled back. At the sound of his soft knock she opened the door to his lovely form – all hers – framed in the doorway. He stepped back in and they shut out the world.

In the studio, with the sulphur-tinged darkness of the city night outside gilding the canal, and the bright task lamp beaming over his shoulder, Luka's face glowed golden in the shadows as he worked on at the dissection tray, a figure from one of Joseph Wright's portraits of Enlightenment experimentation – a tenebrous study of patience, dexterity and wonder.

They went to bed just before dawn and she lay basking in his regard, renewed and infused, in a benign contagion, by his youth and beauty.

12

She continues down Oxford Street which, even at this late hour, is thronging. Thousands of LED snowflakes drift over this busiest, ugliest retail strip in London. Crowds stand hushed and awed, faces shining in reflected light, gazing like medieval pilgrims before candlelit altars into extravagantly decorated shop windows. She catches a glimpse of one display – a long table spans the window horizontally, Last Supper-style, and sitting behind it, apparently enjoying Christmas dinner and pulling crackers, are a number of giant poodle mannequins wearing paper crowns and garish Italian designer clothing. The tableau is no less artful than one of Jeff Wall's staged photographic conversation pieces from the seventies. It's wittier than anything by Jeff Koons, too.

What does the average window dresser earn in a year? £30,000? £35,000? She read recently that one of Koons's *Balloon Dogs*, made under his orders by German fabricators, fetched $59 million at auction.

She would never delegate her work to a fabricator. She's always loved the process and relished the craft. She's good at it. She bumped into Koons a couple of times in New York in the early eighties. A charming snake oil merchant, even then. She didn't think he could blow up a balloon unaided. Eve's assistants were there merely to support her with minor tasks. She, alone, was at the centre of the work.

With Luka's help, she entered a phase of unprecedented productivity. The weeks unfolded — days and evenings devoted to work, nights to love.

Gradually, she became aware that an atmosphere had developed in the studio. It was like low-level traffic noise intruding on an exquisite piece of chamber music; once noticed, it was hard to ignore. For the first few days, taking turns to mix the powdered pigments and handle the formalin, all the assistants wore Abi's masks, gloves and glasses against possible toxic fumes. But putting all the equipment on and taking it off was cumbersome and time-consuming and they rebelled. Soon, only Abi wore the full rig. She was furious.

'If you all want to risk your health, that's fine by me,' she said one morning.

Luka, at the dissection tray, waved his gloved hands at her. 'This will do me, thanks. I don't suppose Leonardo da Vinci and his team went around in HazMat suits.'

Hugo and Matt laughed.

Abi's small face was contorted with injured defiance. 'It might have been better for him if he did. All that lead and mercury didn't do him any good.'

'Please?' Eve said, holding her brush like a conductor's baton. That was enough to silence them for now.

Luka wanted to take over the filming but Josette resisted; this had always been her territory. At one point, she wrested the camera from his hands. These petty quarrels seemed part of a conspiracy to keep Eve from work.

Her irritation was made worse by more phone calls from Ines Alvaro, who wanted Eve's personal approval for the most minute details of the Gerstein hang. Should the new cobra lily piece go at the end of her eighties carnivorous sequence? Or the beginning? Should it hang alone? Ines also insisted on discussing publicity and marketing schedules for the exhibition.

'The *New Yorker* wants to do a profile and *T Magazine* is talking about a photo spread.'

'It's really not convenient now,' Eve told her.

They finished the violet sequence and, as she painted her signature, EL, a black hieroglyph hovering in the lower right quarter of the flower field, she felt a sense of profound significance. This serious enterprise was entirely hers. She had made her mark.

They moved on to indigo. The second canvas was to be filled with a twilight image of the veined bells of *Atropa belladonna*, deadly nightshade, its glossy dark berries with their tangy green tomato scent fatally tempting to children and unwary walkers. Of all the flowers in this florilegium, it was the plainest but it had, as Nancy would say, 'brand awareness'. The name alone, homage to the Greek goddess of Fate, Atropos, announced it as the brightest star in the firmament of poisonous plants. Atropos wielded the scissors that cut the threads of human life.

The flower, and its berries, was responsible for more deaths than all the other plants combined. Its second name, belladonna, acknowledged the pupil-widening effect that it had when a diluted extract was dropped in the eyes of 'beautiful women', or would-be beautiful women – Renaissance predecessors of the Botox sorority who, hoping to acquire a mesmerising gaze, also attempted to harness a deadly poison. Instant beauty was the goal. Who cared how it would pan out? The subject of Titian's *Woman with a Mirror*, whose inky pupils are as big as Venetian ducats, may have used tincture of nightshade. Side effects included heart failure and blindness.

At Oxford Circus, Eve hits pedestrian gridlock. Squeezing through the crowd, she turns right into Regent's Street, whose Christmas lights are outlines of giant Blakeian angels. She cuts left into Great Marlborough Street and even here, in this more lightly populated tributary, she has to weave her way through large groups of nocturnal sightseers gawping outside the 1920s Tudor revival fantasy of Liberty's department store. Having spent her childhood in a Tudor revival suburban enclave, Eve has no affection for the building's half-timbered style and hurries on. She's with Pevsner: 'The scale is wrong, the symmetry is wrong, and those twisted Tudor chimneys are wrongest of all.' Kristof tried to make the case for it, praising its 'exuberance', expressing admiration for its three light wells. He was at his most exasperating when most reasonable. He never believed any of it, she felt. He never believed in *her*.

She began to dread his return from Singapore. She had no idea where her affair was heading but she wasn't ready for its end. The boy appeared committed. His passion was a nightly miracle. But she'd lived long enough, weathered her share of disappointments and was sufficiently rational to know that most things were finite. All things, ultimately. She could only be certain of her work and she went at it with a fervour that matched her hunger for Luka. *Carpe diem.* And *carpe puerum* – seize the boy.

The presence of the other assistants imposed a necessary discipline on the lovers. Ten hours' compulsory restraint fuelled the night's wild release and, back at work each morning, in company, even when occupied at opposite ends of the studio, Eve felt warmed by Luka's force field. The others must have guessed what was going on. Josette and Glynn had a taste for gossip and they were clearly jealous of him. Why wouldn't they be? They were jealous of each other.

Glynn prepared the green ground for the nightshade canvas, laying down the ferrocyanide Prussian blue of a summer's gloaming, while Josette filmed Eve at work on her watercolour, talking through the process and telling the story of Jeanne Baret.

'This is really a bouquet for Jeanne.' She sketched out the dark, bell-like flower heads and lustrous berries – 'death cherries' was one folk name, according to the herbal. 'And for all those female artists and botanists who laboured in the shadows, the Victorian women, rigorous natural scientists doomed to be perpetual amateurs, who passed on their findings to their "professional" male counterparts who took all the credit.'

Fractures continued to emerge among the team and soon they threatened to undermine the work itself. Hugo and Matt took against Luka and joined with Josette and Glynn in cutting him out of conversations. One afternoon, Eve saw Hugo brush past Luka at the dissection tray, causing him to drop his scalpel. Luka coolly glanced at Hugo, bent to pick up the scalpel, and carried on with his work. If only they had all been so focused. Abi was irritating everyone, creating a consensus of sorts. Robed up in her lab coat, goggles, mask and gloves, she continued to lecture her eye-rolling colleagues on studio safety. Luka led the teasing. Was she about to tackle a moon landing?

'You are all so negative!' she said. There was a pitiful throb in her voice.

Luka laughed. 'Look at yourself!'

Again, Eve intervened. 'Can we get back to work? Please?'

Later, she walked in on a heated argument between Luka, Hugo and Matt and, in the moment before they noticed her presence and fell silent, she sensed the threat of violence. Luka's fists were clenched by his side. He was holding his ground and she felt a curious proprietorial pride. That night, when she asked him about the confrontation, he made light of it – 'Male egos,' he murmured.

One morning, while she worked on the bottom half of the canvas, giving the purple flowers and glossy berries the inky tint of graduated evening light, she was distracted by a squall at the far end of the studio. Abi was shouting incoherently. Eve turned to see the girl take off her safety glasses and lab coat, throw them down and stamp off in tears, her oversized brogues squeaking in the sudden silence. She wrenched open the studio door, walked out and slammed it shut behind her. She wasn't coming back.

Glynn and Josette took Eve aside and blamed Luka for Abi's meltdown. It was bullying, Glynn said.

'He was always mocking her,' Josette added.

'Really?' Eve dipped a fine filbert brush in a pool of zinc white to give the berries an animating glint. 'She must have been very thin-skinned, poor thing.'

Hugo and Matt stood conferring in a corner. Only Luka had a proper sense of priorities. He'd returned to his duties.

That night, in bed, Luka reassured her. 'It's really a waste of your energy to think about any of this stuff.

135

They're pygmies these people. You know what's important. So do I. Let's get on with it.'

He took over Abi's role as still photographer and volunteered to help Josette with the pigments and floating herbaria. He was a quick study and the transition appeared seamless. It was a relief not to have Abi there, frowning in her goggles – the girl was a nexus of anxiety.

But two days later, when Luka was out getting lunch for the team (Hugo and Matt had been slow to stir when Josette asked them), Glynn approached Eve. She was on the wheeled platform, working on the top half of the indigo canvas.

'Can we have a word?' he asked.

'Must we?'

She descended the ladder reluctantly. How many more interruptions would there be today?

'He's got to go,' Glynn said.

'Who?' Eve asked, reloading her brush with colour – two-thirds Prussian blue, one-third cerulean.

'Luka. He's a disruptive influence.'

Eve shrugged, intent on her work. 'What's wrong with a bit of disruption?'

Josette joined Glynn.

'He's undermining the team,' she said. There was an unpleasant bleat in her voice. 'We were all getting along fine – it was so harmonious – until he came along.'

'Harmonious?' Eve couldn't hide her irritation. 'I haven't seen much evidence of that. You should know by now, I don't give a damn about harmony. This is an artist's studio. Not choir practice.'

They returned to their work in silence.

That night in bed, Luka seemed distracted. Eve asked what was troubling him and he turned away.

'It's not important.'

'Tell me!'

She raised herself on her elbow and looked at him – his solemn face, the Romantic poet, too sensitive for the world; Wallis's young Chatterton, picturesquely arranged on his deathbed.

'It's Hugo and Matt. The Old Etonian Hell's Angels. They're taking the piss.'

'Meaning?'

'They don't take the work seriously.'

'Look' she said, 'they wouldn't be my first choice as assistants. But they've been useful for the heavy, technical work. Let Josette and Glynn handle them. I really can't get involved with this level of micromanagement.'

'I know, I know,' he said, reaching to draw her in for a kiss. 'I didn't want to trouble you. It'll be fine. The work is all that matters. I know that.'

'The work – and us,' she corrected him.

13

Eve has skirted the hideous Swinging London theme park of Carnaby Street and is now in Berwick Street, where she, Mara and Wanda used to shop for rag trade remnants, bright scraps of silk, velvet and taffeta, plumes of ostrich and peacock feathers, to make wild party costumes, embellished by cheap treasures they found in vintage markets and jumble sales. When they weren't costumed as post-apocalyptic punk warriors, they dressed like odalisques in Aladdin's harem. She remembers a particular morning-after when she had to make her way back on a rush-hour Tube towards Hackney from Gloucester Road wearing nothing but a beltless embroidered kimono and a pair of knee-length boots. Her youthful fondness for costume was one trait she bequeathed to Nancy. That and an impatience with motherhood.

She walks on down Wardour Street, breasting waves of drunks, mostly merry, some wearing inane Santa hats, others paper crowns, and she feels a pang for the bad old days when Soho was a place of real danger rather than a hangout for tourists, office workers and students on a bender. Best not to dwell in the past, though lately it's been more hospitable than the present.

For the first few days after Abi's walkout and Glynn and Josette's attempt to oust Luka, the atmosphere seemed to settle. Eve was back on the platform, completing the nightshade canvas. From this vantage point, with her assistants toiling below, true groundlings, she pressed on with her work. Glynn and Josette went at their duties diligently and, while the silence in the studio may have been loaded, the quiet suited Eve. If she wanted external stimulus, Luka would put on some music, or the radio news – accounts of global conflict and economic gloom usefully gave perspective to any studio spats.

Even Matt and Hugo were amenable, volunteering for errands with implausible eagerness. They assembled the first display cabinet without fuss, poured in the preservative for the herbarium and, once Josette had dropped in the monkshood specimens, they sealed the tank with an acetylene torch. There was a celebratory atmosphere as they crowded round to admire the purple flowers, leaves and seeds shivering in their watery tomb.

Eve went back to the canvas feeling buoyant. With a delicate Japanese sable brush, she layered titanium-white highlights on the phthalo-green leaves. Lunch, ferried without complaint by Matt and Hugo from the deli, seemed a collegiate affair. Then out of the calm, the crisis.

139

They were sitting eating and drinking coffee when Luka jumped up and threw his sandwich across the table.

'Come on. The food's not that bad!' Matt said. He and Hugo were grinning.

'You bastard!' Luke shouted.

'Lighten up,' Hugo said, leaning back in his chair and stretching out his legs, hands clasped behind his head.

Luka walked over to him, fists bunched. 'You just tried to kill me.'

Now Hugo and Matt were on their feet, squaring up. They had the advantage of height and bulk.

Eve had to step in. 'What's this about?'

Luka turned to her. 'They tried to kill me.'

'What the hell are you talking about?' Hugo said.

'He's gone mad. Completely flipped,' Matt said.

'Let's calm down.' Glynn stepped in, placatory palms raised. 'No one's trying to kill anyone.'

Luka reached for the sandwich and peeled it apart. On top of the cheese and salad filling were two purple petals. Monkshood.

Hugo and Matt denied it, of course. But who else could it have been? The amount of aconite used may not have had fatal consequences. But that wasn't the point. The atmosphere in the studio was toxic and this level of disruption was unsustainable. Hugo and Matt had to go.

Josette and Glynn pleaded on their behalf, but Eve was firm. The pair had done much of the manual groundwork required anyway – all the canvases were ready, primed and in position against the walls, most of the display tanks had been assembled and were waiting to be filled and the chemical supplies were set out in order.

'Get out! Now!' Eve told them.

When she was finally alone with Luka that night in the studio, he made light of what amounted to an attempt on his health, if not his life.

'We don't need those two. End of,' he said.

He didn't want to dwell on it. He began to film Eve at the canvas. Josette might try to hog the camera during the day, but at night it was exclusively his.

'We can focus on your work now,' he said. 'Not the egos of those two goons. It's so amazing to be involved in this project. That was the problem with Hugo and Matt – they just didn't get it.'

He was confident he could take over all their roles.

'It's not rocket science,' he said, adjusting the camera's focus. 'I've watched them. How difficult can it be to knock up a flat-pack glass case and shift a few cans of chemicals about?'

She relaxed, marvelling at his competence, and in bed later, there was a heightened passion in their lovemaking.

'I've never known anything like this,' he told her. 'You're better than any drug.'

They lay together, exhausted and exultant. It would have been absurdly reductive to suggest that gratitude played a part in his ardour, but Eve knew that Luka had much to thank her for – for sticking up for him, for giving him a purposeful life. Though neither of them liked to talk about it, she'd also given him a good salary, topping the wage he'd earned from the Old Masters website, then increasing it to compensate for the extra work he'd taken on when Abi walked out. And, with the departure of Matt and Hugo, he was about to take on even more.

The next day she sketched out the watercolour for the blue sequence – aquilegia – while Glynn tackled the ground for the large canvas and Josette, wearing Abi's goggles, mask and gloves, carefully picked out specimens of nightshade with tweezers and released them into the glass tank of formalin.

Eve, watching Luka, noticed Josette bridling when he leaned over her.

'Let me help, Josette,' he said.

'I'm doing fine, thanks.'

'Let him have a go,' Eve said, conscious, even as she spoke, that she sounded like Mara, intervening with her squabbling toddlers, reminding them that it was 'nice to share'.

Josette stepped back, removed the safety glasses and gloves and thrust them ungraciously towards Luka. He ignored her, picked up the tweezers and let the last few plants fall into the herbarium.

'Easy,' he said.

So it seemed. Josette, her arms folded, still sulking – her expertise and authority undermined – asked Eve if she wanted to check the tank before they sealed it.

Eve wasn't interested in technical details. The thing itself, the bright box of anatomised flowers, was what she wanted to see. It looked exactly as she'd envisaged. The nightshade specimens, suspended in their transparent medium, seemed to hang in space, shivering faintly, and the backlit berries glistened like black tears.

'Perfect,' she said.

Before Josette could object, Luka put on the safety glasses, picked up the acetylene torch and, in a spray of sparks, swiftly sealed the cabinet. Usurped again, her jaw set grimly, Josette walked around the tank, leaning in to examine the seams, tapping them with a screwdriver, clearly unhappy that she couldn't find fault with Luka's handiwork.

'That's enough, Josette. Leave it,' Eve said. 'Let's get on.'

Josette dropped the screwdriver on the lid of the sealed tank.

'Watch it!' Luka said, in an unnecessarily teasing tone. 'You'll crack it!'

Josette glared at him.

'Come on, Jose,' Glynn said. 'Let's get these pigments sorted.'

Eve turned on the radio to reports of wildfires in Greece – up to a hundred dead – and she thought of her own wildfires here. No fatalities, so far. But the sparks were spreading. The tension in the studio was palpable – Glynn and Josette now refused to address Luka directly.

Eve reminded herself that tension was good for the creative process. It seemed to be good for the bedroom too.

Glynn had almost finished the base colour for the third canvas and the fresh green field would soon be ready for its scattered blue stars of aquilegia. Josette resumed filming and, with her eye behind the camera, seemed to regain composure, zooming in on Eve as she worked on the watercolour, questioning her further about her methods, filming the extravagant sweeps of Glynn's arm as he laid the chromium oxide wash across the canvas, moving in for close-up footage of the two floating herbaria and the five empty tanks waiting to be filled.

'In many ways, the process is an investigation,' Eve said, as she teased out the delicate spurs of the petals with her finest rigger brush. 'If I want to learn about something, I paint it.'

She noticed Josette was carefully excluding Luka from the film, sweeping past the dissection table, filming every corner of the room except his. It was so childish. She was almost a decade older than Luka yet he had the edge on maturity. Josette may have given up making her own art, but she retained the cliché diva temperament. For almost ten years, Eve had lived with the tidal surges of her assistant's moods but this pettiness was exasperating; if it weren't for her competence and loyalty, Josette would have been banished from the studio long ago.

'What's this one again?' Luka called out.

Josette sighed, a little exhalation of contempt.

Luka ignored her, and so did Eve.

'Aquilegia,' Eve said. 'From the Latin for eagle – the petals are said to look like an eagle's claw. It's also called columbine.'

'Like the massacre?"

She hadn't thought of that connection.

'From Columbus – the dove,' she said.

'So, two birds? One predatory and one peaceful?'

'If you like. The folk name is grandmother's bonnet.'

'Bonnets?' He held up a flower and squinted at it. 'Oh, yeah! I see it now.'

'A pretty wicked grandmother,' she said.

He laughed and she caught a narrow-eyed look of contempt pass between Glynn and Josette.

'How poisonous is it?' Luka asked.

'Well, not as lethal as some.' Determined not to be oppressed by Josette's mood, Eve picked up the herbal and read out: '"Gastroenteritis, palpitations ... used to induce miscarriages ..." Not pleasant, but that manganese-blue pigment we're about to mix is actually more toxic.'

The pellucid powder used by generations of artists to render a summer sky was now deemed so harmful to the environment, and so toxic to humans, that its manufacture had been banned. Glynn and Josette, displaying the resourcefulness that made them indispensable, managed to track down rare illicit stocks. It was helpful to be reminded that those two still had their uses.

'This is getting *really* interesting,' said Luka, looking over at the tin of powdered pigment with a new respect.

Josette picked up the camera again and brushed past him, blocking Eve's view of him. The lens swept the studio, taking in everything except the boy.

14

It's started to rain again. She ducks into a doorway in Frith Street – a boutique hotel which two hundred years ago, in its former life as a Soho boarding house, accommodated itinerant painter and maverick writer William Hazlitt, one of Florian's heroes. Roused to a fury by some slight, or imagined slight, Florian used to quote Hazlitt on the pleasures of hating: 'we throw aside the flimsy veil of humanity ... the greatest possible good of each individual consists in doing all the mischief he can to his neighbour'.

In hatred, as in love and portraiture, Florian was a master, and his most potent store of contempt was reserved for those who had been closest to him: erstwhile friends like Lucian Freud (too successful for Florian's liking); Florian's former dealer (who committed the crime of insisting on his full commission); and Eve herself, the lover who got away.

She searches in her bag for her umbrella as two tourists – Americans, husband and wife, presumably – emerge from the hotel in waterproofs to hail a cab.

'London rain, eh?' says the man to Eve, jovially.

'Yes!' Eve replies with a smile strained by a sense of her own bad faith.

If she had the energy she would have pointed out that no, actually, London has lower precipitation than Paris or New York or even Rome. But reputation is a tricky commodity, another flimsy veil, one that conceals the wearer then consumes her. Let them indulge their comforting cliché of rainy London.

Keen to avoid the crowds, she finds herself in Manette Street, behind the site of the old Foyles bookshop, where some of her more radical art college contemporaries used to go on book-stealing expeditions. This was shoplifting as a political act, they would say. Eve would smile and nod – more bad faith – and make her excuses. As a young student, she was intent on shaking off her suburban roots but couldn't make the leap into larceny and, once more, she hated herself for her bourgeois timidity.

Where were they now, the dashing champions of the revolution? Mara kept in touch with some of them – the most high-profile survivors were gearing up for retirement from senior posts in television, journalism, local government and the law, and, no doubt, they'd ceased to view shoplifting as a brave blow against the iniquities of monopoly capitalism.

Eve always had difficulty reading people and was bewildered by the gulf between expressed intention and action. Kristof was more clear-sighted. Even virtuous Mara could sniff out cant from a hundred paces. And

Luka? He'd scanned and parsed Eve in an instant. For her, though, plants have always been a better bet. Plants and paints.

She had been working so intensely that she failed to see the warning signs. In bed, after a half-hearted attempt at lovemaking, which she put down to the heat and exhaustion, Luka rolled over and confessed.

'No, no. It's not the work. It's not you. It's Josette. She's been trying to sabotage me. Right from the start.'

'Don't worry about her,' Eve said, stroking his face. 'She can be tricky.'

'Tricky? She's a sociopath.'

'Don't exaggerate. She's a good worker. Loyal, too.'

'Loyal to herself.'

He brushed Eve's hand away.

'What exactly has she done to you?' she asked. His petulance was beginning to grate. 'Come on, Luka. Tell me.'

He rolled away from her.

'What's going on?' she asked.

'It's nothing I can't handle.'

'Come *on*,' she coaxed. 'Out with it.'

He turned onto his back and stared up at the ceiling, hands behind his head.

'She's so up herself. Mixed race and gay – she's got everything going for her, hasn't she?'

His sudden fierceness threw Eve. She was unsure how to respond.

'Well,' she said finally, 'you don't have to like her to work with her. I don't come to the studio to make friends. I could have plenty of those at home, if I wanted.'

'Isn't this your home?'

He looked so vulnerable.

'Yes, of course it is. Here, with you, feels like home,' she said gently. 'But outside, in the studio – it's a place of work. Egos shouldn't come into it.'

He frowned again.

'Are you saying I'm egotistical?'

'No! We're talking about Josette. She's a big personality. She's been with me a long time. She's fiercely loyal and she's jealous of you. Don't let it get to you. You're working so well.'

'You really think so?'

That touching insecurity.

'You're a marvellous addition,' Eve said.

He pulled her towards him and they kissed. The moment for passion had passed but there was sensual pleasure in companionship, too.

As they drifted towards sleep, her head resting on his chest, he started up again.

'But Josette. She's *all* ego. Her filming's useless too. So boring. Yet she won't let me near the camera. It's all about her. I don't trust her and you shouldn't either.'

'Shh … Let's get some sleep now?' There was more impatience in her voice than she intended.

He didn't let up. 'I see it. You don't.' He threw off the duvet and sat up. 'I've heard her whispering with Glynn, mocking you, slagging off your work, I've seen her rolling her eyes at you, nudging Glynn, behind your back. You should hear what she says about you. She likes her status in the studio but doesn't value you or your art. She resents what we have, you and me, and she's got it in for me.'

They were both fully awake now. Eve sat staring into the shadows of the darkened room. News of this betrayal was humiliating, and what made it more wounding – the poison on the arrow tip – was that her lover should have witnessed it.

Yet she felt weary at the thought of having it out with Josette. They were in the middle of a complex project. It would be disastrous for the work. Eve had to think this through. Be strategic.

'Look. I'll take her aside,' she said. 'Tell her to go easy on you. To calm down.'

'And if she doesn't?'

'She will.'

'Well,' he said, clenching his fists, 'if she doesn't, I'm not sure I can continue to work here.'

Eve reached over and stroked his arm. 'Trust me. We'll sort it out. Everything will be fine. Sleep now.'

She leaves Charing Cross Road and turns into quieter Denmark Street, the Tin Pan Alley of the sixties and seventies where boyfriends with musical pretensions would hang out in guitar shops housed in eighteenth-century buildings and where the Sex Pistols, who might have been improved by a few pretensions, would rehearse their shambolic sets under the guidance of Malcolm, their wily Svengali. The street has preserved its rackety charm despite the wide-scale demolition and construction going on around it to make way for the new rail service. Kristof talked approvingly of the plans for 'mixed-use development' at St Giles junction and praised the buildings' 'innovative retractable facades'. She concedes it has to be an improvement on the St Giles of the eighteenth century, notorious as inspiration for Hogarth's Gin Lane engravings, his extended study of the evils of poverty and addiction. But as far as Eve is concerned these new luridly coloured blocks – clad in mustard yellow, phlegm green and brick-red grids – are so hideous that they make nearby Centrepoint look like Sanssouci.

She can hear Kristof's chiding: 'The trouble with you, Eve, is you're a traditionalist masquerading as a rebel.'

Ah, if that were her *only* trouble ...

Luka had seen Josette's treachery first and Eve reproached herself for being so narrow in her focus that she'd missed it completely. This omission prompted a serious reckoning; for an artist, whose most important sense was sight, she was guilty of a fatal myopia. Her eye had been fixed to microscope and magnifying glass for too long and she failed to look up. Engrossed in cellular detail of petal and stamen she didn't notice that the flower was withering and beyond it the entire garden had become a wasteland. So it was with the studio. Her marriage too. With most of her relationships, in fact.

Early that morning, two hours before the others were due to arrive, she and Luka began work. She climbed the ladder to start on the blue canvas while he walked towards the dissection tray.

'Eve!'

His urgent shout startled her.

'What is it?' She was already descending the ladder and hurrying towards him.

'Look!'

He was pointing at the nightshade cabinet – the herbarium that he'd finished and sealed so efficiently yesterday. The floor beneath it was glistening with a viscous fluid which was visibly dripping from the tank. Yesterday's translucent box of floating berries, flowers and leaves was a wrecked stew of shrivelled vegetation.

She was furious with Luka. But most of all she was furious with herself. Another failure of perception. Her vision was so foolishly skewed by desire that she trusted this inexperienced, overconfident boy. He looked as if he knew what he was doing. Blinded by intimacy, she encouraged him.

But now, he was pointing again, at the far corner of the display case, the site of the leak. This wasn't an inexpertly sealed seam. It was gaping, damaged: prised open by the screwdriver that lay on the display case where Josette dropped it yesterday, after making such a performance of inspecting Luka's work.

When Josette finally arrived, bursting through the door, a patchouli-scented blur of pink hair and bright drapery, carrying a box of pastries for morning coffee, laughing at some shared joke with Glynn, she made a show of shock and concern over the damaged case – 'God, no! How did that happen?' – and feigned outrage at the suggestion that she was responsible.

'Why the hell would I do that?'

'You tell me,' said Eve coldly.

Then Josette turned to Luka. 'It must have been him.'

'That's pathetic,' he said, shaking his head. 'You fuck up my work, then try to pin the blame on me. We all know you've had it in for me right from the start.'

Glynn stepped forward to intervene.

'Look. This isn't necessary. It must have been an accident. We can start again. If we work on this together, we'll have it finished in a couple of hours.'

'Nice try,' said Luka. 'Sticking up for your friend again?'

Eve knew she had to take control before the argument got out of hand.

'Glynn, this is wilful, criminal damage. We can't just "start again".'

Josette glared at Luka. 'Too right.'

'That's enough, Josette,' Eve said.

'Whatever happened,' Glynn continued, addressing Eve directly, 'whatever's been said or done in the heat of the moment, we can all agree one thing – we need to get back to work here. This is such an amazing project, the culmination of years of work together. We're so lucky to be involved, Josette and me, and we want to be part of it and help you realise your vision.'

Eve was almost persuaded. It would be far easier to forget this, put it down to a fleeting display of temper, start again and move on. They'd been her team for so long, Glynn and Josette. But then Luka broke the silence.

'Oh yeah?' he said to Glynn. 'That's not what you said last week. I heard you – the two of you, sniggering over the canvas. What was it you called Eve? The Princess of Chintzes?'

Eve's faced blazed and her loyal, long-standing assistants stood there, exposed and stricken, their silence an admission of guilt.

'We'd better go,' said Josette quietly.

'Yes,' Eve said. 'I think you'd better.'

Josette bustled out of the studio, a huffing caricature of indignation, as if she hadn't been sacked, as if she'd quit. And Glynn, Josette's faithful lapdog, walked out with her, throwing Luka a final look of frank hostility.

15

Eve and Luka adapted quickly to the new reality. She went back to work on the blue canvas, losing herself gratefully among the frilled sepals of aquilegia while Luka calmly restored the nightshade herbarium, filling it with fluid and fresh specimens and sealing it once more. He printed the aquilegia photographs and set them out on the table before moving on to continue Glynn's work on the green ground for the next sequence. Green on green. Aromatic *Artemisia absinthium* – a neurotoxin, said to cause convulsions, renal failure and epilepsy. Also, in small quantities, an ingredient of the eponymous drink favoured by demi-mondaines and hipsters. She would use chromium oxide green with the cooler green of copper azomethine.

Luka ground and mixed the pigments, set up the cabinet for the next herbarium and filmed Eve at her work. Soon he had quietly and competently taken over all the roles once performed by a battalion of assistants. It made perfect sense. How had she put up with their chattering and bickering for so long? In those moments when she wasn't fixed on her work, Eve looked up and marvelled at her young lover, his face grave with concentration, pretty and potent as an annunciating Gabriel, bringing nothing but good news. All she'd ever needed was Luka. They worked so well together and when he turned on the camera to film her at work, it seemed they were mining a deeper level of intimacy as he moved on from Josette's formulaic questions about process to a serious investigation of Eve's wider vision and reflections on her life.

'In the end,' she told him, 'it's about the impulse to see, to really see, and to make others really see – beauty and atrophy, the dawn of life and its decay.'

Kristof, phoning from Singapore, was so puffed up by his own project, full of news about office politics, budgetary restraints and the latest from Wanda Wilson's 'people' on the Art Ranch project, that he expressed no curiosity about Eve's work or her life. She had a mad urge to break into his monologue, tell him about Luka. Tell him everything.

'I've had a personnel change in the studio,' she started to say.

'Great! Must go. Sorry.'

He would be back next week. Her vertiginous confessional urge was replaced by cold unease. She looked over at Luka. He was assembling another herbarium cabinet, his strong arms, bare in rolled sleeves, beautiful as those of Caillebotte's Paris workmen, the *raboteurs*, whom she and Theo had admired in the Musée d'Orsay so long ago.

How could she replace *this* with *that*? It would be like stepping from a sun-dappled glade into a coffin, lying down and sealing the lid.

'Love you, darling,' Kristof said, before ending the call.

He might, more convincingly, have signed off: 'Thank you for listening.'

As Eve began the green sequence, the pace increased. She and Luka would regularly work straight through until the early hours. This level of industry required stamina. She was less than halfway through the project and knew she mustn't overextend herself.

Luka shadowed her faithfully, filming her at every step, and no task was too demanding or demeaning. Each day at noon he left the studio to buy their lunch and get essential supplies and there was none of the low-level grumbling or dragging feet she'd become used to from the other assistants. He took pleasure in the work. In *her* work.

One bright morning she volunteered to do the errands herself. It seemed an amusing role reversal to leave him attending to business in the studio while she set off for a little light fetching and carrying. She needed a break and it would be good to walk briskly and feel the cool air on her face. She'd been working so intensely, she'd almost forgotten a world existed beyond the studio.

She stepped out into a copper blaze of sun and walked through the deserted business park – its local authority designation a double oxymoron; there wasn't much business going on and the neighbourhood bore no resemblance to a pleasure garden. Once it was part of the second largest industrial estate in Europe, a thronging citadel of factories and workshops on a confluence of canal and river, a useful debouch for toxic by-products in those heedless days. Now the area was silent, those hulking buildings were mostly deserted and, apart from the occasional discarded supermarket trolley or bicycle, the river was cleaner than it had been for a century. The fish were back, it was said, though Eve would take some persuading before she would eat a pan-fried product of this river, whose banks were haunted by junkies and winos.

Kristof bought the lease on the site with a long-term proposal to turn it into a 'technology hub' and there was talk of converting the old flour mill into luxury flats. Plans stalled last year. Their son-in-law, the impenetrable Norbert, was said to be acting as an intermediary with several IT companies which were seeking to relocate their British headquarters. The white heat of technology was not much in evidence at the moment. A couple of Internet fashion retailers inhabited two floors of the flour mill, above a car wash that, judging by the number and demeanour of its clientele, seemed to be a front for a shadier business. Next door to them was a minicab company, an analogue Canute, holding the tide against the digital advance of Uber.

Her studio, it struck her on bleaker days, had something of the medieval Danish king about it too – valiantly standing firm on the shore, producing art for an impervious world, as waves bearing debris from a polluted sea crashed around it. She had to watch for the undertow.

A low, rusty iron bridge crossed the canal. From there, a muddy path led to a flight of concrete steps up to the broad concrete walkway spanning the motorway. She stopped at its midpoint to look down on the lines of speeding traffic sixteen feet below. She liked these impersonal industrial views – the noisy machines streaming in orderly lines like a monstrous piece of op art.

Across the motorway, she descended again and skirted the river, walking through the bank of scrubby bushes – broom, hawthorn and a thicket of lilac hung with small knotted plastic bags heavy with dog shit: a copse of excremental prayer trees. What was that about? The human urge to decorate? One for Wanda.

She turned into the shabby high street. She'd brought Hans here once on some errand – a last-minute present from the deli for his aged aunt – and he'd been appalled: 'This is the *high* street?'

The delicatessen, run by a tenaciously cheerful gay couple, was an optimistic anomaly in a thirties parade of grimy shops dominated by a castellated pub draped with St George's flags. There was a betting shop and a massage parlour, where it was also possible to get tanned and tattooed in a single sitting. Next door to a charity shop – a dispiriting holding pen for the cast-offs of the poor – the small branch library had been turned into a food bank and there were boxes of donations outside: low-grade tins, biscuits, spongy white bread and a pack of disposable nappies.

The deli was empty and she rang the bell on the counter to summon Dino or Thierry. As she waited, she gazed absently at the glass cabinet filled with wheels and wedges of cheese – an Orphist abstract in zinc white and pyrrole orange with a slab of blue-veined Carrara marble. On the counter were bowls of exotic salads. Plump vine leaf parcels made her think of the faecal fruit hanging from the riverbank lilacs and there was a jar of artichoke hearts, pale as pickled embryos in a cabinet of curiosities. Who bought this stuff round here? When she sacked her team, Thierry and Dino must have lost 70 per cent of their custom. Would the cave-aged Roquefort and artichoke hearts end up in the food bank too?

Dino emerged from the back office and took her order.

'How's Glynn?' he asked.

'Fine,' she said. 'As far as I know . . .'

She paid, took her bags and left the shop before he could ask any more. That was enough social interaction for one day. She walked back past the pub, where a hunched figure now sat outside veiled in cigarette smoke.

'Cheer up, darling,' the cracked voice called out.

She looked over and saw that it was a lone woman gripping a glass of urinous-coloured spirits in one hand, a cigarette in the other. Next to her was a supermarket trolley piled high with what must have been her worldly goods, carefully sorted into scores of tightly packed plastic bags.

'All right, love?' the woman said, baring a gargoyle's broken-toothed smile. A jaunty mascot – a grubby naked Barbie doll – was pinned to the front of the trolley like a ship's figurehead.

Eve turned and walked away.

'I said, "all right?", you stuck-up cow!' the woman shouted after her.

Eve hurried on; every step she'd taken away from the studio had been an unnecessary diversion. She needed perspective on her work and now she'd got it. She wanted to run back, to the calm order of easel and canvas, to the clear narrative of film, to the beauty of the floating herbarium, and Luka.

16

The rain seems to have stopped at last. She pauses to fold away her umbrella and sees that she's outside the small Cartoon Museum. Art of a kind, she supposes. Draughtsmanship and wit were involved, at least, and an attempt to address current concerns – qualities absent from any of Wanda Wilson's infantile 'concepts' and sickening confidence tricks.

When Eve returned to the studio after her dispiriting trip to the high street, she sensed that something had changed. Luka's back was turned to her and he was working at the canvas. Painting. But he'd completed the background for the green sequence days ago.

'Luka?' she called out, walking towards him as calmly as she could. He had moved on from wide gestural strokes of chromium oxide and flat green ground. Leaning in, his face inches from the canvas, he was absorbed in detail, using a rigger brush loaded with the milkier copper azomethine green, painting the leaves of artemisia with pointillist precision.

'What the hell do you think you're doing?'

It was as if she hadn't spoken. He glanced at her water-colour, which he'd propped up on the paint table to use as a guide, then turned back to the canvas and stippled at the detail to create a hazy effect.

She grabbed his wrist. 'Enough. You've crossed a line here.'

He laughed, shook her off and reloaded his brush with colour. This was all a joke to him.

'I thought I'd help out. I know we need to push on.'

He was defacing her work and making light of it. How could she have misread him so badly? He was smiling, expecting to be congratulated or thanked. Then she looked at the canvas. He'd made rapid progress. And here was the thing, the second shock of the day – it was really rather good. The delicate fronds, like terrestrial seaweed, were exact reproductions of her watercolour. No one would know the difference.

'Not bad,' she conceded finally.

'Yeah.' He put down his brush and kissed her. 'This is how I used to earn a living, remember? Copying. Belle always said I'd make a good counterfeiter.'

Belle was right. Eve felt such guilt for mistrusting him. She watched in silence as he went back to work, conjuring the plant in quick, economical strokes. His pride was touching. It hadn't occurred to him that she would object. Why should she? He was paying her homage. She picked up another small brush, a sable round, and began to work alongside him. This canvas would be their joint work – her

164

gift to him and an act of trust. Green on green: from the distance an undifferentiated field, close up a subtle tapestry of sixty-seven interlacing plants, beautiful and deadly.

He set the camera on the tripod to film them both at work.

'Tell me about this one again,' he said.

'Artemesia. They use it to make absinthe – that aromatic anise smell. It's also known as lad's love ...'

They kept at it, side by side, engaged in true collaboration. A first, for her. Once, the prospect of relinquishing her autonomy would have been terrifying. Now, working closely with someone who valued her vision and shared her sense of purpose, she found his competence and commitment set her free. Like a soloist tentatively exploring the pleasures of the duet, she discovered the repertoire was larger, the interplay of resonances deeper.

This was work as compulsion, a race against a deadline, though as far as she was concerned, the real deadline for her was death – far closer to her than youth, and more pressing than any artificial cut-off point set by Hans, who wanted to capitalise on the success of the Sigmoid show and the coming Gerstein retrospective. But Luka, for whom death was pure abstraction, sensed the urgency too. He matched her pace, a tireless helpmate, intuiting her needs. For him, Eve knew, it was also about bringing this one perfect work, the product of consummate skill and a unique vision, to an imperfect world mired in the mediocre.

Sometimes they listened to music as they worked – Bill Evans, Couperin, Dollar Brand – at other times they would turn on the news: another terrorist attack outside the Houses of Parliament; heatwaves and wildfires had given way to heavy rainfall, catastrophically in Italy, where a motorway bridge collapsed – forty dead so far – and in Kerala, where more than four hundred died and a million were displaced. Then, when the news oppressed them and the music ceased to transport, they would shut out the world and he would return to the camera and film her.

He liked to hear her reminisce about her art school years, about her early days on the circuit, about her time in New York, about Wanda, the parties at Warhol's Factory, the earnest Fluxus crew and the crazy days with the Viennese Actionists, as he steered the film from an exposition of Eve's singular process to an exploration of her life and work in the context of late-twentieth- and twenty-first-century contemporary art.

His college dissertation on her work had been a useful apprenticeship for their relationship. It was a shortcut too – none of that lying in the dark, tentatively outlining the CV to a new lover. Luka knew it all. And he wanted to get the details, go deeper.

'So what was she like, Wanda? I mean really ...?'

The rhythm of reminiscence complemented the process of work. The broad sweep first, then the detail.

'Really? Well, to be honest ...'

'You were friends, though?'

'You could say that. Once. It was complicated.'

'How complicated?'

He smiled – that alluring grin.

'The usual,' she said. 'Lovers, status anxiety … Wanda was always … hypersensitive.'

He scanned her with the camera – close up, in intimate engagement with the canvas; medium shot, mixing pigment or refining a floating herbarium; long shot, a tiny figure in the vastness of the studio, a miniature peasant in a Claude landscape – and indiscretion was tempting. He urged her to say more, tell all, but she resisted. A lifetime's habit of wariness was acquired for a reason.

'But,' he persisted, 'you did say that thing about her sole talent being for monstrous self-pity?'

'I was misreported,' Eve said. She had, by now, learned to deflect that one. 'A creepy journalist from the *Village Voice* misheard me at a party.'

The camera was on and – even though the final edit would be hers – she didn't want to risk derailing her reputation at this stage by challenging art world shibboleths. Wanda wasn't worth that.

'And you were at her first exhibition – *Love/Object* – in the seventies. That must have been amazing.'

'Amazing. Yes. You could say that.'

As Eve knew from Nancy, this generation had no sense of history, so it was especially flattering that Luka should value Eve's experience, be so curious and know so much about the art scene of the seventies. But you could have too much history.

There was no need to encourage his unhealthy interest in Wanda Wilson, or to tell him the story behind that first pitiful exhibition. How Wanda, naked but for a russet velvet robe draped over one shoulder and a garland of laurel leaves crowning her wild hair, in the guise of J. W. Waterhouse's Narcissus, stood in front of a mirrored wall for two weeks, staring impassively at her reflection for eight hours a day, her attention never wavering despite the distraction of spectators, some admiring, some sceptical, crowding around her. The admission fee kept out mischievous schoolkids but it didn't stop more uninhibited male spectators tugging at her toga, whispering lewd suggestions or, in one case, slapping her dimpled buttocks. Wanda barely flinched, gazed on and was rewarded with more press attention for the stunt.

As a feat of endurance it could hardly be faulted, like those human statues which later sprang up, tourism memes – gold-painted Charlie Chaplins winking in Covent Garden, cloth-draped Mariannes by the Pont des Arts, silver-sprayed Fernsehturms in Alexanderplatz. They all deserved a euro and a commendation for stamina. But Wanda was making bigger claims than that, according to the exhibition's two-page catalogue. She was 'challenging the relationship between viewer and artist, subverting the process of objectification in an alchemical engagement which transforms spectator and practitioner alike'. It was Eve's duty, as a serious artist, to test the hypothesis.

If unfinished business with Wanda over Florian Kiš played any part in Eve's plan, she wasn't aware of it at the time.

And so, in the eighth hour of the final day of the show, she turned up with Wanda's boyfriend, Mike, who, after a year on the wagon, had been talked into anticipating the evening's triumphant closing party by getting stupefyingly drunk. Holding his hand, Eve forced their way to the front of the crowd, right next to Wanda, whose gaze, as she neared the finishing line, now had a desperate fixity. Eve looked into the mirror at her room-mate's reflection. In her wonky laurel crown and toga, staring ahead at her own uncomely image, there was something affectingly risible in Wanda's self-belief.

Then Eve moved so fast that Mike later claimed to have no recollection of the moment she grabbed his crotch with her right hand and pulled him towards her with her left. They began to make out, tongue on tongue, hungrily tearing at each other's clothes as if they were entirely alone. Wanda saw the whole thing, as she was meant to, but stared on, unmoving, even when the spectators cheered and whistled, applauding Eve and Mike as if they were a fitting finale devised by the artist to her *Love/Object* marathon.

Wanda didn't make it to the closing party that night. Nor to any party for the next few months, while Mike and Eve pursued their frivolous affair. Mara attempted to mediate but got only abuse from heavily medicated Wanda, whose six-month crack-up – reprised and amplified when Kristof and Eve got together two years later – became her subject. And look where it got her.

The Three Msketeers fell on their swords and Wanda was now a 'world-renowned multi-disciplinary artist', presiding over a multimillion-dollar industry. She'd exhibited at the Getty, the Whitney and the Pompidou Centre and was credited with, according to one fatuous review, 'transforming the definition of art' with her 'explorations of the body, sexuality and gender' – in other words, she compulsively took off her clothes in public, displaying those parts of the anatomy which, in the absence of lovers, were usually seen by gynaecologists and colorectal surgeons. For this generous spirit, she received countless grants from American arts foundations, held teaching posts at NYU, Bard and San Francisco, and was given an honorary professorship by a university in Estonia.

She moved on to 'immersive art', which saw her taking up residence in institutions and galleries and the homes of the super rich, role-playing – Maries Antoinette and Curie, late-period Colette, Ayn Rand, Frida Kahlo, eccentric housekeeper, vengeful mother-in-law, medieval saint – for weeks on end in pantomimes that had the critics swooning.

'In the age of the Internet and cyber alienation, Wilson offers a thrilling carbon-based durational experience in which the boundaries between art and life are entirely dissolved. Her characters inhabit our space over time, we feel their breath on our cheeks, their touch on our skin, and in a thaumaturgical process, we are transformed by the encounter.' Eve had to consult the copies kept on her phone to remember the exact phrasing of her own positive reviews, but she was word-perfect on Wanda Wilson's.

In May, when Kristof was preparing his brief for the Art Ranch, he showed Eve a *New York Times* piece from last year outlining Wanda's most recent work – *Domestic Intervention I/Mansion* – in which for two weeks she took over the Long Island home of a financial analyst and his wife, trustee of a dozen US galleries, relegating them to the role of uniformed domestic servants who waited on the artist at table, did her laundry and cleaned up after her. The whole piece was committed to film, in which Wanda portentously described her consensual home invasion as 'relational art'. 'In *Domestic Intervention I/Mansion*,' she said, 'the artist is mere catalyst, the spectator takes centre stage and becomes both medium and subject.' The couple, who paid more than a million dollars for the experience, described it as a 'profound, life-changing exploration of empathy'.

Wanda had moved on, in every sense: from angry young feminist *épating* the male bourgeois by flinging a pot of menses in his face, to grande dame of the conceptual art scene, bestriding a billion-dollar hokum industry.

She now had studios in New York, Berlin and Rome, as well as her Double U Art Ranch in Connecticut – a boot camp (tastefully spartan dorms at luxury-spa prices) where acolytes from all over the world were inculcated in the 'Wilson Technique', a gruelling series of fasts, eye-gazing workshops, group screaming, 'creative role play', and 'backwards hiking' through prepared trails holding rear-view mirrors, to prepare them, in a pyramid scheme of abominable pretension, to go forth and spread the Wilson word to a gullible public.

Yes. Wanda had a lot to thank Eve for. But Luka didn't need to know all that. Dissembling as best she could, Eve reminisced more generally about Wanda, about Bradley, whose career stalled before he made a lucrative comeback twenty years later playing twinkly silver foxes in porn movies – 'let me help you with that, young lady' – and Mike, poor Mike, and the whole crowd, the bio-art, the smeared body fluids and self-inflicted wounds, Fluxus and those sadomasochistic bozos, the Actionists. But she held back on the true story of Wanda, the neediness and tantrums, the adolescent howling and heartache.

Nor did she mention her conviction that Wanda's success was a practical joke played on the art establishment, that it was a case of the Empress's new clothes, in which the cheering crowds were also naked. For Luka, despite his passion for Eve's work, subscribed to the conventional hare-brained view that Wanda was some kind of pioneer. So Eve went along with it. Yes, she knew

172

the great Wanda Wilson, yes, she was close to her, yes, they shared an apartment, and, occasionally, lovers … it pleased Eve to please Luka and so she continued to talk, answering his questions as best she could without alienating him, the art world or posterity, giving a diplomat's version of her personal history as the camera rolled.

Besides, to tell the story of her New York days, even in sanitised form, was to reclaim her youth, to live it again, as it might have been, without the anxiety, the feuds and self-doubt. In those early days, blundering blindly, still reeling from her bruising entanglement with Florian, she could have no sense of the trajectory of her work. She might have baulked if the veil had parted and she'd seen the years of disappointment ahead, as the art world turned its back on her, belittling her while canonising the megalomaniac mediocrity Wanda.

But then, if Eve had been able to see even further into the future, flashing forward through the wilderness years of marriage and obscurity, if she could have glimpsed herself that afternoon in her studio, her beautiful young lover next to her, engaged in the finest work of her career, all the discouragement of those hard years would have seemed a minor inconvenience. The grunt work was done, the pigment mixed, flat ground painstakingly laid on canvas, against which her achievements would finally shine like pole stars in the void.

17

She passes Bloomsbury Square and waits to cross at the junction of Southampton Row. During the day, the road is a busy midtown intersection but tonight it's quiet, apart from occasional taxis and night buses which pass by in a spray of rainwater. Next to Eve on the pavement, an East Asian couple, a young man and woman, possibly Chinese, also wait to cross. A breeze gets up, sending debris – fast-food cartons, free newspapers, brochures and handouts – scudding down the street. Eve stands there, buffeted, and remembers reading Jeff Nuttall, a counterculture guru of the sixties and seventies, who mocked the conformists – 'straights' was the term – who would wait on an empty road for the traffic lights to change before daring to step out. Nuttall, like all those *soixante huitards*, was a man in a hurry. Eve is killing time, though she has far less of it to spare these days. She stands with the Chinese couple, waiting for the signal before crossing ...

It had all been going so well. Hans phoned. He wanted to see how the project was progressing. She told him that she'd pared back her staff.

'I heard,' he said. 'As long as it's not interfering with the work.'

He arranged to visit the next day. When he arrived, four watercolours, four sets of photographs, three monumental canvases and three floating herbaria were ready and the artemisia sequence was almost complete.

'You're managing all this without Josette and Glynn?' He turned away from the canvases to hold the nightshade watercolour at arm's length.

'Luka does more work than all of them put together. And his temperament suits me.'

'I imagine it does,' Hans said, appraising Luka with a connoisseur's stare.

His expression remained neutral as he walked round the studio, left arm folded across his bon viveur's paunch, right fist under his chin, taking in the canvases properly: the long view from ten feet away; close up, lifting his glasses to inspect the brushwork, leaning in, nose against the canvas as if he were smelling the painted flowers. Then he paused briefly over the dissection tray and the photographs before peering into the illuminated cabinets of flowers trembling in preserving fluid.

He said nothing and it was hard not to read his wordless scrutiny as criticism. He had never tried to steer Eve in any way, for which she was grateful. But she felt a new impatience with him. For form's sake, in front of Luka, he could at least say something. This silence was humiliating.

While Hans continued his mute patrol of the studio, Luka set up the computer to screen the monkshood life cycle film. Eve moved over to the desk with Hans and they stood behind Luka as he pressed command. The computer's whirr sounded like an old movie projector as the sequence began to play.

'No, Luka. Stop it there,' she said, with a prickle of irritation. 'Rewind. Something's gone wrong.'

The film was playing in reverse; fallen brown petals were infused with colour and flew up to reattach themselves to a bent, desiccated stem which grew erect, surged with glowing sap and stretched towards the light. Freeze-frame – the dead flower, sere and broken, was transformed into an incandescent purple wand.

She reached over the keyboard to stop the film.

'No,' Luka said, gently holding her wrist. 'Wait!'

He was contradicting her – in front of her dealer. She watched, helplessly, wondering what her next move should be – a public row would be undignified – as the petals flared in their imperial glory then folded away, vivid silks crammed into small green purses which shrank into the stem's verdant vigour. Freeze-frame again. The plant paled, wavered and coiled downwards, a cobra retreating into a snake charmer's basket, then one poignant tiny leaf seemed to give a last defiant wave before sinking below the soil.

'Interesting,' said Hans, nodding slowly.

'We need to play it again. The right way,' said Eve. 'The cycle. Life to death … No freeze-frame.'

176

'No need,' said Hans, holding up his hand. 'Leave that to the wildlife documentary – predictable, commonplace. This is art – from death to life. Much more interesting.'

Luka was looking at her, his eyebrows raised quizzically.

'You really think so?' said Eve. She castigated herself for sounding so uncertain. 'I mean, I know …'

'Really!' said Luka. 'You're challenging the tired old certainties. It's a brilliant, subtle twist.'

Eve flushed. He'd planned this, ignored her instructions and gone his own way. But then there was Hans's response. And Luka was at least giving her the credit. Before she could formulate a reply, Hans spoke again.

'You've moved on to a new plane here, Eve. A profound interrogation of the big questions. Remarkable. We can really do something with this.'

'I can email you the video file to show to clients, if you'd like,' Luka offered.

Hans nodded. 'That would be very helpful.'

Eve reached across Luka and switched off the computer. Then she smiled at him. He smiled back.

On Clerkenwell Road she pauses before the miniature basilica of St Peter's, the Italian church, with its mosaic friezes: the miracle of the loaves and fishes; St Peter receiving the keys to the Kingdom of Heaven. Ornate black-and-gold railings protect the memorial to the 471 Italian civilians who were deported from Britain during the Second World War, destined for internment camps in Canada, but died when their prison boat was torpedoed by the Germans. The railings also deter any rough sleepers – immigrants or indigenes – from bedding down for the night in the twin-arched loggia. No loaves and fishes here. No keys to any kingdom. Another sanctuary barred. She walks on, head down against the biting wind ...

She always knew that, once Kristof got back from Singapore, she would have to return to Delaunay Gardens. She never guessed quite what a wrench it would be, like stepping out from the jewelled colours of a Matisse into the monochrome gloom of a Motherwell. Her first evening farewell to Luka, after another long and productive day, was strained. He was so depressed, almost tearful, and she found herself blindly reassuring him that they would be together soon.

'Properly?' he asked, brightening.

'Properly,' she lied.

'How soon?'

'Soon.'

In truth, she had no idea where, or how, this was going to end. Shared meals with her husband in their cavernous basement kitchen were, in the first week after his return, like board meetings – members' reports, matters arising from the last meeting, any other business. She felt no ill will towards him. She felt nothing at all, in fact. If 'apologies for absence' were on the kitchen agenda she could have cited herself. She felt curiously disembodied, moving weightlessly around the ample space and luxury of her family home, longing for the cramped intimacy of the studio's living quarters.

A new routine began to take shape. In the morning, she would leave home early, before Kristof woke, and arrive at the studio to find Luka already up, gilded by morning light, a young Medici nobleman busy at his tasks. Together, side by side, they would work on intensely until the late evening, their collaboration an act of love more consuming, and transcendent, than mere physical congress.

Kristof, meanwhile, wasn't curious about her late-night returns and early-morning departures – he had work of his own to attend to. He was about to sign the deal on the project for Wanda's Art Ranch, and his design for a new tower next to Sydney Harbour was likely to be approved next year.

But a week after he got back, he asked her to accompany him to dinner at the home of an important new client.

'I know you're busy but I'd really appreciate it,' he said. 'Everyone's bringing their partner.'

She'd assumed her days as a company wife were over.

'It's the worst time for me,' she said. 'I've got so much on at the studio. Ines, the Gerstein curator, is coming back to rummage through my old stuff. And Hans is very excited about this new piece, says there might be a bidding war. I've got to move fast.'

'Please,' he said, reaching out to take her hand.

Kristof's client, Albrecht Bernoise, a Swiss hotelier, had approached him to design a new property in the Middle East. An evening of tedium was guaranteed. But, said Kristof, it would seem like a snub, professionally damaging for him, if she stayed away.

'Couldn't you spend the weekend at the studio to catch up?' He pleaded. 'Can't you allow yourself one night off this week?'

She held back from pointing out that a night away from work and love, demurely supporting her husband in his business aspirations, was not her idea of 'a night off'. But he was always so genial when they coincided at Delaunay Gardens, and he made so few demands on her, that she found it hard to refuse him. Besides, the promise of an unbroken weekend with Luka, without any need to make excuses, was irresistible. She smiled, nodded, and squeezed Kristof's hand.

'I owe you,' Kristof said.

'You certainly do ...'

18

She hated leaving work early that Thursday evening. She hated leaving Luka more. He'd made a start on the background wash for the next canvas, the fifth, and planned to work through the night on it.

'It's my tribute to you – my way of being with you, even in your absence,' he said.

But when the moment came for her to go, he pulled at the zip on her dress and drew her teasingly towards the bedroom. They'd been so busy that they hadn't made love in days and now, with her cab waiting outside, she felt the rip tide tug of desire once more. If she succumbed, that would be it. She'd never leave the studio.

'No. No. I've really got to go … I can't bear it either. I'd much rather be here with you. But it's for work …' she said. 'Our work. I'll be back as early as I can tomorrow.'

She was only partially lying. It was Kristof's work. But she'd learned that Otto Stoltzer, an important Zurich gallerist and collector, would be there too, with his boyfriend, a young Italian artist. 'So it won't all be architects and money men,' Kristof had reassured her. He added that Stoltzer was 'on a buying spree', itching to divest himself of his vast reserves of capital.

In the cab on the way to Knightsbridge, Eve received three texts, framed by affectingly childish *x*s, from Luka, reminding her that he would be waiting for her when she got back. The journey away from him took her seven and a half miles west, spanning London's socioeconomic spectrum, from the hard-pressed east of Dickensian poverty, through pockets of youthful bohemianism, past down-at-heel neighbourhoods where the few visible women in the streets were shadowy figures shrouded in black, along a noisy, neon-lit thoroughfare where drunk girls in short skirts and high heels struggled to stay upright as they queued, shrieking, to get into a nightclub, all the way to the plutocratic mansions of the west with concierges, security and valet-parked supercars.

She put her phone on silent as she walked into the penthouse. Its central water feature and marble floors could have been prised from one of the owner's hotel foyers. She arrived forty-five minutes later than agreed and immediately saw her calculation had been correct – the awkward introductions were over and champagne was already defrosting hosts and guests. Sober and composed, Eve was at an advantage.

'Ah, my wife!' said Kristof, getting up as she walked in. 'My late wife!'

There was a susurration of appreciative laughter. The threshold for wit was going to be low tonight. Otto

Stoltzer nodded curtly to her and turned back to his boyfriend. She was of no interest; he would not be calling Hans in the morning to arrange a purchase. The evening was, she could tell already, a colossal waste of time. How many hours of this would she have to endure? The rest of the gathering was as dispiriting as she'd feared – two middle-aged men working in finance, hospitality and property development with their younger second or third wives, docile and decorative. The most interesting man in the room was her own husband. It was that bad.

The host, Albrecht, led her towards the dinner table. 'So you're an artist? My wife, Laura, is an artist too. And there's Otto and Enzo. We're all great patrons of art here.'

Eve had done her research. Enzo, sleek and feline in a velvet smoking jacket, had built an international reputation with his giant erotic collages made from candy wrappers. Madonna was said to be a fan. Eve and Enzo would not be swapping artists' shop talk on technique and vision.

Stretching across the table was an extensive arrangement of orange gerbera and ornamental cabbages. Eve saw immediately that her place in the seating plan, marked out with handwritten cards tucked in a cabbage leaf, was doubled-edged – an insult and an honour. She was seated opposite the host, at one end of the table, with no neighbour on her left.

The starters were served by an obsequious waiter who kept one arm behind his back, as if concealing a knife.

183

Eve struggled to make conversation with Albrecht and it became apparent that he only had one subject – the hotel business, and in particular the new site he'd just acquired in Doha.

'We're planning a thousand-bed *Kulturhotel* – concerts, exhibitions, performances – which will draw in the world's elites ...'

Eve gazed at her plate, striving to summon another question: 'And how is your *Kulturhotel* in Austria faring in the current economic climate?'

The pink mousse – smoked salmon, at a guess – was framed by oily green apostrophes, as if the chef was making a visual joke on the notion of 'food'.

'Given the constraints and uncertainties, it has been remarkably successful,' Albrecht was saying. 'Turnover is excellent and our wellness programme has attracted a lot of media coverage ...'

Wellness ... another of Nancy's watchwords – the telling combination of consumerism and narcissism.

On Eve's right was Clive Etchinghall, a wealth management consultant and board member of Albrecht's hotel business. He was tentatively poking at his mousse with a fork as if it might go off in his face any minute. He was plump and ruddy-cheeked, with a rasping voice that suggested a staple diet of brandy and cigars and gave an insinuative edge to his most banal remarks. Eve thought it might have been cocaine, rather than a problem prostate or gastric revolt against the fussy food, that drove him, twice, to get to his feet suddenly without apology and head for the bathroom.

His wife, a slender cipher in a cashmere sheath, was opposite Kristof at the other end of the table. They seemed to be engaged in animated conversation. He would be delighting her with details of his own professional achievements.

Having exhausted Eve's questions, the hotelier turned to his neighbour – in her forties, with a startled stare and buck teeth that brought to mind one of Barry Flanagan's dancing hares. This was Albrecht's wife, Laura. Had there been a placement accident? A wrongly distributed name card, for which someone would have hell to pay later? Or had jittery Laura insisted that her husband take the seat next to her as a buffer against possible hostile forces. She was, Eve was told, a 'society jeweller' and, if her calling could be described as art, by the look of the clunky gold chains and brutalist pendants resting on her freckled décolletage, she drew inspiration from the hardware store. Clive was attending to his social duties on his right with the gallerist's candy wrapper boyfriend and Eve, now unoccupied, listened in, with an all-purpose social smile, to the hosts' marital conversation.

'We're planning a thousand-bed *Kulturhotel* – concerts, exhibitions, performances – which will draw in the world's elites and ...'

The wife pushed her untouched starter aside and nodded, wearing her own strained version of Eve's facile smile.

Clive held out his glass for another refill. He was clearly done with Enzo and turned back to Eve.

'A very good Friuli,' he said, gulping the wine. 'Herbaceous, buttery, with a tang of tea leaf. From Albrecht's vineyard.'

'Hmm,' Eve said. She sipped her drink, unimpressed. 'And have you been there? The vineyard?'

Her question, she knew, was hardly interesting, but its plodding politeness was entirely in keeping with the rest of the conversation so far. Clive clearly thought otherwise and ignored her. He leaned across her towards Albrecht, raising his glass again.

'*Prost!*' he said.

'*Prost!*' Albrecht said, lifting his own glass.

Eve caught Laura's eye and realised they were mirroring each other's tightening smiles.

'Good to have the Russkies on the run in Doha!' Clive said.

'They just weren't up to it, were they?' Albrecht gloated.

The main course was served – slivers of unidentifiable flesh set in a fuchsia sauce and garnished with a rosebud carved from a radish – as Albrecht and Clive continued to re-enact highlights of their latest deal.

'They really thought we were going to walk away! And then you …'

'… His face! I never thought he'd go for it. But I guessed, after the Kohler business, that he …'

Laura Bernoise turned from her husband to her other neighbour, Otto Stoltzer – silver-haired and impeccably suited, his Mondrian-patterned pocket square a discreet declaration of aesthetic tendencies. Perhaps Laura was harbouring hopes of an exhibition in Zurich of wearable gold plumbing equipment. Eve's neighbour made another hasty visit to the bathroom and she was marooned, alone again.

When Clive returned to the table, he judged that the social preliminaries were over and he was free to get down to real conversation. He pushed out his chair and twisted round, giving Eve a three-quarter view of his back. Laughing at some wan joke of Kristof's, he leaned behind Enzo. For Clive, gay men obviously fell into the same category as women – at best, they were decorative adjuncts to civilised life, like those ornamental cabbages and gerbera. His voice grew louder – he really did seem high; why else would you find anything Kristof said funny? Kristof seemed surprised by the unfamiliar sound of laughter greeting his unexceptional remarks and, with a fevered gleam, rose to the occasion.

'Why don't architects get to heaven?' Kristof said. 'Because Jesus was a carpenter!'

A joke? Kristof never told jokes. Did he get it from a cracker at the last office Christmas party? She would have to warn him later before this wisecracking got out of hand. But if Clive was guffawing sycophantically at Kristof's attempts, he was laughing even louder at his own feeble repartee.

187

'No point in arguing with the contractors,' Clive wheezed. 'You just get bogged down in ... cementics!'

'That's so great!' Enzo said. 'Your contractors are interested in semantics! Have you met Noam Chomsky? We had dinner with him and Wanda Wilson in the Village.'

Eve began to plan her exit. She needed to think of an excuse that would allow her to leave Kristof there while she caught a taxi east. An accident, not too serious, at the studio – a burst pipe, a small fire. She reached into her bag and took out her phone. Four more imploring messages from Luka, more garlands of kisses.

She was texting him back – 'me too x' – when a fluttering movement in her peripheral vision drew her gaze upwards, diagonally across the table to Otto Stoltzer, who was gesturing at her with his index finger. She gave him a little wave back. She'd written him off too soon. His head was cocked and his left eyebrow was raised interrogatively. They exchanged a smile of recognition – a meeting of kindred spirits in an alien setting.

They were too far from each other, across the savannah of oriental cabbages, to speak. She pulled out a business card from her bag – contact details for her and for Hans – and leaned across the greenery to pass it to him. He could, she tried to signal, email or call her tomorrow, once this dreary evening was behind them. But Otto was waving now. Waving away her card and waggling his index finger again. Waggling and pointing. At the wine. She passed him the bottle.

19

She turns onto Old Street, once a dead zone poised between the cold commerce of the City and the human shambles of Hackney and the old East End. Now, with its nearby clubs and bars still thronging at this hour, in this month of frenzied celebration, it's a chillier, windier combination of Las Ramblas and Rio. Presiding over the party is St Luke's Church, with Hawksmoor's stark obelisk spire, lit blue at night and pointing heavenwards, a neon admonishment to Eve and to the clubbers wandering the streets in search of the next thrill.

For an atheist, Eve is something of a connoisseur of churches. Her parents' mild Anglicanism rarely involved churchgoing but she had a brief and embarrassing passion for brass rubbing in her early teens – touring London's historic parishes with rolls of paper and balls of wax, patiently harvesting the imprints of engraved monumental plaques. Though her interest in mere copying, rather than creating, soon faded, she continued to take pleasure in the buildings themselves – Larkin's 'serious houses on serious earth'. The yearning for grandeur again.

That was something else she and Florian fought about. He loathed all religion and thought her appreciation of a quiet nave, a baroque choir loft and a carved baptismal font betrayed a superstitious nature. He couldn't have been more wrong. To Eve, each church was a novel, or a series of novels – a Trollopian box set – written by many hands over the centuries, remnant of a time when it was easier to place your bets on an invisible world than on the tangible, visible world around you. A rolling programme of hope and grief, down the years — all that marrying and baptising and burying. Kristof later opened her eyes to the architectural complexities. St Luke's, in its current incarnation, was a secular music venue and they went to several concerts there – the LSO, Patti Smith – even though Kristof bore a grudge against the place; in 2002, he'd submitted designs for the church's conversion and lost out. He took it hard. He was competitive about his work and he hated to lose. Another thing she and her husband had in common.

After the excruciating dinner party, as they stood in the street waiting for a taxi outside Albrecht's apartment, Kristof was in high spirits, confident that he'd secured the Doha deal. Eve took advantage of his drunken triumphalism and told him outright that she wouldn't be going back to Delaunay Gardens that night.

'I should go straight to the studio to catch up on lost time,' she said. 'One of the herbaria needs to be sealed urgently tomorrow morning – Ines Alvaro is coming next week – so I might as well spend the night there and get up early to do the job.'

'Can't Glynn do it? Or Josette?'

He'd forgotten her new arrangement. If he'd ever taken it in. She didn't bother to enlighten him.

'No. I've got to deal with it myself,' she said.

'You've been working too hard,' Kristof said woozily, handing her into a separate cab. 'Isn't it time you got yourself another assistant?'

She stared out of the taxi window at the wet city streets slipping past, sliding down the social scale at twenty miles an hour – the same route she's taking now, six months later, on foot – and she began to have doubts. Perhaps it would have been better if she'd gone back to Delaunay Gardens. She was feeling so diminished by the evening, so old, unattractive and marginal, and she didn't want Luka to see her in that state.

But when she opened the studio door and found her lover still up, sitting at the computer, she felt a rush of relief. He'd finished the green ground for the next painting and was uploading the latest film footage. He turned towards her, welcoming her with that seraphic smile, and led her towards the bedroom. Redemption. He restored her to herself.

There was no time for more physical intimacy over the weekend. There was too much to do. He had to finish the artemisia herbarium and then they could move on to the yellow sequence. She started her drawing of a gelse-mium flower – the deceptive five-petalled star, fragrant as orange blossom, innocent in appearance as a child's painting of a summer sun. She would apply the water-colour later. Luka began to mix the oil pigment for the canvas – aureolin yellow with potassium cobaltinitrite and Hansa arylide – then he returned to the dissecting tray with some specimens.

'So, this one?' He twirled the flower in his gloved hands.

'An interesting one,' she told him. She opened the herbal manual and read aloud: '"Cold war politics … said to have been used in assassinations by Chinese and Russian security services."'

'Like those Russians in Salisbury?'

'If you insist,' Eve said with frank irritation. 'You know I'm not interested in banal commentary on current affairs. This project's focus is planetary and timeless.'

But he wasn't listening.

'Slip it in a sandwich …' he hypothesised, 'what happens then?'

She sighed and picked up the book again: '"convul-sions, paralysis and fatal asphyxia"'.

'I could think of a few candidates for that …' he said, bending to his task at last.

'Now can we get back to work?'

Once the weekend was over, the charade of her married life continued. Luka stayed on in the studio at night while Eve, after a full day's work, returned dutifully to Delaunay Gardens. Ines came to the studio to look through Eve's old work and exult in the new, but the curator's enthusiasm was oppressive and did nothing to raise Eve's spirits. How long could she sustain this split life? And how long would Luka tolerate it?

Later that week, she seemed to have her answer. After he'd filled and sealed the artemisia herbarium, Luka told her he was going back to his sister's flat.

'Just for a few nights. It's lonely in the studio without you,' he said.

Eve smiled to hear this admission but said nothing. The situation was hard on him. His growing insecurity was undermining their lovemaking. Sometimes their nights seemed to be more about reassurance than sex. His return to his sister's flat was an ultimatum and Eve couldn't blame him for giving it. She must make a decision but she feared the consequences, either way.

Towards the end of Old Street, she skirts the roundabout – an infantile name for a hellish pedestrian-hostile tangle of traffic; didn't Kristof have something to do with one of these hideous biscuit barrel buildings? – and crosses into Shoreditch. When she was a young student living in a crumbling shared house with Wanda and Mara, the area was known for its dilapidated social housing and squats. By night it was bandit country, haunted by the twentieth-century equivalent of footpads and vagabonds.

And now? Newly built blocks, some of them Kristof's, were selling for millions to overseas investors, and industrial warehouses and Victorian banks had been turned into fancy clubs, low-lit twenty-first-century versions of Gin Lane, with champagne, cocaine and surround-sound music.

Five years ago, when these pleasure grounds were in their infancy, her godson Theo worked as a DJ in one of the new clubs – a glorified illegal rave legitimised by cash. He told her about his job with the pride of a young musician announcing he'd just secured a season at Wigmore Hall.

Outside the clubs tonight, junkies and alcoholics without the income to sustain their habits linger, badgering the wealthy incomers.

'Help the homeless?' A skinny old man in a tattered coat extends a hand seamed with dirt. He has picked the wrong prospect. She shakes her head, draws up her collar and walks on.

After Luka's first night back at Archway, they met the next morning at the studio door. Eve asked him lightly about his evening but his answers were terse and evasive.

'Fine. Yes. I saw her. She was fine.'

He opened the fridge, took out some gelsemium samples and carried them to the dissecting tray, moving through his tasks in silence.

'What's wrong?' Eve asked.

'Nothing.' He picked up a flower with tweezers and walked to the herbarium.

'Tell me.'

'I said, nothing!'

There was anger in his voice and, as he waved her questions away, the tweezers slipped from his grasp and fell into the cabinet, splashing preserving fluid across his ungloved hand.

'Careful!' she shouted.

'Fuck!'

He was shaking his hand, blowing on it, looking around for something to wipe away the corrosive liquid. She picked up a clean rag, quickly poured water on it and went to help him. He shook her off and, still clearly in pain, hurried to the sink to run his hand under the tap. His anger seemed directed at her. This was unfair. It was his carelessness, not hers.

If he didn't want her help there was plenty to occupy her elsewhere. There was work to do. She switched on the news. Another weather front on its way ... 80mph storm ... Power cuts ... Danger to life from flying debris. So, turbulence was general. She put on some music instead – Lester Young, at full volume, hoping those free-floating sax riffs would lift her mood.

She climbed the ladder to start work on the yellow canvas. Unobserved, she looked down on him as he poured out the powdered pigment. He was still sulking. It was like dealing with Nancy, who expected you to spend your time trying to read her feelings, wondering whether you'd accidentally inflicted some injury. He mixed the colour – a quivering slick of egg yolk – put on the gloves and returned to the herbarium.

By early afternoon, she wearied of the music. The news – American sabre-rattling and Brexit scaremongering – was no better. It was Ines Alvaro's misfortune that she should choose this moment to phone. She wanted to follow up on her visit to the studio.

'I'm wondering again about the cobra lily,' the curator told Eve. 'I'm thinking maybe your old *Amaranthus* – love-lies-bleeding – might work better in that spot.'

'Really, Ines. I don't have time to deal with these details,' said Eve, with a terseness that was perhaps ill-judged. 'That's why I have an agent. Call Hans.'

She turned off the phone. Luka's continued silence pressed in on her again and her composure began to crack. She and Kristof were scheduled to meet Nancy and Norbert that evening at a launch for one of Nancy's affiliate partners – a fair trade 'luxury loungewear' company. Mara, such a loyalist, though not an obvious champion of luxury loungewear, would be there with Dot. Mara's daughter Esme, Nancy's IT adjutant, was coming too. Eve would have traded an evening with all of them for an extra hour at the studio with Luka, even in his current mood.

She had to leave. Her absence would raise suspicions at home – Kristof had insisted: 'you have to support your daughter' – and Eve didn't want a confrontation. But she despaired at the thought of a sleepless night, tormented by thoughts of Luka. Unspoken questions and self-hating answers flooded in to fill the silence. Had he tired of her? Why wouldn't he? Was it over? Why wouldn't it be? What was he doing with her in the first place? Perched on the stepladder in her paint-smeared overalls, thinning hair uncombed – when was the last time she'd been to the hairdresser? – streaks of yellow pigment on her tired and, yes, old face, did she really expect the beautiful boy below, bent over her work, to desire her?

He was at the dissection tray again, frowning. She climbed down the ladder to reload her brush with colour, working the bristles back and forwards in the thick golden cream. In a neutral voice, she asked him if he was returning to Archway that night. He shook his head and picked up the still camera. He and Belle had quarrelled, he said.

'It was a major row,' he added. 'We're not speaking.'

'Why?' she asked softly. She didn't care about the details. The only thing that mattered was that he was angry with his sister, not her.

'She told me I was a waster. Couldn't stick at anything. Need to get a life.'

He worked on, methodically photographing each plant part in turn.

'Why don't you tell her you've got a life? A perfectly good one?'

'I kind of did. But she's just full of all these big ideas and thinks everyone else has to be on board with her programme.'

Eve went to him and reached for his hand – still raw and inflamed from the formalin – lifted it to her lips and kissed it.

'Ring her now. Bring her here. This evening. Before I leave. Show her your life. Our life. I'd like to meet her, anyway.'

It was an impulse partly prompted by guilt over his mishap with the formalin – as if it were her fault, somehow – and partly by gratitude to his sister for being the cause of his moodiness. Eve wanted to make him feel better, too. Let Belle see her brother flourishing, in good hands. Eve knew the invitation was irrational, that her affair with Luka was still clandestine, that she was asking for trouble. But there was some part of her that was seeking trouble. She needed an invigorating jolt. No good art ever came out of complacency.

20

A crowd blocks the street outside Shoreditch Town Hall. She picks out French and Spanish accents, possibly Russian and Italian too – all well-heeled, milling around, embracing, waiting for cabs, too absorbed in each other to notice the lone woman pedestrian trying to make her way through. They have been to the Michelin-starred restaurant which now occupies a wing of the pale Italianate building, once the seat of local government. She steps off the kerb to walk round the crowd and looks up at the tower – the fierce stone woman brandishing a torch is named on the plinth as Progress. Nearby is a stained-glass window engraved with the old municipal motto – 'More Light, More Power'. Now there's a maxim to live by.

Belle was poised and pretty, though her looks wouldn't last – no bone structure. Her hair was hennaed and she had a churlish lipsticked pout. A tattered fox fur was draped round the collar of her unseasonal tweed coat, which she unbuttoned and handed to Luka. He took it, with its dangling dead vermin, as if he was her valet. Under the oversized coat, she was gamine, a panto principal boy up for some spirited business with Buttons in leopard-print jacket, leather miniskirt and fishnet tights. The look – ironic tart – was complemented by clumsy lace-up boots. This was fashion as oxymoron. Only the young could get away with it. Belle was a clichéd throwback to the days of the Sex Pistols and the Clash, the edgy London of power cuts, demonstrations and Rock against Racism – more than a decade before she was even born. Eve had lived the real thing. She'd done it all. Worn it all. Now the young, intellectually and culturally enfeebled, were condemned to rummage in the dressing-up box and recycle insipid versions of their elders' countercultures.

Eve poured Belle a glass of wine and noticed the girl had the same small tattoo as Luka – the grinning Mexican skull – on her right hand between thumb and forefinger.

'There must be a gene for tattoo selection,' said Eve.

Belle frowned. 'We got them done at a festival.'

Either she hadn't grasped Eve's mild attempt at a joke – a social overture – or she'd taken offence. This generation, as Nancy regularly demonstrated, was uniquely good at taking offence.

The girl looked up, glass in hand, taking in the enormity of the studio.

'Cool. I've seen photos but there's nothing like being in the physical presence ...'

'You won't have seen photos of *this* work,' said Eve. 'No one's seen it yet except my dealer.'

'And me,' said Luka.

'And Luka,' Eve corrected herself.

'Fantastic,' said the girl, in a flat voice.

Luka led his sister to the dissection tray.

'This is part of what I've been doing,' he told her, picking up a scalpel and swishing it through the air. 'Stripping the plants right back to their elements, then I photograph them and drop them into preserving fluid in these herbariums – herbaria – along with the whole specimens, so you can see the entire life cycle.'

His excitement about the project was not shared.

'And here,' he said, leading her over to the artemisia canvas. 'I worked on this painting with Eve. Can you tell my work from hers?'

Belle shrugged off her jacket. Her black lace shirt was unbuttoned almost to the waist and a tangle of cheap costume jewellery was looped over plump breasts brimming in a red bra. She could have been a shop girl at Vivienne's Chelsea boutique in the seventies.

'Is there any more wine?' she asked, holding up her glass as if proposing a toast.

What was it with these young women – self-described feminists all, demanding their right to dress like old-school prostitutes? 'Look at me!' they yelled. 'Look at me! Don't look at me, you sexist pig!'

Belle wandered away, glass refilled, walking past the glowing canvases as if they didn't exist, gazing up at the girders in the studio's darkest corners. She was the younger sibling but she was clearly the dominant one.

Luka danced around her, trying to ingratiate himself, to win her approval. The more he advanced, the further she retreated.

If Belle had been more congenial, or enthusiastic, if she'd even made an attempt at polite interest in the work, Eve might have opened another bottle and ordered a food delivery. She was dreading Nancy's party; an evening of shrill vacuity and bad wine. But if the alternative was several hours in the company of the unpleasant Belle, Eve was glad to be leaving.

'Luka can show you round. Stay as long as you like,' she said.

The wail of an approaching emergency vehicle starts up. Someone's merry evening – an office party, perhaps – has ended badly. Eve puts her hand against her ears to shut out the noise as an ambulance flashes past, its blue lights oddly festive, merging with the Christmas decorations flickering from shops and flats around her.

As young teenagers – fifteen and sixteen years old – Eve and her brother would sometimes walk the city at night. Not the tourist routes of London but the ugly twenty-five-mile link road fringing the city's bleaker suburbs – the North Circular. This wasn't sightseeing. The act of walking, aid to conversation and reflection, was the spur – the chance to talk and think, unhindered, outside the stifling bounds of home. Back then, there was no awareness of the health risk of traffic fumes. Their main impulse was to flee the contaminating mental sickness of their mother, a bitter spectre, her pallor ghastly in the light of the television set which was always on, long after the service shut down. Amazingly, Eve and John were only challenged once – a police car stopped to check on them as the lorries hurtled by, somewhere outside Wembley, and having established that they were siblings out for a blameless, if eccentric, late-night stroll, the two bemused policemen drove on. It had been, she could see now, a preparation for the flight of adult life – a willed act of self-propulsion into the future.

They were close then, Eve and her brother, but she was aware that, though their sibling relationship wasn't as obviously unhealthy as Belle's with Luka, it didn't bear close examination. She always held the upper hand. Poor John. Like Magnolia Boy, he never stood a chance.

It started young. Family dynamics were forged in the womb. In Eve's case, her resolve and tenacity rushed in to fill the cavity left by her parents' emotional absence – her mother's thwarted ambitions, her father's dogged adherence to rules and routine. There were a few missteps in her teens and twenties, when she confused sexual hunger with love; Florian exacerbated that confusion. What her childhood did give her was a rare talent for solitude, even in company. She always knew that she was on her own, even through the most social years of art college, New York and the best, early times with Kristof. The sealed capsule in which she made her way through life became her protective armour, and then her skin.

John shared her taste for solitude but he never acquired a carapace. From the start, he was rubbed raw by life. For him, that absence of childhood warmth led to a lifetime of yearning. For unloving parents and a bossy sister, he swapped bossy, unloving wives – two of them, the second worse than the first. They reinforced his sense of guilt that he could never do enough for others. This was his doomed vocation – to bring happiness where there was misery. So he sought out misery and in the process visited even more of it on himself.

The temperature has dropped and the rain has turned to sleet. Eve shivers and looks around at the sparse passing traffic, hoping to see the friendly yellow light of a black cab for hire. No luck. She takes out her phone to summon an Uber. But to get in a taxi would mean social interaction and even the most basic level – 'Had a good night?' 'Going home?' – would be more than she could stand. If the driver were to start on the subject of Brexit – they talked of little else – she'd be tempted to unclip her seat belt, open the door and hurl herself onto the road. Besides, a cab, with or without political commentary, would deliver her to her future too soon. She isn't ready. Better to shiver outside on a wild night, alone with her thoughts.

As they worked on, Luka began to tell her his family history. It was Eve's turn to ask the questions, though she had little interest in the precise details – the dead mother, the lonely years at boarding school, the hastily remarried father and the wicked stepmother who, eventually widowed, cut Luka and Belle out of the family fortune. It was like listening to the synopsis of a soap opera she had no intention of watching. What drew her in was Luka's urge to confide; it bound him to her even more. His loneliness touched her, and mirrored her own. They were kin and she could save him from bitterness.

They made such progress with the *Florilegium*, and were so mutually enraptured, that it became difficult for Eve to remember that she had a life outside the studio. She began to get careless. She stayed overnight at the studio and texted late, lame excuses to Kristof. He was preoccupied with work – a firm of German architects had come in at the last minute with a counterproposal for the Wanda Wilson project, forcing him to cut his fees – and he didn't challenge Eve about her absences.

After a lifetime spent struggling to achieve some equilibrium between domestic life and the call of work, Eve went with the work, loosened her grasp and leapt, relishing the sensation of free fall, a delicious swoon into herself. All the calls of convention and conscience could go hang. This was what mattered, where she wanted to be – at the surging confluence of creativity and sensuality.

One night, in play, Luka hid her mobile and by the time he gave it back to her the following morning, she saw she'd missed three calls from Kristof. She built up a story about a mislaid phone – that much was almost true – and a studio emergency. Her husband had never been the suspicious type, a fact that had irritated her wildly in the past when she embarked on her retaliatory affairs. But, though he bought her story about the lost mobile and a studio power failure, he seemed to withdraw from her.

Discovery was inevitable. She'd been seeking exposure all along. The invitation to Belle was the first step. The following week, after two nights' absence without explanation, she returned to Delaunay Gardens. Luka, as if he knew what she was about to confront, sent her off with a tender farewell.

'You, me and the work – that's all there is,' he said.

Kristof was waiting for her, his face taut with anger. 'I know something's going on.'

He wasn't a violent man. She wasn't afraid of him, as she had been of Florian, who would lash out without provocation and was roused to fury by the perceived crimes of mediocrity and insubordination as much as by any imagined betrayal. But then Florian was a genius at loving reconciliation, too.

'Tell me!' Kristof shouted, thumping the kitchen table with his fist.

For a few seconds, she considered denial. It was not too late to save herself, to return to the floating, sensationless medium of her marriage. It would have been easy. All she had to do was flip the switch and shut down. But she didn't want to shut down. She didn't want ease. She wanted difficulty – passionate, consuming difficulty.

So she told him.

Kristof's challenge had the stinging force of a slap. 'Are you serious?'

He was belittling her.

'I've never been more serious!'

She even used the word 'love', which she'd so far withheld from Luka. It felt good to say it, to give weight to their commitment. Yet still it was all in the balance. She could, if she wanted, repent, row back, and resume her old life. There was time.

As Kristof harangued and pleaded, she saw two futures, a vivid diptych: one a *tableau mort*, in which she lay frozen in the mausoleum of her marital bed; the other a *tableau vivant*, with the tumbled sheets and ripening fruit of life with Luka. It was no coincidence that, since her sensual self had been unleashed, she was producing the best work of her life. She knew it. Luka said so. Even Hans said so.

To betray this new love would be to betray herself. Even the word love – cover for so much sentimentality and bad art – was an inadequate description of her bond with Luka. He was her psychic twin. His ambitions, vulnerabilities and darkest urges reflected hers. He saw through her to her core, as she did to his. For the first time in her life, she was understood and appreciated, as an artist and as a woman, and she felt invincible. Emboldened by Luka's belief in her, she could step out of the shadows and claim her place as an artist ablaze with potential.

'He's a boy,' Kristof said. 'You're making a complete fool of yourself.'

'No more than you did with the luscious Elena.'

'Precisely!'

Eve knew, even as she said it, that hers was a weak rejoinder. That the name of the vapid girl, troublesome for a few months, who vanished from their lives long ago, should spring to her lips, came as a surprise to her. To Kristof too. He thought Eve was over it. So did she.

They sat in the growing gloom of their kitchen, lobbing insults, summoning ancient slights and injuries unexpressed for years, so intent on retribution that to get up and put on the lights would be a banal interruption to an enthralling drama which promised victory at last to the righteous. Each was amazed by the pettiness of the other. The grudges of decades, nurtured in darkness, had borne monstrous fruit. As night fell, the green winks of the kitchen timer displays grew brighter – coffee machine, microwave, cooker and hob counting down the seconds – and it seemed they were in the cockpit of a spaceship hurtling towards the black extremities of the galaxy.

21

Is that singing she hears? Not a gaggle of drunks but a tuneful little choir. Carol singers? Here? There are six of them, young, ethnically diverse, arms linked and advancing towards her with broad smiles. An ambush of goodwill. Alcohol may have been involved – they seem impervious to the sleet, which is gusting into their faces – but it hasn't impaired their skilful harmonies. Local music students on the razzle? Or stragglers from some church event, who've taken literally the injunction to 'let nothing you dismay'. They look too well adjusted and playful to be bona fide believers. They walk on past her, broadcasting tidings of comfort and joy. A more fitting musical accompaniment on this Via Dolorosa, Eve reflects, would be 'In the Bleak Midwinter'.

When the truth about her affair was out, she was relieved to the point of elation. She wanted to see Kristof suffer and found a giddy joy in provocation as she listed the flaws of their marriage and pronounced it dead: their non-existent sex life, his arrogance, his lack of interest in her work, his constant absences. He gave as good as he got, citing coldness, self-absorption and *her* lack of interest in *his* work. In this exchange of historical indictments and spiralling recriminations – an arms race of obloquy – she wanted not just to burn her bridges but to strafe the approach roads. If she and her husband were both to perish in the firefight at that moment, so much the better. There was no going back.

'And let's not forget Mara ...' she said. She paused for breath and it was Kristof's turn to rant.

He coldly recounted some unwifely business of nine years ago – support not given, enthusiasm not shared, attention elsewhere – then turned to her failures as a mother.

'You have no interest in our daughter. Never had.'

Eve could take no more. She left the room, walking into the bright glare of the hall, leaving him fulminating behind her in the dark.

'And as for our grandson ...' he shouted. 'What's *wrong* with you?'

Upstairs, she packed a few clothes and toiletries in an airline carry-on. It was so easy. In this new phase of life, it would be hand luggage only.

By the time she came downstairs, Kristof was pouring a single glass of wine. He'd had enough too.

'I've ordered your cab,' he said. 'The studio, I assume.'

'That's good of you.'

If there were obituaries for marriages – summarising the good points, glossing over the bad – this would be theirs: even *in extremis*, they could revert to chilly civility.

Her husband's face was haggard in the half-light as she stood at the door.

'Eve,' he said softly, 'are you sure you know what you're doing? What you're turning your back on?'

She knew exactly what she was doing. All she could do was submit to the pull of gravity and fall towards her future. One step and a delicious, tumbling surrender.

More sirens sound in the distance – another ambulance, or a police car. The noise bears down on her and she ducks into a quiet side street where the slate face of a new luxury apartment block glowers across the road at the festering concrete of a low-rise council estate. She walks on and sees, before it's too late, a group of people standing in the shadows ahead. They are all, as far as she can tell, young men, and there are about eight of them. She slows her pace. Can she shrink back, undetected? To turn and run would be provocation. All evening, she's been struggling against a dragging sense of terror. Now she's swamped by it; terror is all there is. The luxury apartments look empty and defended against outsiders. Should she cross into the council estate and hope to find help there? Or at least a witness?

Her saviour, it seems, is a car that comes speeding along from the other end of the street. It brakes noisily by the group and they go over to it, surrounding it, leaning in to talk to the driver. The car starts up again and they step back. Now the car pulls up alongside Eve. The driver lowers his window and holds up a small plastic bag.

'You buying?' he asks her.

She shakes her head and he drives off.

The group of young men have dispersed to their private pleasures. She thinks of Theo, her godson, the radiant boy who chose a half-life in the shadows. Another vote for mediocrity. Such a denial of talent and autonomy. She turns and heads back to the main road.

A week after her confrontation with Kristof, two letters arrived at the studio – the first from him, a handwritten, wheedling and reproachful request for her return, warning of the consequences if she stayed away; the second, official, with a central London postmark, was, she assumed, from the lawyer he threatened her with. She didn't answer the first or open the second. She didn't have time.

She went back to the canvas and Luka began to film her as she painted another gelsemium flower.

'Tell me about Florian Kiš,' he said.

She sighed.

'Not now, Luka.'

'But when?' There was an unattractive whine in his voice.

'Don't you think the world has heard enough about Florian Kiš? He was in my life for a matter of months.'

'Okay, okay. I get it. Then tell me more about your influences.'

This was better. She'd never had the chance to speak about all this in any depth before. She put down the magnifying glass and spoke directly to the camera, describing her visit to Karnak, and the Temple of Thutmose III. Luka didn't need to know that Kristof had taken her there on honeymoon.

'The bas-relief carvings of nearly three hundred plant species date from the fifteenth century BC. Human preoccupation with this branch of the natural world is not new. What *is* new is our increasing *lack of* interest. Plant blindness.'

She spoke about the medieval herbals, the Renaissance Italians who used flowers as allegorical adjuncts in religious art, and the Dutch *stilleven*, with a sense that her exposition was a fitting commentary on the magisterial, time-transcending nature of her work.

'The whole tradition of still life – *nature morte*, inanimate or dead nature to the French – sprang from the human impulses to display and to classify. There's a preoccupation with the richness of the natural world and the fleeting quality of life. By fixing in perpetuity the velvet bloom on a fat grape, the dewdrop on a petal, we cheat time.'

Luka stood, rapt and silent, as the camera did its work.

She told him about the *xenia* paintings: 'gifts for visitors – groaning boards of native country produce, beakers of wine, luscious fruit, cheese, game and flowers from the boastful host's estate; and the *vanitas*, like *xenia*, with the addition of a skull to remind us that we go to the grave empty-handed'.

Only once before did she have such a captive audience. In Paris, long ago, Theo had been so eager for details of the tradition she drew on in her work.

'Then there were cabinets of curiosities,' she continued, 'exotic plants brought back from the new colonies, the medieval herbals and botanists' encyclopedias, the fruit and flower images used by painters of religious scenes – the Annunciation lilies – and by the *rhyparographos* – painters of filth.'

'Filth?' Luka said, a sudden brightness in his voice.

'Not that kind.' She laughed. 'Sordid or vulgar, meaning commonplace, subjects – nature brought into the everyday human context, the single stem of mallow in a jar in the tavern, the scattered posy of wild flowers by the cobbler's last; pleasure in the humdrum and the domestic, once God and his cohorts were out of the picture.'

'Right.'

'The Dutch market scenes are another example ...' She could see he'd lost interest.

'What about the critics?' he asked.

She looked up sharply, from lens to cameraman.

'What *about* the critics?'

'Those people, reviewers, who say you're playing safe? That it's all just decoration? Copying?'

His interruption was an affront.

She turned her back on him to load a squirrel-hair liner with colour and began to conjure the flower's bamboo-like leaves with light strokes. When she finally spoke again, her voice was cool.

'There were those who thought painting should only cover religious themes. Then the mortal human form became an acceptable subject, but *nature morte* has always been a poor relation. Mimesis, the skilful rendering of the natural and material world, was dismissed as mimicry, though Caravaggio said it was as challenging to paint flowers as it was to paint figures.'

'And today's critics?' He wasn't going to let this go.

'Today's critics think seeing, and the precise rendering of what we see, is redundant; it's what the artist *feels* that matters and how much of themselves, fanny and fundament, they're prepared to expose in the funhouse.'

'But Florian Kiš —'

'Luka!' She put down her brush.

'It's all part of your work, your story,' Luka protested, following her with the camera.

This conversation was over, as far as she was concerned. But Luka pushed on.

'Well, Brian Sewell, for instance. Didn't he say your paintings were "Seductive trivialities. Women's pictures"?'

What hurt was not Sewell's old barbs but the fact that Luka had seen them and committed them to memory.

'He was no friend to women artists.'

Luka didn't let up.

'And Ellery Quinn. Didn't he write that you were "an ape of nature" and your work was "slavishly mimetic, fit only for children's books, haberdashery and the wrapping paper industry"?'

Eve glared at the camera, as if the inanimate box of circuitry, not her lover, was generating these offensive questions.

'You read Quinn's review of my Sigmoid show?' she said, retrieving her brush. '"Not art imitating life, but life itself." He finally got it.'

Luka adjusted the focus.

'But he's your dealer's latest lover. Or occasional lover. He would say that about Hans's client, wouldn't he?'

Eve threw down her brush again.

'Luka, stop that now. What's got into you?'

He fixed the camera back on the tripod.

'Sorry. I didn't mean to wind you up. These are the sort of questions people are going to ask. This stuff is out there. You might as well tackle what they say head-on. Besides, I want to know how you handle all that.'

She picked up the brush, dipped it in turps and cleaned it off with a rag.

'A lot of people say a lot of things,' she said. 'But you've got to be tough, build a carapace, stay true to your vision and keep going.'

'Did you ever have doubts?' He was filming again.

'About my work? No never. It's not a small undertaking – opening the eye to the intricacy and wonder of the natural word in a plant-blind age.'

'Maybe you should explain plant blindness more fully at this point?' he suggested.

She was glad to be on sure ground again.

'No one truly *sees* flowers any more,' she said, addressing the camera. 'They're not big enough, showy or threatening enough to demand our attention and they're vanishing from our view. Their names are vanishing from our culture too.'

'Which names?'

'Bluebell, buttercup, catkin, cowslip …'

He paused the camera.

'What's a cowslip?'

She was relieved to see he was laughing.

22

The following morning, another letter arrived in the studio. It was a personal invitation from Wanda Wilson for the opening of her show at the Hayward. Even after the long passage of time, Eve recognised the loopy hand-writing. Well, at least Wanda was addressing her directly and acknowledging her autonomy at last. All must be forgiven.

'Do come!' was the scribbled note on the back of the printed invitation. *The Five Ages of Woman*, first shown at the Whitney fifteen years ago, was being revived in London and, the invitation stated, it was 'one of the most hotly anticipated cultural events of the year'. Eve threw the card in the bin. Luka, looking down and recognising the gallery's logo, fished it out.

'You can't turn this down!' he said. 'Invitations for her shows are gold dust.'

Eve shook her head.

'I don't have time. And neither do you.'

'Oh, come on!'

She didn't tell him that she would rather have a tooth extracted than turn up to one of Wanda Wilson's shows.

'Seriously, Luka, we have too much to do here.'

'You're ashamed of me. You don't want to be seen out with me. I know.'

'Oh, nonsense,' she said, leaning towards him for a kiss. 'Of course I'm not ashamed of you.'

He averted his face and shrugged her off. She watched him return to the herbarium with the heavy steps and hunched shoulders of a sulky teenager.

Then it occurred to her: why not go to the Hayward? They'd been cooped up, working hard for so long. It would make him happy. This would be her response to Kristof's letters. She'd be curious to see Wanda again close up. Clearly, the old fraud no longer bore a grudge against her after all these years. Wasn't she working with Kristof now on her Art Ranch? Eve would go to the ridiculous show. With Luka on her arm. Time to come out of the shadows.

On the night of the opening, however, her defiance ebbed away in the horizontal rain. She walked with Luka to the front of the long line outside the gallery, pushed through the doors into the foyer, shook out her sodden umbrella and showed her invitation to a burly man with a headset and a sheaf of paper. He looked for her name on his list and shook his head.

'VIPs only,' he said, waving through Solokoff, the Russian oligarch, and a fresh batch of lingerie models.

He directed Eve back outside to rejoin the end of the queue.

'It doesn't matter. Let's do it!' said Luka, opening the umbrella again.

There should be an upper age limit on queuing – say, twenty. The last time Eve could remember standing in line was as a student in her late teens, hoping to get into a Covent Garden club. Most of this crowd, jostling under umbrellas, were in their twenties and thirties – younger and, she was peeved to observe, hipper than the crowd that attended her own show.

The patrons, critics, sponsors and gallerists who were at the Sigmoid would be at the Hayward for Wanda too, but they'd skip the queues and be ushered straight into her presence. Perhaps this was Wanda's revenge after all – consigning her old rival to the role of humble congregant, milling at the back of the nave with the multitudes.

They inched through the puddles towards the entrance, Luka as excited as a child on his way to the circus, Eve fuming. A breathless young man in his twenties wearing an orange sweatshirt with a 'DOUBLE U' logo walked down the line handing out flyers for Wanda's next show – *Artist on the Edge/The Death of Mimesis*. 'A multimedia durational work. The artist as catalyst, medium and subject. Pioneering relational work to be presented simultaneously at leading European and American venues. Summer 2019.'

More tosh.

'That'll be amazing,' Luka said.

Once they got to the door, things looked up; Eve was recognised by a pale, wide-eyed young woman with a pierced lip who was directing the queue. She was wearing an ill-fitting vintage frock and neon-pink baseball boots. An art student.

The girl gushed, apologising to Eve for the wait – 'I'm so sorry you've had to stand out there in the rain.'

Champagne, and a little respect, eased the discomfort.

In the first room, on three walls, floor to ceiling, a silent video collage showed hundreds of infant girls of all hues and ethnicities: in nappies or naked; some smiling, their hands clasping and unclasping like fronds of sea anemones; some wailing, faces contorted, pumping their fists with helpless fury, as if the veil had parted and they'd glimpsed the indignities that lay ahead – No! No! No! Over this kaleidoscopic baby dumbshow was a soundtrack of the amplified discordant tinkling of a child's broken music box. 'Für Elise'. As the spectators walked round the gallery, their heads were brushed by thousands of pink dummies suspended from the ceiling on pink ribbons.

Luka was enchanted.

'Wow!' he kept saying as he gazed at the videos then up at the ribbons. He raised his arm and ran his hand through them, setting the dummies swinging and spinning.

'Wow!'

Through the crowd, Eve glimpsed Hans with Ellery Quinn and made her way over to them. She looked back to see Luka talking to a sleek young redhead in a persimmon suit. She looked like a stewardess on a budget airline. The girl turned and waved to Eve. It was Belle. What was she doing here? And what was she wearing? Her clipboard and 'Double U' armband suggested some kind of official role.

Eve turned back to Hans. Her brief eye roll was met with his arched eyebrow. Quinn nodded towards the video collage of baby pictures.

'An infomercial for contraception?' he said.

They laughed and walked together into the next room, where their feet crunched over sugary gravel; tens of thousands of pastel Love Heart candies which, the exhibition notes revealed, would be gradually crushed to powder by visitors' feet and replenished every two days. More silent videos were projected on three walls: a collage of teenaged girls pouting for selfies, applying cosmetics, giggling, swooning over photos of pop stars, trying on clothes.

The soundtrack was of amplified gasps and sighs – teenaged girls, one assumed, engaged in sex. From the ceiling, hanging from lengths of string, were thousands of red-stained tampons: not Wanda's own, as they would have been in the old days. Wanda was long past the sanitary-product years and had moved on from her signature 'bio-art' – exemplified in her nineties *Curse* exhibition, with nude self-portraits crudely rendered in the artist's menstrual blood.

Wanda would have needed to enlist an army of young women to produce the quantity of gore required for this show. There were certainly enough potential recruits, legions of gullible female art students like the girl on the door with her perforated mouth. But, in these hygiene-obsessed days, gallery health and safety regulations would be unlikely to permit verisimilitude. No, the dangling tampons were bright, clean, unsoiled – a rich alizarin crimson rather than the haematite-tinged real thing Wanda had displayed to an admiring audience thirty years ago.

Luka caught up with Eve.

'Amazing!' He gazed up at the encrimsoned curtain above their heads.

'Mmm. Was that Belle?'

'Her temp job. Arts marketing and events.'

'I didn't recognise her in her corporate outfit.'

He laughed.

'She scrubs up well, doesn't she? That's her thing. She's got her costume and she's playing her part.'

'Well, if she's getting paid for it ...'

'It's the best gig she's had all year. Meeting and greeting ... Wanda Wilson.'

'Lucky girl!'

23

Under a railway bridge, Eve stops to retrieve her umbrella. The sleet has reverted to drenching rain. The graffiti arabesques on the red-brick walls remind her of the eerie prehistoric caves in Patagonia, where early men and women left their marks by stencilling round their hands with paint sprayed through a pipe. Eve steps over a pile of filthy rags, which begin to stir, and realises she's intruding in a dormitory for the homeless. She hurries on.

The theme of the next room at the Hayward wasn't hard to guess, the amplified groaning and yelling declared it before they walked in: motherhood. The centrepiece was a life-size plaster Madonna and Child, plundered from some decommissioned church. Once more, three walls of silent film: childbirth – a blur of flesh and blood and agonised maternal faces, in contrast to the serenely saccharine centrepiece. And above them? Suspended from the ceiling were thousands of soiled nappies. Again, in her early days Wanda would have gone for the real thing but here the nappies were stained with sloppily applied Vandyke brown and ochre gouache.

Eve spotted Ines Alvaro in the far corner of the room, gazing upwards, as if contemplating the ceiling of the Sistine Chapel. Ines caught Eve's eye and waved. She was coming over.

'Are you done?' asked Luka, who was less enchanted by the stained nappies swinging, pendulum-like, above his head.

'Let's get out of here,' said Eve. 'That woman, Ines, she's a stalker.'

They moved into the next room and found they'd entered a sealed gallery – a black box, silent but for the steady whirr of two industrial heaters. No videos, no caterwauling soundtracks, no apparently insanitary objects. Nothing but the stifling heat – a woman's middle, invisible years once her biological destiny has been fulfilled, when the hot flushes are a cruel mockery, the last hurrah of those dwindling inner fires. Cunning old Wanda – she'd monetised her menopause, and at no effort at all. Here was nothing, a vacancy bounded by plain walls, presented as art. Some wealthy patron, Solokoff perhaps, would pay an absurd sum to recreate this experience of female midlife sensory deprivation in an unused room in his Holland Park mansion.

Eve was glad to get out but there was one more room to endure before they could have another drink.

The massed choral music was absurdly portentous, and familiar – the soundtrack of a suburban Black Mass, or the signature tune for a meeting of the Croydon branch of the

Aleister Crowley Appreciation Society: *Carmina Burana.* Here was Death, or particularly, Woman's Death. Still images (it would have been hard, even for Wanda, to get clearance for videos hot from hospice or mortuary) of the dead and dying in drawings, paintings and old photographs. From Millais' flower-strewn, semi-submerged *Ophelia*, Salgado's *Vanitas*, with smug angel supervising a heap of gold trinkets and human skulls, and Posada's *Calavera Catrina* engraving, a 1913 skeleton parody of fashionable womanhood, to Frida Kahlo's self-portrait as fatally wounded deer.

There were murders and martyrdoms, ingenious in their methods of torture, of saints Agatha, Agnes, Catherine, Maria Goretti, Martha and Ursula. Inevitably, the *pièce de résistance* was the old exhibitionist herself: Wanda, photographed, po-faced in magenta robes, in the guise of St Lucy; eyes shut, eyeballs, acquired from an accommodating abattoir, proffered on a plate. Over this image, suspended from the ceiling on wires, tinkling like a diabolic wind chime over Carl Orff's choral medieval pastiche – 'O, Fortuna!' – were thousands of bones, sterilised animal femurs donated, according to the programme notes, by that same friendly slaughterhouse.

Luka was marvelling again, pointing admiringly at the stock shots of Mexican sugar skulls – inspiration for his asinine tattoo – and, though Eve knew it was unfair, she couldn't help thinking less of him for it.

Back in the crowded foyer, he fetched more champagne and led her towards another queue. This one, contained by ropes and supervised by self-important young marshals wearing the orange 'Double U' livery, snaked through the building like an airport security line. At the head of it, behind a table stacked with hardback copies of *The Artist's I*, Wanda's latest manifesto, Eve made out her old adversary's unmistakable froth of hair, now white, evoking an eighteenth-century monarch in powdered periwig, and that frightening mask of a face – frozen by nerve-paralysing toxins, swollen by chemical gels and stretched by surgery – with its expression of astonished hauteur. She was seated in a high-backed chair which, in the context, gave the illusion of a throne.

'Come on!' said Luka, taking Eve's hand.

It was his touch – a reminder of their intimacy – that drew her in. Why else would she join a receiving line to pay homage to her old room-mate whom she hadn't seen for more than three decades, by choice? Eve still, pathetically, wanted to impress her young lover and this, it seemed, was what it took.

They shuffled forwards in silence as in a New York immigration line and, as they neared the head of the queue, Eve's misgivings grew.

'I'm not sure about this, Luka. It's been so long since I've seen her. Maybe I'd rather meet her privately.'

Luka gripped her hand tightly.

'Come on, Eve. Please. This means so much to me.'

Another marshal came over. 'One at a time please. Miss Wilson only gives individual audiences.'

Eve was led up to the table and Wanda was before her, a shamanistic figure with a scarab clip in her wild hair, swathes of scarlet pleated silk covering her bloated body, a ruby-topped cane in her left hand. Eve had seen her photographs over the years but even so, close up, the effects of her cosmetic surgery startled. Only Wanda's eyes were the same, deep-set and darting. They stared out anxiously from their new waxy mask, above a whittled, upturned nose, and inflated lips that suggested freakishly distended labia.

By Wanda's side a goateed acolyte, a Van Dyck courtier, passed Eve a copy of the book then extended his hand. 'That'll be £25 please.'

Eve fumbled in her bag for the money and handed the book to Wanda, who sat, looking frankly bored, pen in hand.

'Who shall I sign it for?' she asked, looking up at Eve briefly then down at the book, which she opened on the title page.

'Luka,' said Eve, seething at the boy for forcing her into this role of supplicant.

'How are you spelling that?' asked Wanda, pen already at work.

Eve looked round. Luka was standing several feet back and hadn't heard their exchange. He'd been joined by his sister and they were talking excitedly, filming the encounter on their phones.

'Hi, Wanda,' said Eve, in a clearer voice. 'How are you?'

She looked up. 'Do I know you?'

Eve leaned across the table and murmured into the artist's blank face.

'Come on, Wanda … You know very well it's me, Eve … Hornsey? Hoxton? Avenue B?'

She frowned.

Eve hissed: 'Mike … Kristof … Florian … Remember?'

That did it.

'Ah yes! Of course! How *are* you?'

Wanda bent to sign the book, snapped it shut and handed it back to Eve. 'How's the flower business?'

Eve had no time to respond – a photographer asked her to pose for a picture with Wanda, who beckoned star-struck Luka to join them. Wanda declined to stand – the ruby-topped cane, some temporary infirmity, was her get-out – so Luka and Eve were pictured stooping low over the artist, two serfs grinning sycophantically at the shoulders of a taciturn tsarina.

Within seconds, another marshal ushered them away – the queue was building – and Luka was 'wow'-ing again.

'Let's get out of here,' said Eve.

She was longing for her studio. Longing to get back to work. Her lover held her hand and they walked out of the gallery, just as her husband walked in. They exchanged cold glances. Kristof looked from her to Luka, taking in his rival, showing disdain with a faint retraction of his upper lip. Eve drew herself up, defying Kristof to challenge her. Luka grasped her hand tighter.

'Come on. We've got so much to do in the studio,' he said.

They walked on towards the river and Eve looked back to see Belle, with her officious clipboard, greeting Kristof at the door. No queues for him. His commission for the Art Ranch was probably sealed by now and, if age had compromised Wanda's memory for names and her consummate networking skills, Belle would be there to prompt her.

They worked late again – Luka spurred by exhilaration, Eve by anger and the conviction that her only defence against the affront of the evening was her work. She started on the sketch for the orange sequence – *Arum maculatum* – while he mixed the pigment for the canvas's green ground. The penultimate canvas.

He was cleaning brushes and tidying the studio before they went to bed when Eve remembered Wanda's book. It must have been a masochistic urge that led her to retrieve it from her bag. She read the dust jacket: 'Wanda Wilson, world-renowned multidisciplinary artist, has challenged taboos and transformed the definition of art with her relational art and deep-immersion encounters, in which she transforms the lives of spectators in a groundbreaking discourse on the social corpus.'

Though Eve, for her own reasons, had never been a fan of Brian Sewell, she delighted in his review of Wanda's show at the White Cube in the 1990s – 'The ravings of the archetypal madwoman. Euthanasia would be a kindness,' he'd written. He couldn't be wrong *all* the time. She kept a copy of that review on her phone, too. Eve turned to the book's title page. There was the dedication – not to Luka.

'Fuck you, Eve! See you at my next show ... WW'

24

Her walk has brought her to Victoria Park. The gates have been locked since dusk – hours ago. Perhaps a twenty-first-century magnolia boy and girl are kissing under bare branches at the park's northern corner. She turns right, skirting the park's iron railings and the canal, which is oily as pitch. Most of the houseboats look deserted but, judging by the fairy lights looped round a few windows and the plastic Christmas tree ostentatiously fixed to a prow, some are inhabited. Maybe a narrowboat and a mooring here wouldn't be such a bad end.

Orange. Luka mixed the pigments. Perinone orange veers towards pink when mixed with zinc white. The addition of cadmium orange and quinacridone gold gives it heat and luminosity. She completed the drawing and watercolour of two specimens of *Arum maculatum* at different stages of their life cycle: the spring form with purple spadix framed by a green hood, and the summer clusters of orange berries on a pale poker stem. Now Luka was at the dissection tray, twirling a spring specimen between his fingers, preparing to photograph it.

'I've see this one before. In the wild?'

'That's right. Cuckoopint. It's a woodland plant. Lords and ladies is another name for it. A shade lover.'

'It's kind of phallic.'

'You wouldn't want to bring that one into the bedroom,' she said. 'Unless pain's your thing … It burns the mouth – one seventeenth-century herbalist recommended it, sprinkled on meat, as a cure for unwanted guests. It shuts them up and they never come back. Plays havoc with mucous membranes.'

He dropped the specimen in the tray.

'Could be a cure for unwanted lovers, too, I suppose,' he said.

The following morning, he set up the video camera on a tripod and joined her at the canvas, taking over the top half of the green field and covering it with identical oil iterations of her watercolour cuckoopint.

Absorbed in their work, they were startled by the dentist's drill drone of the intercom. Only couriers pressed the buzzer and no deliveries were expected that day. The studio's few visitors – Hans, Ines, on the days when Eve would let her into the studio – knew to knock. This afternoon the sound seemed particularly malign, as if announcing a police raid.

Luka opened the door to an angry emissary of Eve's old life – her daughter. Nancy walked in, pug in arms, a self-righteous Boudicca in frayed denim, throwing a cold glance at Luka. He smiled, grabbed his jacket, murmured some excuse about getting supplies, and left the studio.

'Was that him?' Nancy asked, nodding towards the door.

'Luka. His name's Luka.'

'He's a kid. Is it even legal?'

'Don't be ridiculous. A "how are you?" would have been nice. How are *you*? Daughter?'

Nancy's face darkened and she tightened her grip on the pug.

'How do you think I am? My father's in pieces because my mother's just run off with someone half her age – a student. How am I *meant* to be?'

'A student!' Eve laughed. Her daughter always had a genius for exaggeration. 'You've seen him, Nancy – Luka's a mature, independent young man.'

'Independent? I very much doubt it. And mature? Hardly. You're sixty. Remember? He's my age, for God's sake.'

Eve lowered her brush with a sigh. 'Can't you see I'm working? I don't have time for this.'

Nancy stroked her panting dog. She really believed that the two of them made a winsome picture – Singer Sargent's portrait of Beatrice with her toy terrier, perhaps. Only George Grosz, or maybe Diane Arbus, could do this pet and owner justice.

'This isn't about me,' Nancy said. 'It's about you, and about Dad.'

'Is this a first? My daughter is actually concerned about someone other than herself?'

Tears began to seep from Nancy's eyes.

'Oh, Mum ...'

Eve always winced at that diminutive. As a new mother, she made the case for 'Mor' – the Danish word, with its apt suggestion of Oliver Twist and the empty bowl. She could even have coped with the chilly, timeless Mother. She settled for Mama – international and not completely unsexy. But Nancy had, as Nancy continued to do, responded to peer pressure, and every time she reverted to 'Mum' it seemed to Eve an insult; a deliberate suburban belittlement.

A year and a half ago, when Nancy announced her pregnancy, Eve got in early and told her that she would veto Grandma, Granny, Nana or any other crone designation. When Nancy's baby finally spoke, Eve insisted, it would call her Eve. And now the baby, little Jarleth, that plump, caterwauling, twenty-three-pound sack of needs, would never call her anything. Her name would be excised from the family record, her statue toppled in the domestic equivalent of *damnatio memoriae*.

Her daughter's shoulders were heaving and she was holding her dog against her cheek – was she wiping her tears on her pet?

'You've seen the press, I suppose?' Nancy said, struggling to compose herself. 'The diary stories?'

'No. I'm working.'

'They're mocking you,' Nancy said, with a glint of sadistic pleasure in her eyes.

Eve turned back to the canvas.

'If you'll excuse me? As I said, I'm working.'

The cuckoopint, as Luka noticed, had a sub-pornographic *Carry On* sauciness – particularly in its spring form, with the purple phallus of the spadix nestling in the vulva of its false flower. Some artists would play up that connection. Eve chose subtlety, always harder to master.

'A grandmother!' Nancy continued. 'Ditching her successful husband for a toy boy.'

'That's pathetic,' Eve said, over her shoulder. 'One of those trashy papers you read, I suppose?'

'One of those trashy papers *everybody* reads – the *Daily Mail*. Twitter's full of it, too.'

Eve dropped her brush in a jar, wiped her hands and turned to face her daughter again.

'Do you really think I care what a bunch of envious imbeciles think about me?' But her voice betrayed her. She took a breath and spoke more softly. 'Now I see what's upsetting you. What other people think. All you've ever been concerned with is surfaces – reputational damage. Damage to *your* reputation, that is ...'

Nancy was crying openly now. But these were tears of anger.

'You don't see it, do you? What you're throwing away – Dad, me, Jarleth, Delaunay Gardens, all the rest. That whole life you built together. And for what? A dumb pretty boy with his eye on the main chance.'

'You know nothing. Nothing about Luka, nothing about me.'

'I know enough to see an old woman about to trash what's left of her life for a gold-digging gigolo who'll dump her as soon as she's no longer any use.'

Eve didn't flinch.

'Really? Why would I value your opinion on anything? Look at you! You can't even dress properly. Those jeans? With your thighs?'

Usually, a remark like that would provoke an aggrieved outburst from Nancy. But she stood her ground, tears dripping on the wrinkled head of the pug, whose bulging eyes widened further, as if taking offence on his owner's behalf.

'Don't try to change the subject. I'm here for your sake, as well as Dad's. I'm trying to pull you back from a disastrous decision.'

Her voice was measured. Her equanimity was almost admirable. How little they knew each other. And now, they would always be strangers.

'You know nothing, Nancy. Never have. Never will. What are you doing here? Don't you have an important dispatch to write? "Scarves – In or Out?"' "Hemlines – Up or Down?"'

Nancy shook her head. 'You have no idea what it looks like, do you? You, with that *boy*.'

'Maybe not.' Eve paused, then smiled and lowered her voice: 'But I know what it *feels* like.'

Nancy groaned. 'You disgust me.'

Those were her daughter's final words. She walked out of the studio and Eve stood for a moment, listening to the fading reverberation of the slammed door, before returning to the canvas.

The late-summer form of the cuckoopint was another beast altogether, its toxic berries bright as burning coals. She cleaned her brush and worked it through the orange paint. Then it struck her – Nancy had been in the studio for a full twenty minutes without demonstrating the slightest curiosity about the giant, colour-saturated canvases lining the studio walls, about the herbaria, the photographs, the watercolours. She'd never had any interest in her mother, or her work. Good to get that straight.

Luka returned ten minutes after Nancy's departure and they went back to work without a word. She was still seething at her daughter's visit and appreciated his silence.

Outside, night was falling and the street lamps came on, ochre auras staining the growing darkness. In the studio, the orange berries of Eve's cuckoopint seemed a light source all of their own. Luka sealed the herbarium and uncoupled the video camera from its tripod.

'Do you ever think,' he asked, levelling the camera at her, 'that it's all a bit tame?'

'Tame?' Eve held her brush mid-air.

'Don't you ever get tired of it? Isn't it sometimes like working in a florist's.'

'No, I don't tire of it,' she said, glaring at him. 'And it's never like working in a florist's. You know that.'

What had got into him? He plunged on.

'Or, that you're one of those women in a TV costume drama? All you need is a bonnet and a basket. A grand-mother's bonnet?'

He'd gone too far. He was sending her up now. She stabbed her brush into the pool of colour.

'We don't have time for this. Put down the camera and help me here. I need you to mix more pigment.'

He reattached the camera to the tripod and walked over to measure out the powder.

'What about Florian Kiš? He wasn't exactly a fan of your flowers, was he?'

She froze. 'Fuck Florian Kiš.' She dropped her brush on the table. 'It's a completely different aesthetic. He found ugliness in the beautiful and beauty in the ugly. I choose beauty, unmediated. This is about me, not some ancient art world behemoth. Now, let's get on. Unless you've had enough of floristry …'

Was that a smile on his face? He bent over the grinding slab, working at the new mix of cadmium and quinacri-done with what seemed like parodic zeal. What was up with him? She expected abuse from her daughter. But her lover? She picked up her brush and returned to the canvas but her anger and confusion gave a shaky imprecision to her line. It was no good. After another hour, dismayed by her own shoddy work, she dipped a hog-bristle brush in the colour and painted over her afternoon's work. Tomorrow, she would have to start again.

They went to bed in silence and through the night Eve lay awake while Luka, his back turned to her, slept on like a contented child. She stared up at the ceiling, rerunning their exchange, recalling his cruel words, making excuses for him; they'd been cooped up together for so long now, he'd been so diligent, she'd been heedless of his needs and insecurities, something had to give. She countered each excuse with rising indignation – How could he? How dare he? – before rerunning the loop of excuses. It must be the strain of work. Eve was used to the long hours, the skipped meals, this degree of feverish concentration as a project neared its end – she'd trained for it all her adult life – and she hadn't considered that it might take its toll on him. It had certainly taken a toll on their physical relationship.

Every night lately, he'd retreated to his side of the bed, falling into instant and profound sleep. Neither of them had the mental space or energy for the consuming intensity of sex. It was always hard to imagine quite how ordinary life could resume once the final frenzy of work was over. All that extra adrenaline can't be turned off like a tap. It has to be processed somehow. The *Florilegium*'s end was in sight and, though it wasn't going to be easy to let it go, once the work was done, physical passion could reclaim its place.

25

The bridge over the canal is covered with low-grade graffiti – crudely inscribed nicknames (Sax, Piq, Rok), expletives, sexual boasts and insults. Whoever dignified graffiti with the term 'art' had a lot to answer for. These scrawls were 'street art' just as the scribbled obscenities in public lavatories – in the days when there were public lavatories – were 'toilet art'.

There was a better case for the aesthetic value of ghost signs, the palimpsests and faded lettering of old adverts once painted directly onto buildings by skilful working men on ladders with brushes, enamel paints, measures and mahlsticks to steady their line, who saw themselves as craftsmen rather than artists. These ghost signs are ubiquitous round here, if you look closely enough – elegant typographical phantoms with illustrative flourishes declaring the merits of long-gone tobacco brands, soap, beer, fountain pens, horse-carriage services, coal merchants, and haberdashers selling uniforms for maids and cooks. This is true street art, addressing the ordinary stuff of life – subject matter of the *rhyparographos* – conjuring a vanished world across time.

This has, in one sense, been her own project – to leave a mark, to give a sense of today's increasingly fragile world to future generations. Should there be any future generations. Her fear, the artist's fear, is that despite the effort expended in her mission and the monumental nature of her work, no one is looking. Luka, with his careless burst of mischief, played right into the heart of that anxiety.

The next morning, over coffee, he seemed contrite.

'I can't wait to finish it. To step back and celebrate,' he said.

As an apology, that would have to do.

They continued to work on the arum canvas and by the afternoon it was almost done. Eve stood at the far wall to take in the painting in its entirety and was dissatisfied by the detail in the top left of the painting – the scale was wildly off. She was particularly vexed that it was her own work rather than Luka's.

He turned on the video camera as she climbed the ladder to fix the problem.

'So,' he called up to her, 'in the past you worked with an army of assistants. And now you're alone.' Then he corrected himself: '*We're* alone. How do you feel about that?'

Not a bad line of enquiry, she thought. She forgave him yesterday's silliness and wanted to reclaim their easy, affectionate alliance. Once again, using a broad hog-bristle brush and a fresh batch of the green ground mix, she began to excise the offending plants.

'The artist is always alone,' she said as she painted. 'Even in company.'

'In what way?'

'Florian would always say, when you address a new piece of work, the studio is crowded.'

'Florian Kiš?'

Which other Florian would it be? But the surprise in Luka's voice was excusable. This was the first time Eve had brought up the name of her famous lover and she invoked it in a spirit of generosity. That's what they all wanted to hear. Let Luka have it. In the substantial space of her studio, surrounded by her finest work, at the peak of her career, she had no need to feel defensive.

'Crowded,' she continued, 'not just with whatever personnel the artist has hired – fabricators and administrators to help realise the project, or in Florian's case, a single assistant and the sitter – but your past is there too, the ghosts of your family, friends, enemies, critics, supporters, and all your clamorous, competing ideas. Then you start to paint and they all begin to leave, one by one, shutting the door gently behind them until you're left standing there, finally alone – just you and the work. Paint and a passion, that's all you need. And then, if it goes well, you leave the studio, too, and shut the door behind you.'

'He said that?'

She nodded, climbing down the ladder to fetch a new brush, fresh paint.

'What about *Girl with a Flower*?' he asked. 'How do you feel when you're described as Florian Kiš's muse?'

Now she regretted her generous impulse.

'It wasn't exactly an exclusive club. In some circles you'd be hard-pressed to find a female art student who hadn't posed for and slept with Florian.'

'Wanda Wilson?'

The name, in this context, made her recoil. Was he provoking her again? Wanda, a blabbermouth on the most personal subjects, had been discreet on this one – probably because it didn't pan out too well for her. She'd been just another art groupie, vainly hoping for promotion to muse.

'Possibly. Though there's no evidence of it. I doubt she was Florian's type.'

In the press and on-screen, Wanda's compulsive name-dropping had always seemed a subset of Tourette's. She was an assiduous cultivator of celebrity, and her circle included rappers, tech innovators and reality TV stars as well as gullible intellectuals – writers, fashionable philosophers and politicians – seeking to extend their demographic reach. Was Wanda now, late in the day, bidding for artistic credibility by claiming a special relationship with the great Kiš?

'Amazing to have been part of that circle,' Luka said. 'Kiš's and Wanda Wilson's. Did you feel you were part of an important movement at the time?'

He was testing her patience again.

'God, no. Why would I feel that? Come on. Put that camera down. Your last flowers? Top-right corner?'

'What about them?'

'The scale's off.'

He was indignant. 'No it isn't. It's a perfect match.'

'No really. It's wildly out. Can't you see? You'll have to do that whole section again.'

He sighed and meekly went to work.

She watched him, trying to shut out memories of another artist at a canvas. All those years ago, after her final bathroom exile – the meditative forty-five minutes while Florian pleasured himself with his visitor – Eve heard Florian's summoning knock and emerged into the studio, which was suffused with a familiar resinous musk.

Four decades later, in her own studio, standing before her own work, Eve felt too distracted by this slideshow from her past to paint. She would deal with some head-clearing administration – the latest batch of unopened letters, including several from her husband and his lawyer. It was quite a pile. She felt sufficiently detached from Kristof, at least, to tackle them. She opened the most recent first.

It was bad. Kristof intended to keep Delaunay Gardens, 'the marital home, which you deserted', the barn – her barn – in Wales, and the Tribeca apartment. In exchange, he was offering her 'half a lifetime share' in the studio and a lump sum, barely enough to match the cost of their international travel over the last few years, 'in full and final settlement'. She could stay on in the studio, partly as his tenant, in a grace-and-favour arrangement in the new 'technology campus' at Bartlett Business Park, as long as she managed to remain alive; if she didn't – and she imagined vengeful Kristof was now praying for that outcome – it would revert to Kristof or, in the event of his own death, the beneficiaries of his will: Nancy, she assumed, and her baby. Kristof, with the help of his expensive lawyer, was ensuring that Luka, or any future lover of Eve's, would never get his hands on the studio.

She tore up the letter and went back to work in a fury. The proposed arrangement infantilised her, treating her like a feckless child, as if she hadn't been an equal partner in their marriage, as if her sacrifice hadn't increased the store of his success, as if her decision to strike out on her own was foolhardy caprice. Luka was on the platform, painting the last canvas with its green base ready for the red sequence, and she picked up her final subject – a spray of castor oil plant, *Ricinus*, with its perky scarlet pompoms. She forced herself to narrow her vision and focus on this one, still, small object of beauty.

It was no good. Her attention was shot. She felt hatred towards Kristof, not for his insulting proposal – so petty and predictable – but because he'd thrown her off course with her work. He'd robbed her of the composure and pinpoint concentration required to tackle her new subject. She went to the grinding slab and spooned out more quinacridone gold. She would retouch the orange canvas, an exercise in Zen repetition, until she felt ready to move on to the final sequence.

Luka shinned down the ladder and began filming.

'So the three of you in New York? You still see Mara Novak? Tell us about her.'

All her irritation with him had gone, replaced now by gratitude – sensing her distress about Kristof's demeaning letter, Luka was bringing her back to her own history, to her secure, unchallenged place in the world. Kristof could never take that from her.

They worked on and talked through the night, their edges blurred by wine and exhaustion. When they could work no longer, they went to bed and made love for the first time in days, re-energised by pent-up hunger. They were back on track.

'This time I really need a lawyer,' Eve told Mara over the phone the next day.

'I heard. I was about to phone you.'

'How did you hear?'

Mara, her old countercultural compatriot, reinvented as a lesbian feminist therapist, shunned the art world, didn't read the *Daily Mail* on principle and had never been on Twitter in her life.

'Everyone knows. You're the talk of London. An achievement, of sorts ...'

Sarcasm was no way to treat an old friend in crisis. Eve bit back her anger. She needed Mara. She needed her expertise in matters of family breakdown. They agreed to meet in a bar on the South Bank that evening.

She left Luka tidying the studio ready for their advance on the *Florilegium*'s final sequence. By the time she arrived at the National Theatre, Mara was already there, sitting at a table in the crowded foyer, bundled up like a babushka against the cold, warming her hands on a cup of green tea. Eve queued at the bar, bought herself a gin and tonic and joined her friend.

'He's trying to screw me financially,' she told Mara.

'Who?'

Was she being deliberately obtuse?

'Kristof. I'll be left with nothing.'

Mara sipped at her tea. She seemed strangely distracted.

'You could look at it that way,' she said. 'Or you could look at it as recognition that you're an independent woman with a successful career in your own right.'

This even-handed therapy-speak was maddening.

'I'm going to be penniless – he's giving me a lump sum that will barely keep me in pigments and brushes, and a half-share in the studio for my lifetime, unless Google or Amazon want to take out a lease there.'

'Why do you think you need his handouts?' Mara said in that infuriating voice of reason. 'You're at the peak of your career – the Sigmoid show was a great success. You've got the Gerstein coming up in January. Your stock in the art market has never been higher. Kristof is just a glorified builder with an injured ego. Move on.'

This wasn't helpful.

'He's punishing me,' Eve said. 'Punishing me for humiliating him, for choosing passion over respectability.'

Mara put down her cup.

'Well, let's face it,' she said, dropping her neutral tone, 'this peccadillo of yours – it's not the first time, is it?'

Eve flinched. There was hostility in Mara's tone.

'What do you mean?'

'It seems to be your thing. Uncorrupted young flesh … At least your current victim is above the age of consent.'

So that was it. The civilised veneer they'd maintained and polished over decades had finally cracked.

'If you're talking about Theo, that was years ago. You know that. A moment's folly.'

'Folly? That would be a kind way of putting it.' Mara's voice was hard, accusatory. 'He was a child. You were a predator.'

'That's ridiculous. Theo was sixteen. It was perfectly legal.'

Mara was looking at her with open hatred.

'Actually, he was fifteen, if you remember. A week away from the birthday that you took him to Paris to celebrate.'

Eve pushed away her glass.

'Oh, for God's sake, Mara. You know that's just pedantry. Why bring this up now? There's no comparison. I thought you were fine with it. You had Kristof – I had Theo.'

249

'Actually, I didn't know — until two weeks ago. Theo told me in a rambling phone call from Thailand.'

Astonishingly, Mara began to cry. Eve, embarrassed on her friend's behalf, leaned over to pat her hand. So Mara hadn't known. Eve never expected Theo to keep their secret — what teenage boy could resist boasting of his first serious sexual encounter? — but apparently he had. Until now. Eve's satisfaction at her exquisite revenge, all those years ago, had been misplaced; Mara hadn't been sent reeling by the news that her beloved son was the subject of a retaliatory seduction. Nor had she turned a blind eye to the affair, accepting that her own behaviour justified Eve's response. Mara never saw a thing. All the same, even if she'd only just found out, her response to this old story seemed over the top. Did this new emotional lability signal a mental breakdown — maybe she and Dot had split up — or even herald dementia?

'I can't believe you're bringing this up now,' Eve said, chiding her softly. 'You know I was fond of Theo. You know I did everything to help during his difficult teens, paid for his rehab, got him an internship at a recording studio, sent him back to Paris ...'

Mara, her eyes puffy and bloodshot, withdrew her hand sharply and looked directly at Eve.

'Did it ever occur to you that his teens might not have been so difficult if he hadn't been thrown off course by a powerful older woman who exploited his innocence?'

Eve reached for her glass. She could match anger with anger. She wasn't taking this from Mara, the friend who betrayed her and did her best to wreck her marriage.

'That's ridiculous,' Eve said. 'Theo was perfectly mature. Maybe you don't want to hear this, but it was an innocent, beautiful thing, an intense physical relationship between emotional equals. And he wasn't a virgin. He's not saying that, is he? Blaming me for his derailed life?'

'He's not saying anything any more.'

'What do you mean?'

'He died of a drug overdose in Thailand last week. They're flying his body home on Tuesday.'

Eve rocked back in her seat and closed her eyes. 'No! … Theo? … God …' She shook her head. 'I'm so sorry.'

She leaned across the table to grasp Mara's hand, as much for her own comfort as for her friend's. This time she was swatted away.

'Yes. You probably are. But you'll never be sorry enough.'

Mara's chair scraped noisily as she got up to leave. 'You'd better find your own divorce lawyer.'

26

Eve's heart starts to thud, it seems, even before she hears the sound. It's a lone vehicle whose distant whirr becomes a whine and then a soft roar as it approaches her. A moped. Once seen as an effete mode of transport – the 'mobile hairdryer' of parka'd mods, dwarfed by the Harleys and Nortons of the 'ton-up boys' – now, in this context, a real threat. She'd heard the news – moped-riding thieves were the vicious new highwaymen plaguing London streets. 'Your money or your life.' Sometimes '*and* your life'. She grips her bag tighter, knowing that the wisest thing would be to let it go. Just give it all – cash, cards, phone, keys – to the thief who might slash her with a knife or douse her with acid.

Just as she fears, the moped stops right by her.

'Excuse me,' the lone biker calls out.

She walks on, sick with dread but defiant. Tonight she's facing a greater reckoning than mere robbery and violent assault.

'Excuse me, miss.'

Was this politeness irony? She turns to face her tormentor, to challenge him with her anger, knowing that, after a series of fantastically stupid missteps, this might be the most stupid thing she's ever done.

He lifts his helmet so she can see his face – pale, acne-scarred, ludicrously young.

'Can you tell me the way to Sewardstone Road?'

She looks again at the moped, sees the logo on its storage box, and directs the pizza delivery boy back towards the bridge over the canal. She walks on. The rain is beginning to seep through her coat.

In the days after Eve heard the news from Thailand, work was a balm. Luka had calmed down and his silent presence was a solace as she fussed at the edges of the orange canvas. Soon she would be ready to tackle the red sequence. She was less than a week away from completing the *Poison Florilegium*.

One morning, she received a terse text from Hans. He was on his way to the studio. Luka was setting up the camera when there was a soft knock at the door. Hans barely looked at him as he walked towards Eve. His expression was solemn.

'I wanted to speak to you in person.'

Eve picked up a rag to wipe her hands.

'I'm almost done! I was going to invite you over to raise a glass when we'd finished.'

She gestured round the studio – by a trick of light you could almost believe that it was the glowing canvases, not the setting winter sun, that burnished the room and turned the canal outside into a river of blood. The watercolours and photographs were neatly laid out on the table and the six sealed herbaria were lined up, side by side, against the east wall like display cases in a jewellery store. Only one watercolour, one canvas and one herbarium to go.

But Hans's glance seemed perfunctory and impatient. He wasn't here to appraise her work.

'It's the Gerstein,' he said. 'They've cancelled the retrospective.'

'What?' Eve balled the paint rag in her fist. 'They can't do that!'

'Well, they've done it.'

'Why?'

He flung a newspaper across the table. 'You've not seen it?'

The paper was open on the unmistakable Kiš portrait, *Girl with a Flower*, spread across two pages. Next to it was a grainy snapshot of a young man, bare-chested on a beach, hair tousled by a sea breeze. Theo. The headline read 'VILE PREDATOR KILLED MY BROTHER'. Under it, in smaller type, were the words 'Famous artist's muse was paedophile, says dead DJ's family'.

Eve reached out to steady herself against the table. Esme had taken her revenge. And there she was, the grieving sibling, photographed for the article, beefy arms folded confrontationally in a button-down shirt. Under her picture was the caption: 'Eve Laing destroyed innocent Theo, says IT consultant Emmet.'

There were two more pictures – one of Eve and 'current toy boy, Luka Marlow', flanking Wanda at the Hayward, the other of Eve smiling and apparently serene on Kristof's arm at the Sigmoid opening. The caption read: 'In happier times: alleged child abuser Laing with her estranged husband, millionaire architect Kristof Axness.'

'Absurd!' Eve said, tossing the paper back towards Hans. 'Malicious nonsense. What's this got to do with my New York retrospective?'

'The official line is that it doesn't fit the Gerstein's schedule any more.'

Eve was suddenly conscious of Luka's presence.

'That's not good enough,' she said to Hans. 'What are they playing at? They can't just scrap the show like that. How could they have got their scheduling so wrong?'

Hans shook his head. 'The scheduling is a fiction. They've pulled your show. Because of this.' He pointed at the newspaper. 'There's the Twitter business, too ...'

'What Twitter business?'

'About you and ...' Hans nodded in Luka's direction.

There was contempt for her as well as Luka in that nod.

'Luka's his name. Come on, Hans. Twitter? *Really?* Another meaningless moral panic. Since when did the art world get all puritanical about extramarital affairs?'

She looked over and saw that Luka was back at the camera, filming their exchange.

'Well, it's not just about him, is it?' continued Hans. 'There's the dead boy. Theo Novak.'

She felt a rising panic.

'But that was decades ago, when we ... when I ... knew him.'

She sensed the camera implacably recording her confusion.

'Turn that damned thing off,' she told Luka. 'Aren't there some supplies you should be getting?'

'Sure.'

He took his jacket and left the studio.

'Eve,' said Hans, 'you know I've never pried into your personal life.'

'It would be a bit rich if you did, Hans. I've heard the rumours. The cottaging, the heath, the clubs ...'

He winced. When he next spoke there was a brusqueness in his voice.

'No one's interested in me,' he said. 'And besides, I was always careful to keep within the boundaries of the law.'

'This is ridiculous, Hans. It was half a lifetime ago. I haven't seen him for years. I was a young woman, lonely, hurt by my husband's infidelity. He was a sweet, loving boy. It was real passion for both of us. Different times.'

'That's not the line they're taking on social media. Or the press. They're laying responsibility for his death at your door.'

'Theo became a junkie because of the crappy youth culture. Drugs killed him. Our brief fling, two decades ago, had nothing to do with it.'

Hans sighed. 'I'm afraid the world takes a rather different view. In this new climate, there's no statute of limitation on sexual misdemeanour.'

'I can always deny it,' she said. 'They can't prove it. It's my word against his. And he's dead.'

'Your word against his sister's – his brother's.'

'Esme? That little freak?'

'That little freak, as you call him, knows how to orchestrate a social media campaign. It's global, thanks to your husband's profile. Your daughter's been spreading the word, too.'

Eve shook her head. So this Oedipus was a woman, intent on murdering her mother.

Hans walked towards the door: 'I'm sorry, Eve.'

'Can't you do something?' she called after him. 'Persuade the Gerstein to reconsider?'

'They've moved fast. Damage limitation. They've already rescheduled. They're running a new immersive piece by Wanda Wilson, a pop-up curtain-raiser for her summer *Artist on the Edge* show.'

Eve's unconvincing laughter echoed in the silence of the studio.

'A video walk-through of her latest colonoscopy? With music by Satie?'

Hans turned back to her. He wasn't smiling. 'Wanda Wilson is the greatest artist of her generation.'

'You don't believe that, Hans, I know you don't. Tell me you don't believe that.'

He opened the door letting a pale strip of light fall across the gathering gloom of the studio.

'I've got a lawyer weighing up your options but I don't fancy your chances.'

'*Our* chances.'

'Yours. You're on your own with this one, Eve.'

Once Hans had left, she switched on all the lights, found her phone and rang Ines Alvaro's number. It went straight through to voicemail. She left a message asking her to call. What else could she do but return to work? Luka too, when he came back from his convenient errands. He didn't ask about Hans's visit and kept his distance. He moved the camera tripod and they tidied the studio, cleaned the brushes, muller and grinding slab, and set out the powdered pigments in preparation for the concluding sequence.

Red. They should have been exultant. Instead, the studio seemed as quiet and heavy with sorrow as a funeral parlour. Her thoughts returned to that other studio, years ago, with its tall sash windows letting in the northern light, chilling her naked body sprawled at Florian's feet.

As she took comfort in the rites of process, sharpening pencils, laying out watercolours, putting brushes in a jar of fresh water, Luka filmed her.

Now she could begin. She selected a pencil – 3B, a balance between softness and precision. Bent over the vellum, she began her preparatory sketch for the *Ricinus* watercolour. It was hard to focus and remain purposeful without asking: 'What is the point? Who is this for?'

She began to resent Luka's tiptoeing silence and the pitiless scrutiny of the camera and snapped at him: 'Turn it off!'

He mimed an apology, hands up, and went back to the herbarium.

'So,' he called to her in a bright shot at conciliation, 'tell me about this one?'

He was waving a branch of *Ricinus*, its twin scarlet pompoms grotesquely festive. He was trying to lift her mood, or at least to distract her. Perhaps this was what she needed. As she reached for the herbal manual he set up the camera and tripod next to the herbarium and adjusted the focus.

'"Ricin. The deadliest of them all ..."' she read. '"Used by the Soviets to assassinate exiled dissidents."'

Oddly, she read, it was also said to have been used by Cleopatra to whiten her eyes. Another dicey beauty regime.

He whistled, releasing the plant into the formalin with comic reverence. She returned to her watercolour, teasing out the seed capsule's scrotal delicacy with a fine brush.

Her phone rang and, in her haste to answer, she trailed drops of vermilion all over the watercolour. Blotting desperately at her work with a rag, she saw the call wasn't from Ines, but from Hans. He must be feeling guilty about their sharp exchange: it had all been a mistake; the Gerstein board members had changed their minds; the retrospective was going ahead.

But Hans was sombre.

'No. Their decision is final.'

There was worse. The offers for the *Poison Florilegium* had been withdrawn.

'That's it, I'm afraid,' he said. 'And there's growing pressure on the Dallas Museum to take down the *Urban Florilegium.*'

'Pressure? Who from?'

'The Twittersphere … An editorial in the *New York Times …*'

Into her stunned silence, he sounded a tentative note of hope.

'I did receive one offer,' he said. 'From Wanda Wilson. Her people have been enquiring about using images from *Rose/Thorn.*'

Eve squeezed the sodden red rag in her hand. What did he mean by 'using images'?

'Reproduction rights. She wants to use them in her Gerstein show, an "art banquet" – an extended feast, with music, food and wine – open to spectators …'

'They're trading the *Poison Florilegium* for that? What's it got to do with *Rose/Thorn* anyway?'

'She wants to print the images on the tableware – plates and cups, drapery.'

Eve threw the rag across the table.

'Hans, I'm an artist, not an interior designer. You know that. Wanda knows that.'

He ignored her sarcasm. 'She says – Wanda Wilson's people say – *Rose/Thorn* will be an integral part of the work.'

'You're telling me my best hope is a joint show, featuring printed reproductions of my old work, alongside a new piece of nonsense from Wanda Wilson?'

'Not exactly. Your work would be what they describe as an adjunct – an accessory – to Wanda's show.'

Eve looked over at Luka. Was he listening to this? He was at the computer, editing footage.

'How long have we worked together, Hans? Twenty, twenty-five years? This year, we had the show at the Sigmoid. Only a few weeks ago we were talking about potential buyers for the new *Florilegium* – the Middle East … Russia … China … And now you're honestly advising me that my only hope is to help out in Wanda Wilson's immersive restaurant experience?'

'Eve, you don't seem to understand the gravity of your situation.' There was exasperation in Hans's voice. 'Your reputation is in tatters and the value of your work has plummeted. Whatever animus you have towards Wanda Wilson, this is your best – perhaps your only – chance. It's a generous offer. If I were you, I would snatch at an invitation to play a part in her new show. It's a serious piece of work that's already attracting international press attention.'

'You're not me, Hans. If you were, you'd know I'd rather die in obscurity than join Wanda Wilson's circus.'

'I've given my advice –'

She cut him off. It was all over with Hans.

Numb with fury, she never wanted to see him again. She would walk away; she was good at walking away

– from her parents, her brother, from Kristof, Nancy …
One step and then the next. Repeat. Until you're out of
sight and earshot. She'd turned her back on Theo, too.
It seemed easy, measuring the distance in footsteps, a
leisurely stroll towards the horizon. Easy at the time.

She'd also turned her back on Florian, though that had
cost her more. She'd had to cut him out of her life like a
canker, anaesthetised by rage.

She returned to her drawing but it was impossible; her
hand was shaking. Maybe it was all over with her too.

27

The wind has got up and she's alerted by a sudden movement – a low silhouette is slinking from a side street
towards her. She stops; it's a fox, dragging its flapping prey.

A night bus flashes past, each lit window framing an
Edward Hopper profile – thumbnail studies of urban
loneliness. The fox walks into the road, illuminated by the
bus's tail lights, and Eve sees that the quarry is not a fatally
wounded puppy or kitten struggling in its last throes, but
a bag of rubbish plundered from a nearby dustbin. She
puts up her collar against the wind and walks quickly
on. The past is no comfort. She's not outrunning her
thoughts. Nor is she hurrying back to the studio. She's a
woman pursued. Pursued by her future.

Half an hour after Hans's phone call she opened
a bottle of wine and turned on the radio. She returned
to her drawing while Luka attended to the camera and
cleaned the studio. The news was of refugee convoys,
more catastrophic floods, deadly wildfires and impending
economic doom. But nothing could quell her thoughts
of that last time with Florian, when he'd banished his

visitor, knocked on the bathroom door and asked Eve to come and resume her pose. As she stretched out on the studio floor for him she noticed that a small canvas – 30cm by 30cm, less than half the size of her portrait – had been brought out from the stacks against the wall and was leaning against the sofa. She stared at it absently. The painting was an incomplete nude study of what appeared to be a Neanderthal fertility goddess in a state of abandon, her torso ringed by bands of subcutaneous fat, splayed legs revealing the frilled viscera of sex organs, her dark hair a wiry halo. It was repellent…

By the time Luka opened a second bottle, Eve had somehow managed to complete the watercolour. He returned to the herbarium and set up the video camera. She began to organise the brushes and pigments for tomorrow's assault on the final canvas. She knew what was required but she couldn't unseat the question that now squatted like a malevolent demon over the enter-prise: what was all this for?

Luka seemed to read her mind. He turned on the camera and asked: 'Do you ever wonder what all this is about? I mean, what's it saying? Who actually likes this stuff? What's the point?'

Was he being hostile or just obtuse? If he was looking for a confrontation, he could have one. It would at least take her mind off the chasm yawning at her feet.

'If you want to leave, there's the door,' she said. 'I'll get on fine without you. You might find it tricky, though, without the salary or the status. What's your future? A dazzling career copying French Impressionists? Designing greetings cards? Pet portraiture?'

He kicked the herbarium and the plants shuddered in their oily bath. He was angry too. But he knew she was right. He had come this far. He was as committed to the project as she was. He had to see the *Florilegium* through to the end. Perhaps it would be their end, too, but they could address that later. They must work now.

Slowly, he measured out the pigment and mixed the colour. They worked at the canvas in sullen silence, side by side. By the time they were too exhausted to carry on, they'd almost finished half the *Ricinus* painting. Even as enemies, they worked well together.

It must have been 4 a.m. when he made up a bed on the studio couch. She went to the bedroom alone and woke just before dawn, three and a half hours later, wrecked by lack of sleep and too much wine. She felt an undertow of fear – about Luka, about Kristof, Florian, Theo, her reputation, everything – but she had to get back to the canvas. Another day would do it. Then she could collapse, take stock and decide her next move.

Luka was already up, sitting at the computer, editing footage. He made coffee and went to grind more red pigment in silence. When she was ready to start on the painting he returned to the herbarium and set up the video camera next to it, angling it on her. She leaned close into the grain of the canvas, her brush clotted with glutinous carmine. The spiky red seed capsules were so hard to render – they had a party piñata quality, but in another light, they suggested the lethal flails of medieval warfare. The colour wasn't helping. On the canvas it was flat, lacking depth and luminosity.

He was dropping the last of the *Ricinus* seed capsules and leaves into the herbarium's preserving fluid when Eve called to him.

'Can you take another look at this mix?' she asked. 'The colour seems a bit off.'

It was as if he hadn't heard. He continued to drop the plant parts in the herbarium, one by one, watching, as if in a trance, each twirling, rippling, slow-motion fall.

'I said, can you do this red again? The mix isn't right.'

He looked up, a strange smile on his face, and didn't move.

'Hans was right,' he said. 'You should listen to him.'

'I don't go to Hans for advice. How much of that phone conversation did you hear?'

'Enough to know that you're crazy to turn down a chance to take part in Wanda Wilson's new show.'

'If I want your opinion, I'll ask for it. Now shut up and get on with your work.'

He wasn't finished with her.

'It's a one-off New Year appetiser for next summer's big multi-venue relational show that everyone's talking about. Should be fun. There'll be round-the-block queues, a buffet provided by the most fashionable chef in Manhattan, themed tableware, dinner jazz. She's calling it *Best Eaten Cold/Revenge*.'

Eve looked at him in disbelief. The unkind light of the grey winter's morning stripped him of his beauty, giving him the look of a gleeful cadaver. She turned away and picked up her brush. It was shaking in her trembling hand. Close up, staring at the warp and weft of canvas showing though the lurid red, she thought again of that small, unfinished portrait in Florian's studio, of how her eyes had narrowed, sharpening her gaze, and moved from the ragged wound of vagina and labia to the crude blur of facial features framed by a dark fright wig. A moment of mild curiosity was followed by a shock of recognition: it was Wanda. Unmistakably.

'Back to work then,' Luka said. His voice was louder, a yobbish jeer. 'Your public's waiting ...'

He was openly goading her. She wiped her hands on her overalls. She'd mix the colour herself if she had to.

'Either get on or get out,' she said.

He rolled his eyes, a delinquent child defying tedious elders, and with a camp flourish of the tweezers, dropped another *Ricinus* bauble in the tank.

'If people like these flowers so much, why don't they just grow them?' he said. 'Or maybe buy them and put them in a vase? At least they can sniff them, touch them, poison their enemies with them, if they want.'

'You don't mean that, Luka,' she said quietly.

Even now, in the face of his blatant derision, she was willing to give him another chance. He was all she had. But he stood there, his face twisted with an ugly sneer.

'I mean, who would prefer a photo of reality over reality itself? People want the real thing – authenticity. What are you adding to the story, two degrees removed from nature, with your pissy paintings that look like photographs of the real thing?'

'What's got into you?' she shouted. She felt an urge to slap his insolent face.

'What was it Florian Kiš said?' He was holding up his phone. 'I looked it up … Here we are. "Pointless whimsy. A shameful squandering of talent for which the artist should be horsewhipped with a bouquet of her ghastly flowering blackthorn."'

She smacked the phone from his hand and it fell to the floor.

'Florian was angry,' she said. 'Angry that I left him. Angry that I was going my own way, that he couldn't have me any more.'

Luka laughed, a cruel snigger, picked up his phone and stood there gloating, delighting in her rage.

The memories threatened to derail her altogether. When she discovered the portrait of Wanda, she said nothing to Florian. Nor did she challenge Wanda, who was still up and wearing an expression of feline satisfaction when Eve finally got home that night. But something had shifted for Eve. Spurred further by her inconvenient pregnancy, this was the beginning of the end with Florian.

As for Wanda, Eve knew then that she must play a long game. Whatever Wanda Wilson might be saying now, she never meant more to Florian than a quick fuck – late-night fast food consumed in a frenzy of greed and disgust. In a hopeless bid to win Eve back, he consigned Wanda's portrait to the backyard bonfire in one of his culls of second-rate work. It was *Girl with a Flower* that had survived.

All at once, it was clear to Eve. Why try explaining to Luka? He wouldn't understand anyway. It was a case of mistaken identity. She thought he had the intelligence, seriousness and talent to be a partner in work and life. She'd got it wrong. She was on her own. This clarity was all she needed. Luka had been a necessary part of the process. 'You start to paint and they all begin to leave, one by one, shutting the door gently behind them until you're left standing there, finally alone – just you and the work. Paint and a passion.' The crowd had gone. It would soon be time for her to leave too.

Confusion and anger began to drain away, replaced by a focused calm. Time was running out and she must be an automaton for her art. Her hand was steady again and she turned away, picked up her brush and applied herself to a single red seed capsule. She would outline the form and get the colour right later. The rest would follow. Nothing else mattered as she dabbed and incised, striving, as she had for so many years, to bring the illusion of life to the flat plane of canvas. With each painting, you finally master it and then you have to learn how to do it all over again with the next.

A gust of air and a sudden clatter broke her concentration. Luka had thrown the tweezers at her, missing her by inches.

'The only way I could get your attention,' he said, leaning over the herbarium, grinning like a malign child.

'That's it!' Eve said. 'You can leave right now.'

'I'll go when I want to. When you pay me for my half-share of all these.' He gestured towards the canvases.

She lowered her brush. 'You have no claim on anything.'

'I guess they're worth less now than they were last week,' he continued, with that provoking smirk, 'before the papers and the Twitter storm and the fallout. But you never know – things could pick up; your stock could rise again. Maybe you can rehabilitate yourself. Charitable work for Boy Scouts?'

His transformation was complete. Her Botticelli angel was revealed as one of Bosch's tormenting demons. How far he had fallen, and how swiftly.

'Get out!'

'This is my work, as much as yours,' he said.

She laughed. 'No one will believe that. You're a nobody. A lightweight peddler of cheap fakes.'

He was pointing at the red canvas. What did he mean? His finger stabbed towards the right of the painting, where she would put her signature once she'd completed her work. But there was something already there – a fist-sized black smudge. She looked closer and saw that it was an ink drawing. A grinning Mexican skull.

'I've left my mark,' he said. 'On all the canvases.'

Appalled, she glanced around the studio and could see, even from this distance, that it was true. She'd been so agitated by lack of sleep and by his vicious taunts, she'd narrowed her focus to a single seed capsule and hadn't looked up and taken in the outrage – a black smear marked every painting like a disfiguring sarcoma.

Her response was instinctive. Any artist whose work was so brutally defaced would have done the same, or worse.

Replaying the scene as she walks through the night, she struggles to recall picking up the big hog-bristle brush. One second she was holding it and the next she felt it leave her hand. She must have drawn back her arm to hurl the brush with some force but she has no memory of it. All she's left with is an impression of controlled calm the second before she released the brush from her grip, and the appalling moment of impact – the silence followed by the scream …

The brush landed with a splash in the floating herbarium, sending up a spray of viscous liquid. His howl had a guttural, animal quality as he desperately rubbed at his face.

'My eyes! What the fuck have you done?'

She led him to the bathroom, filled the sink with cold water and told him to keep splashing his eyes. In the bathroom, standing behind him as he bent over the sink, she caught a glimpse of herself in the mirror and recoiled – hair like dried sweepings from the dissection tray, eyes shrunk to lustreless beads receding in their folds of flesh, bloodless mouth a puckered gash in a grisaille morgue portrait. She ran the tap again, held a clean rag under it and told him to use it as a compress. Then she took him to the bedroom and left him lying on the bed, still whining.

'It'll be okay,' she said. 'Just keep rinsing the rag in this bowl of fresh water. You'll be fine.'

Back in the studio she put on gloves, fished the brush out of the herbarium with tweezers and washed it. She checked her written formula for the green ground. Phthalocyanine green with cadmium. Two parts to one. She spooned out the powder on the grinding slab, poured on linseed oil then worked in the mixture with the glass muller. How long was it since she'd done this herself? That was another thing about having assistants to take care of business – they robbed you of agency and rendered you helpless. Paint and a passion – that was all you needed. Florian got that right. The ritual of process was profoundly satisfying and offered another, deeper way into the work.

She jabbed a smaller brush into the puddle of green paint then, turning to the unfinished red canvas, she tapped at the disfiguring mark. After four light strokes with the hog-bristle brush, the skull disappeared. Within half an hour, Luka was erased from all seven canvases.

Now she could begin. Her hand was steadier. It had to be. She mustn't falter.

28

The road has widened. It's getting busier. Six lanes of clamorous traffic, more lorries, giant bellows discharging toxins into the cold night air, conveying their burdens to points north and east. Looming ahead are brutalist high-rise Himalayas of social housing and shopping malls. There is little pleasure in this kind of walking. She heads down a short flight of steps to the canal, which is bounded by another squalid gallery of graffiti. Two figures walk towards her, pulling a wheeled suitcase which rumbles noisily on the potholed tarmac. As she approaches them, she sees that they are children, brother and sister, perhaps – both with wide pale faces and tousled fair hair – maybe thirteen or fourteen years old. They smile nervously at her as they pass. They are as uneasy about her as she is about them. Are they running away from a troubled home? Or running towards a more terrible fate? They could be Eve and her brother, half a century ago.

If he were here now, John, bristling with social concern, would intercept these runaways, ask what they were doing, check that they were okay. Eve turns, wondering whether John's instinct would be right – should she go after them? But they've walked on, out of earshot, relieving her of responsibility.

She feels an urge to speak to her brother, to hear his familiar voice. He was always a good listener. He would be concerned about her, but then for him concern was always a cheap commodity, indiscriminately distributed. The purist anchorite, wherever he was, at the peace camp or on his croft, had no phone. He only spoke to her on his terms, with a borrowed mobile or from a rare public call box, when it suited him. When was the last time? More than eight months ago. Before the fall. He was too busy saving the planet to find time for his imperilled sister. She walks on, ricocheting between numb horror and panic.

Red – symbol of life and of death, carnival and carnage – was always the most difficult colour to get right. She couldn't blame Luka for that. She was at fault for asking his help in the first place. She needed no one: Luka, Josette and Glynn and the whole team, her family – they were all a distraction.

As Luka lay whimpering in the bedroom, she prised open the jar of benzimidazolone maroon and scooped two measures of the fine powder onto the grinding slab. Precision was essential.

A sudden commotion broke her concentration. He was standing by the door, still holding the compress to his eyes.

'I need to go,' he said.

'Go ahead. No one's stopping you!'

She measured out a quantity of vermilion, undercut with pulverised mercury.

'I need to see a doctor,' he said, running his hands over the door, searching for the lock.

'Come on. You're making too much of this. Just keep swabbing your eyes with water. It'll soon clear up.'

He found the handle and tugged at it but the door was locked. The key was on the table, right beside her, next to the grinding slab.

'I just want out of here!'

'You know what?' said Eve, reaching for the small jar of naphthol red. 'I want you out of here too.'

Now he was scrabbling helplessly at the door.

'Just let me go!'

Eve was trying to keep track of the pigment mix. She mustn't overdo the naphthol or she would have to start again.

'Please. I need to go!' he said, his whine cranking up to a shout. 'Now!'

She sighed, put down the jar and wiped her hands on her overalls. 'Okay. Where's your mobile? What's your passcode? I'll ring your sister.'

He handed her his phone then slumped on the floor, head in hands, dabbing at his eyes with the rag.

She found Belle's number. It rang out. Eve began to type in a text when she noticed a message sent by his sister an hour ago.

'I warned you. If you let us down now, the deal is off,' it read.

Belle's text was a reply to a message from Luka, half an hour before:

'I'm out of here. Can't stand another second.'

Now he was shouting again. 'Tell her to hurry!'

Ignoring him, Eve stared at the glowing bar of his phone in her hand as if it was radioactive. Then she thumbed through his messages and there it was. How could she have been so stupid?

'Please, Eve,' he moaned.

'Give me a moment. She didn't pick up. I'm trying her again.'

She scrolled back.

Luka, 19 April – *Think she took the bait.*

Belle, 19 April – *Of course! How could she resist?*

Belle, 20 April – *Any photos? Film? Remember – documentation vital.*

Luka, 29 April – *Going to need chemical assistance. Those blue pills.*

Belle, 29 April – *No worries. Whatever it takes.*

Luka, 30 April – *Deed done. Yuck.*

Belle, 30 April – *[thumbs up emoticon]*

Luka, 1 May – *She's a monster … Can't believe you talked me into this.*

Belle, 1 May – *Close your eyes and think of the money.*

'*Eve!*' Luka pleaded.

'I'm doing my best.'

Luka, 3 June – *She's doing my head in. Husband away. Need more blue pills.*

Belle, 4 June – *Don't mess up. Get those assistants out of the picture.*

Luka, 16 June – *Sorted! Just me, G and J, and the PoC now.*

Belle, 17 June – *[three grinning emoticons]*

Luka, 18 July – *I'm going mad with this.*

Eve shivered. She felt cold to her core. The blue pills. The old man's friend. The old woman's too, it seemed. But the PoC? She looked back through the messages and guessed the truth seconds before she saw the text from Luka to his sister on 28 July.

'More aggro from the Princess of Chintzes. If I see another fucking flower I'll kill myself.'

He was on his feet again, feeling his way round the table, trying to reach the door.

'I need to get to a hospital.'

'I can't reach Belle.'

He screamed: 'Get me a cab!'

'You've been lying to me.'

'No!' he protested, screwing up the wet rag and pressing it into his eyes.

'I've seen your messages!' she said.

'No! Give me my phone!'

'I want the truth!'

'Please.' He was wheedling now. 'I really need to see a doctor. Everything's blurred. It's agony.'

'I'll bathe your eyes again.'

He let her guide him to a chair. She tilted his head and squeezed fresh water into those lying blue eyes, now veined with red. Then she soaked the rag again.

'So?' she prompted. 'Tell me. You and Belle ...'

'It was her idea. Nothing to do with me,' he groaned.

She folded the rag and draped it over his face.

'It's all been a lie?'

He flinched as she began to tie the wet fabric round his head like a blindfold.

'She talked me into coming here.'

He lifted his head to let her knot the rag.

'Why?'

He was mumbling: 'One of her performances.'

'Performances?'

She tugged at the knot.

'Don't! That hurts!'

She relented and loosened it.

'Better?'

He was suddenly defiant. 'Don't pretend you didn't get anything out of it.'

'How dare you!'

'I need to go,' he said. He struggled to his feet, holding the back of the chair for support. Blindfolded, he was a caricature of justice, helpless and blundering.

'One more thing,' she said. 'Your dissertation?'

He ripped the rag from his head and threw it on the table.

'I didn't do a dissertation. I began it but I dropped out.'

'It wasn't about my work, was it?'

'No.' He was smiling now, taking pleasure in her unease. 'It was on a *real* artist – Florian Kiš.'

Eve felt a swoon of sickness.

'And Belle?' she asked, her voice a whisper. 'What was her interest in my work?'

He was rubbing his eyes again.

'She was never interested in you. Wanda Wilson was her thing. Immersive work, relational art ... that's how she got the scholarship to the Art Ranch.'

Eve gripped the table.

'I'll get your taxi.'

She picked up his phone. But instead of calling a cab, she opened his email account. His answers had raised more questions.

29

The home stretch. Not long now. And then? Denial is an underrated survival strategy. She's desperate for distraction, looking around like a tour guide, explaining the city and its history, her history, to herself as if to a coach party of curious travellers. She's nearing the Olympic Park, built on the site of another defunct industrial estate. Stadium and velodrome, skate park and aquatics centre, funfair and running track, bounded by flower meadows and a vast shopping mall – all human needs, bar art and love, are met here. It was renamed to mark the Queen's jubilee, like the new 'super hospital' in Glasgow that Kristof advised on. Glaswegians, who'd voted to detach Scotland from the United Kingdom the year before the futuristic Queen Elizabeth University Hospital opened, renamed the hospital the Death Star. In the pre-dawn dark of a winter's morning, there's something of the graveyard about Queen Elizabeth Olympic Park, and the hulking silhouette of its stadium makes a convincing Death Ship.

She scrolled through his emails with shaking hands and found the thread. It went all the way back to April.

[Attachment symbol] From: BelleAmie@BelAmi.com
To: Luka@LukaM.com
2 April 2018
I've told her about you, shown her some photos.
She's on. All you've got to do is bone up (ha!) on EL's
work (document attached) then show up at the studio.
£200,000. Straight split. It'll be the easiest money
you'll ever make.

From: Luka@LukaM.com
To: BelleAmie@BelAmi.com
3 April 2018
What if E doesn't buy it?

From: BelleAmie@BelAmi.com
To: Luka@LukaM.com
3 April 2018
Wanda knows her subject. Says you'll be irresistible.

Eve thumbed forward.

From: Luka@LukaM.com
To: BelleAmie@BelAmi.com
11 May 2018
She's completely insane. Thinks her perfect flowers will
save the world. Insatiable in bed. It's grotesque. Can't
stand this much longer.

[Attachment symbol] From: Luka@LukaM.com
To: BelleAmie@BelAmi.com
3 July 2018
This is the only footage I could get so far. Josette blocking me.

From: BelleAmie@BelAmi.com
To: Luka@LukaM.com
3 July 2018
'Get rid of her too, then!' Wanda says. Take control!

From: Luka@LukaM.com
To: BelleAmie@BelAmi.com
28 July 2018
Done! Just me and her now! Creeps me out …

[Attachment symbol] From: Luka@LukaM.com
To: BelleAmie@BelAmi.com
14 August 2018
Attaching latest footage. She's still cagey on the New York stuff.

From: BelleAmie@BelAmi.com
To: Luka@LukaM.com
15 August 2015
Don't let me down. Raise your game. Don't fuck up. Bedroom footage?

From: Luka@LukaM.com
To: BelleAmie@BelAmi.com
17 August 2018
Bedroom footage my red line. What about privacy?
Aren't there laws about this?

From: BelleAmie@BelAmi.com
To: Luka@LukaM.com
18 August 2018
Wanda's people will take care of that.

[Attachment symbol] From: Luka@LukaM.com
To: BelleAmie@BelAmi.com
3 September 2018
Latest footage. Comedy gold at 13:50, when she has
tantrum over critics.

Eve glanced over at him. He was wailing now – her
Ariel finally revealed as Caliban.

[Attachment symbol] From: Luka@LukaM.com
To: BelleAmie@BelAmi.com
12 October 2018
Daughter footage. WW will love this. E chucked me
out but I kept the camera running.

[Attachment symbol] From: Luka@LukaM.com
To: BelleAmie@BelAmi.com
8 November 2018
Footage – showdown with the dealer. It's all over for her. More to come.

From: BelleAmie@BelAmi.com
To: Luka@LukaM.com
8 November 2018
[a line of emoticons shedding tears of laughter]

    Luka's shrill shout startled her. 'Where's this fucking cab?'
    'On its way,' she lied.
    Her thumb froze as she saw Kristof's name flash up …

From: BelleAmie@BelAmi.com
To: Luka@LukaM.com
13 November 2018
Yeah. Kristof wasn't in the script. But I might have a bit of fun with this.

    And again.

From: BelleAmie@BelAmi.com
To: Luka@LukaM.com
15 November 2018
Wanda wasn't sure about the Kristof thing at first. Now she's totally on board.

Another familiar name was there too. Near the end of the thread.

From: BelleAmie@BelAmi.com
To: Luka@LukaM.com
20 December 2018
Wanda thrilled. Theo N an 'unasked-for gift' she says. One more batch of footage and we're done.

The last message had been sent early that morning.

[Attachment symbol] From: Luka@LukaM.com
To: BelleAmie@BelAmi.com
21 December 2018
More footage. Meltdown. One more day, one more round of filming, then I'm out of here …

There must have been thirty emails. On all of them, the subject field was *Artist on the Edge/The Death of Mimesis.*

So Wanda had played a long game too. Eve's hands were trembling. The only way she could restore her composure was to turn to her work. That was all she had left. She stood staring at that unsatisfactory red pigment congealing on the grinding slab as if it held the key to her current turmoil. Then she carefully measured out more naphthol red and sprinkled it over the mix. Still the colour wasn't right. Perhaps some cadmium barium would add a plasmic depth.

She shut out the sound of Luka's moans. She needed to work. She reached for another jar of pigment.

Now he was yelling.

'Where's that taxi?'

He was wringing the rag in his fists. His eyes didn't look that bad.

'Can't you see I'm working?' she said, measuring out half a spoonful of the plaster-pink powder.

'I need to leave. Now!'

'Just as soon as I've finished my work.'

'You and your fucking worthless work! Give me my mobile and I'll call my own cab.'

She picked up his phone and threw it into the open herbarium. He watched, mouth gaping, as it sank with a graceful pirouette to rest at the bottom of the tank.

'You bitch!'

He grabbed the scalpel from the dissection tray and lunged at her.

What else could she do to defend herself but throw the powdered pigment in his face?

He howled, clutching at his eyes with his left hand. But he was, somehow, still coming for her, scalpel flashing in his right fist. She stepped back and he cornered her against the canvas – the final, red canvas – and slashed at her wildly in blind rage. She tried to defend herself with her arms. The blade nicked her shoulder and blood began to seep through her sleeve but she felt no pain. She ducked past him and he started on the painting, ripping at it in a frenzy. She hurled herself at him and, using both hands, grabbed his right wrist, desperate to hold and twist it and make him drop the scalpel. For a moment she had him, her hands shaking as she fought to hold him back. But he was too strong for her and she had to leap away as she let go. It was over in seconds.

She still wasn't sure how it happened, how their struggle, a grim recasting of their early passion with hatred standing in for desire, ended like that – his right hand, suddenly released, catapulted forward with all the force intended for her, plunging the scalpel deep into his left wrist. His scream was one high note of horror as the hot jet of blood spurted from the wound with shocking force, soaking her throat and shoulders, his blood on hers, and spattering the canvas. For a moment she froze, a powerless witness of unfolding atrocity. What should she do? Who should she call? Sense and feeling returned in the form of trembling panic. There was no time for phone calls. She looked around helplessly then picked up his discarded blindfold to use as a tourniquet. Her hands shook as she tried to tie it round his arm but he thrashed and pulled away from her. Then it was too late. The fountain of blood became a trickle. He slumped back against the canvas and slid to the floor.

He lay stretched out under the painting and in the stillness she knelt beside him, fumbling for a pulse.

She touched his lips to feel for a whisper of breath. Then she lay down and put her ear to his heart. Silence. Minutes passed – two lovers in repose, her head resting on his stilled chest. She struggled to her feet and her stunned gaze turned from Luka's corpse, with its faint, pretty dusting of cadmium on the eyelids, to her work.

Then she picked up her fine sable brush and knelt again to dip it in the pooling gore, a thick, rich cinnabar vermilion with a haematite depth.

She stood before the canvas and began to paint. This was it: the telling hue she'd needed all along, the colour that conferred the third dimension, bringing the plants springing out into relief: you could prick your fingers on the barbed seed capsules.

It was, she knew then, her best work. It might not attain the universality of, say, Munch's *Scream*, familiar even to the art blind. But the *Poison Florilegium* told a beautiful, painful truth about the potency and fragility of life. The colour alone, in the final canvas, would be her legacy – that visceral Eve Laing Red.

In the preternatural calm of the studio, she worked on until she was done. She reconciled herself to the wide gashes underscoring her signature. They were part of the painting's story and gave the work a savage authenticity. The boy beneath the canvas was beautiful again in his gaunt pallor. She would leave the phone in the *Ricinus* herbarium; that was part of the story too.

As she sealed the cabinet, she noticed that the camera was on. It had been running all this time, filming the final sequence for Wanda's summer show. Evidence of Eve's innocence. Luka's death was an accident. But the film would also be evidence of her achievement as an artist. Let skill, imagination and – now it could be said – genius be her final rebuke to Wanda Wilson's feeble posturing. Not the *Death of Mimesis* but the *Death of Deconstruction*. Wanda's show will be Eve's triumph.

She lifted the camera from the tripod and walked round the studio, irradiated by the setting sun, filming the completed work: from the delicate watercolours laid out next to the black-and-white photographs on the table, to the floating herbaria with their seeds, flowers and leaves, glowing and undulating in their watery element like liquid stained glass. She stood by the door to get a wide-angle shot of the studio, a mighty cathedral of colour, its brick walls breached by the luminous canvases, then focused on each painting – from the meadow of violet monkshood, through the entire prism, to the blazing red finale, under which Luka lay, a beautiful martyr for art.

She turned off the camera and went to take a shower. Then she must tidy the studio, always a pleasurable ritual after completing a major piece of work. Later, she had some phone calls to make. But, before she moved irrevocably into her new life, she had to revisit the old.

And so she found herself travelling west on the Tube, a ghost of her former self, haunting her old home, now inhabited by Kristof and his new lover: the redhead, coiled and complacent as a marmalade cat in the armchair, entirely at ease. Her hand, with its small but unmistakable death's head tattoo, gripping the wine glass. The ambitious Belle playing her finest role, staging her immersive artwork in the smoking ruins of Eve's life.

30

She's returning east now, to the studio, to the cold body of the boy spread-eagled beneath her magnificent new work. She knows that she's achieved everything she spent her life working towards. Her *Poison Florilegium* isn't art imitating life, but life itself. She's moved beyond doubt to that region rarely inhabited by the true artist: certainty.

She's on familiar ground – home territory – and walks along the shabby parade of shops. The deli is boarded up. Dino and Thierry have relocated to Germany, a country more hospitable than England to European immigrants selling artichoke hearts and stuffed vine leaves.

The high street is deserted – all life seems to have been swept from it and deposited in the pub, which, though long past closing time, is glowing and thrumming like a nuclear installation. Through the window she sees a scene of wild carousing that could have been lifted from Bosch's *Last Judgement*. She walks on and, looking back, notices for the first time, a ghost sign, a secular Turin shroud, on the pub's gable end – the faded remnants of a painted advertisement for a long-vanished brewery: 'Take Courage'.

It's snowing lightly as she turns into the strip of scrubland – *terra incognita* – by the river, between the high street and motorway bridge. No man's land. No woman's either. Paris, that week so long ago, *À mon seul désir*, was a no man's land, too – a liminal hyperspace without constraints of time and place, a realm of pure connection where all the diversions of the city around them shrank away into a soundless, two-dimensional backdrop. But that no man's land was also *terra vetita*, forbidden ground. Theo was a boy. A beautiful, tender boy who loved her. And she loved him. So long ago.

Her feet crunch over broken glass and in the sulphurous half-light the shrubs rustle ominously. As she passes the lilacs they shiver with their incongruous burdens, now dusted with snow. She hears, against the background roar of the motorway, another sound – a human cough or rasp – and makes out a hunched figure sitting on the bench looking at the river.

'All right, love?' the figure calls out to her.

It's the old woman drinker from outside the pub. Was that really four months ago? Another seeker of solitude.

'Fine,' Eve answers. 'You?'

'Not so bad.' The woman stares at the river and puts a bottle to her lips.

Eve joins her on the bench and they gaze out at the water in companionable silence.

'Happy Christmas!' says the woman, passing Eve the bottle.

Eve shakes her head, smiling, and asks, 'What brings you here?'

'What? Here? Now?'

Eve nods, and sees for the first time that this old woman is probably younger than her, though ravaged, like a Brueghel grotesque, by poverty and drink.

'Nature. Peace and quiet. Just like you,' says the drinker.

'Just like me.'

'Beautiful, isn't it?'

Eve stares up into the blind opal eye of the full moon.

'Beautiful,' she agrees.

'Such a waste. I could do with a new one.'

Eve is puzzled, then sees that her companion is looking not at the night sky, but at an upturned supermarket trolley half submerged in the river, glinting like a silver spider's web in the moonwake.

'My old chariot's getting rusty,' says the drinker. She pats her trolley. Tied to its front is a plastic Santa.

The snow is getting heavier. Soon it will settle, erasing everything, the beautiful and the ugly, with its achromatic mantle. Eve gets up to leave and the two women exchange goodbyes.

'Take care of yourself, love,' the cracked voice calls as Eve walks on up the steps.

Halfway across the motorway bridge, she stops to look down at the speeding traffic. Is there a lonelier, lovelier sight? Those headlights hurtling through swirling snow towards fixed points, towards friends, family, work

– streaming galaxies, pulses of heat and light in a black, indifferent universe.

And her fixed point? A dead boy and a reckoning.

But there is her work. That will always be there. One perfect work. Paint and a passion. That's all you need. And if it goes well, you leave the studio, too, and shut the door behind you.

Her hands tense on the rail. All she can do is submit to the pull of gravity and fall towards the future. One step, a delicious, tumbling surrender, and the old life will be over, rushing past her as she plummets. How easy it is to let go.

Freeze-frame. Then rewind.